LOST IN THE LAND OF THE MIDNIGHT SUN

CHRISTINA CATTANE

M
Meno
Publishing

GET FREE BOOKS AND MORE

Receive free book offers, get exclusive behind the scenes content, and be the first to hear updates about upcoming books, release dates, and events, all by joining Christina Cattane's mailing list.

See the back of the book for details on how to sign up.

To My Daughter Amber
Who never fully understood grace,
Until the moment she truly needed it.

PROLOGUE

September 28, 2225

The wind raged against the waters of Redoubt Bay. The waves clashed with the wind, churning and foaming and throwing slush into the air. In the midst of the storm, a salmon trawler fought its way towards the mouth of the Drift River, tossed by the wind, deluged by the waves, and frozen from the elements.

Winter comes quickly in the land of the midnight sun, and this late September was no exception. The air temperatures were hovering right at thirty-two degrees. Sleet peppered the rigging with slushy pellets. Though the fate of the little boat seemed precarious, the danger to its frame paled in comparison to the jeopardy the lives of its passengers were in. For looming above it, a Navy Cruiser moved ever closer as they desperately tried to outrun it.

"You must protect the book son, no matter what happens, no matter what you see or hear, stay hidden and protect the book, it's the last of its kind, and there are evil men who will stop at nothing to destroy it."

The boy held his breath, gasping periodically to squelch

the urge to cry out. His heart raced. The tightening in his chest left him feeling nauseous and weak. He had been asleep in his bed when his father roused him, told him to get dressed, and dragged him into the icy rain that stung his cheeks. He'd tucked him into a pile of rigging to hide, whispered words of love and reassurance, and left him there with a promise to return quickly.

For what seemed like an eternity the boy shivered in his hiding place, soaked to the skin for so long that all he felt was a strange warm stinging where his wet clothes rubbed against damp flesh. He knew that somewhere ahead of the ship lay land and the snow-capped peaks of the Alaska Range. They only needed to stay ahead of the destroyer and make it to an old filling station at the end of an ancient pipeline. Someone would meet them there to guide them through the mountain passes. There they would join other fugitives like themselves.

The pins and needles in his fingers made it impossible to grip any longer, so the boy tucked the book up under his coat and pulled his hands into his sleeves to warm them. Suddenly the ship lurched and the popping of gunfire filled the air, followed by the clamoring of boots across the deck. A voice cried out. The boy squeezed his eyes shut and silently prayed.

SOMETIME LATER HE realized that the gunfire and shouting had stopped. The ship's engine was silent. Funny how quiet the roar of waves and wind seemed. A silhouette of a man came slowly across the deck toward the rigging where the boy was hiding. Relieved, the boy jumped up and cried out.

"Dad!"

The sneering stranger's face that greeted the boy revealed his error. The boy tried to run, but his feet got tangled in the rigging and he fell. The ship was sitting at an odd angle in the water and he began to slide across the deck. He reached out to grab onto something, anything that would stop him from sliding off the edge and into the frozen waters of Cook Inlet. As he frantically tried to get his stiff fingers around a stray rope, the book he had tucked into his coat landed with a wet smack on the deck.

With one last burst of strength the boy grabbed hold of the book at the same moment as the sneering stranger. Now they were both sliding toward the railing, each refusing to release their half of the volume. The boy slid over the edge, and for a fraction of a moment, he hung in mid-air, holding tight to the flimsy pages. He watched helplessly as the pages began to separate from the binding, until it came apart, and the boy fell into the icy water, the pages still gripped in his fingers.

Sometime later, he had a vague awareness of being pulled from the water, and men's tinny voices from far away. He felt pressure on his fingers as the torn Bible was pried from them. A strange warmth enveloped him, and he felt sleepy. He let himself sink back into the pillowy darkness of oblivion.

ONE

April 22, 2625

Angelica watched the bald eagle soaring above the village. Tucked into a valley between vast mountain ranges, Turquoise had been home to Angelica and her people for hundreds of years. The bird moved in slowly tightening circles around the tabernacle, eying the blood-soaked altar. Swooping low across the market square, he caught Angelica's eye.

Always watching me, aren't you?

As if to prove her wrong, the eagle pivoted away and landed nimbly on a fence rail.

Angelica turned back to the doll she held in her hands. Its bronze skin and straight black hair were perfect. She paid the toy-cart woman, putting the doll in her bag.

"Angelica," called her Grandma. "Come now, hurry."

Angelica picked up two cages, each containing a plump white ptarmigan. She hurried over to where her grandma stood in line at the tabernacle door, handing one of them to her.

"Little old for dolls, aren't you?"

Angelica shrugged. No need to tell her Grandma she was buying it for a sick child from the untouchable camp. It would only earn her another lecture. As the line got shorter Angelica turned her attention back to the market square. There were carts with cured meats and vegetables, some with items of clothing or linens, the toy cart, and then there were those selling ptarmigans for the sacrifices. She clenched her teeth and turned away, determined not to think about all those birds destined to have their throats cut. But her eyes fell upon her very own sacrifice in the cage at her feet, and guilt enveloped her. She turned to let her eyes rest somewhere- anywhere else.

They came to rest on Donavon, who was standing at the temple door, inspecting the sacrifices for purity. He was tall with straight black hair, bronze skin, and shoulders that were strong and wide. The girls in the village giggled when they saw him, whispering behind their hands, and doing anything they could to catch his attention. She didn't share their attraction. The sight of him somberly performing his duties as he checked the birds for defects caused her mind to wander back to a conversation with her father only a week ago.

THE SABBATH WAS ABOUT to begin - she'd come running into the yard just as the sun was touching the horizon.

"Sorry I'm late," she'd murmured, standing before her father with her head bowed. He'd offered no response, no familiar lecture about needing to grow up. He'd only reached out and picked a stray leaf out of her disheveled hair, flicking it away.

After sabbath prayers, they sat down to the meal, which stretched out into endless silence. Finally, her father set his knife and fork down and cleared his throat.

"Angelica, you were late this evening."

"Father, I know, but-" Her father had only to flick his eyes up to meet hers to silence the interruption.

"Daughter, you need to grow up. And you will soon have no choice but to do so. When you're married, there will be no time for running around in the forest."

"Married," said Angelica in dismay. *Not yet. I'm not ready.*

"Yes," Angelica's father continued, "You will be eighteen soon. Donavon's father and I both agree it is time you two were officially betrothed."

NOW, as Angelica watched Donavon arguing with an old man at the door, her stomach twisted, and she felt her face growing hot. She supposed he was pretty enough on the outside, but she'd seen the inside far too many times. Donavon was shaking his head and pointing to the market square. Tears were rolling down the old man's cheeks. Angelica swallowed hard. Donavon was rejecting his sacrifice. Angelica knew how hard the old man must have worked to catch that bird as a chick and raise it carefully so that it would be without blemish. It was likely he couldn't afford to buy a new sacrifice and would end up in the untouchable camp. The place they sent those who were unclean. She also knew that the rejected bird would be kept by the ptarmigan sellers, only to be resold to the next guy whose sacrifice was rejected. No doubt part of that money ended up in Donavon's pocket.

It isn't right. It isn't fair.

Angelica wished she could confront Donavon, tell him to show a little mercy, but she knew it would do no good. She looked down at her own sacrifice, chosen by her father. Her sacrifice would not be rejected. She was the high priest's daughter and Donavon wouldn't dare. A lump formed in her throat. She didn't deserve to be treated favorably just for who she was. Unable to bear the trembling of the old man's lips as he begged Donavon not to reject his sacrifice, Angelica grabbed her cage and pushed her way to the front of the line.

"You can have my bird," she said. "My father picked it out just this morning."

Donavon pursed his lips and his eyes narrowed. The muscles in his jaw twitched. He glared at Angelica, but she glared right back, ignoring the whisper of warning in the back of her mind.

"Very well," he said, waving the man through, his eyes never leaving Angelica's. The scowl on his face spelled out just how he felt about her defiance. She gave a tight smile, bowed, and rejoined her Grandma.

Her Grandma grabbed her arm, squeezing tightly "That was very unwise." she whispered, pulling at Angelica's arm when she didn't reply. "Angelica, you need to watch what you say and do, you're playing with fire."

The urgency in her Grandma's voice made Angelica turn and look at her. She was usually so even tempered. Nothing seemed to phase the old woman. She rarely smiled, but she also rarely got upset, worried, or afraid. It set off little alarm bells when Angelica saw the worried look in her eyes.

"I'm sorry," Angelica mumbled, "I just couldn't bear to see that poor old man be cheated."

Her Grandma released her grip on Angelica's arm, patting her shoulder and saying softly.

"You can't save the whole world Angelica."

Angelica didn't reply, she wasn't trying to save the whole world. She just couldn't bear the thought of seeing others treated unfairly.

As they reached the front of the line, Angelica handed the cage with the old man's sacrifice to Donavon. She looked him straight in the eye as he took it from her. *Reject it,* she thought, *declare it unworthy*. Instead he went through the motions of inspecting the offering before handing it back.

"Pass." His eyes were hard, and his lips pressed together in a thin line. A flutter of disappointment coursed through Angelica. She wanted to challenge his acceptance of her sacrifice, but this time the warning in her mind was more than a whisper, She took it from him, moving to the inner courtyard to wait yet again, this time for her turn before the high priest.

Angelica's stomach roiled as she waited for her turn to approach the altar. She looked down at the bird in her cage. He looked at her with trusting eyes, happily pecking at the seeds on the floor of his cage.

"I'm sorry," she whispered, sticking her fingers through the bars to stroke his downy white feathers. "I should have let you be rejected."

When the time came, Angelica approached the altar on trembling knees. The smell of roasting flesh and burnt feathers assaulted her nostrils. Her father turned to face her, his white robe stained and his fingernails black with blood. As her father recited the customary questions, Angelica's stomach did a flip.

"Do you atone for your sins?"

"Oh great High Priest, please present my sacrifice before Almighty God, that he may forgive my sins."

"May your sacrifice be acceptable to God, and your sins be atoned for."

Angelica swallowed the lump in her throat. Her father lifted the ptarmigan into the air and slit its throat with a long-curved blade. Blood sprayed, adding another layer of stains to his robe.

Angelica closed her eyes, willing herself not to throw up. *I'm so sorry,* she said in her mind, wondering if the bird's spirit would hear. She heard the sizzle, smelled the pungent odor of feathers burning. Her mouth began to water as the contents of her stomach crept toward her throat. When it was over, she forced herself to walk calmly toward the exit, hoping nobody would notice her distress.

Such a waste, so unfair, to take a life for nothing. Tears burned behind her eyes.

An innocent creature had died because of her, a sacrifice to a God who wouldn't accept it. He hadn't done so in twelve years, and Angelica didn't have much hope he ever would. She'd tried, she'd prayed, she'd cried out for mercy, but God remained silent, and her prayers unanswered. She grabbed hold of the jade eagle on a cord around her neck, gripping it to give her strength.

The moment Angelica's feet touched the dirt of the market square, she ran. She ran until she reached the edge of the trees, where she stopped, doubled over, and emptied the contents of her stomach into a bush. When her stomach was empty, she sat on a nearby log, tears coursing down her face, and thought about that day all those years ago. The day that still haunted her, the guilt of it never giving her a moment's peace. She replayed it in her mind yet again, knowing in her head she was only a child, but unable to convince herself she wasn't to blame.

TWO

It was a bath night. Mama slipped into the tub Angelica had just climbed out of. Grandma added boiling water from the kettle until it was steaming hot once more.

"It's like heaven," Mama said, closing her eyes and sinking into the water. Angelica pulled the towel closer around her, grateful for the heat of the stove, while Grandma knitted her long dark hair into a thick braid. Mama's clothes lay neatly folded on the table. Lying on top of them was a jade bird attached to a leather cord. The firelight glinted off the polished green surface making it appear to be dancing. She picked it up and ran her fingers over its hooked beak and spread wings.

"What is it?" Angelica asked.

"My lucky eagle," Mama said.

"Like the one who lives in the tree that grows in the middle of the river?"

"Yes. Like Him. The eagle is a symbol of the one who guides me. Keeps me on the right path, and always leads me home."

Angelica imagined the eagle swooping down from his

nest and leading Mama home from somewhere deep in the forest. She liked that idea. She held the necklace up and let it swing from its cord, imagining it flying through the sky.

"I like him."

"I like him too. He was a gift from Grandpa, and he is special to me." Mama flicked drops of water at Angelica from the tips of her fingers. Angelica giggled.

"Come get dressed," Grandma called. Angelica hid the necklace in her palm as she rose to obey. After Grandma tucked her into bed and closed the door, Angelica put the eagle on her pillow, set exactly right so he was looking at her. The jade was cool against her fingers. She pressed it on her cheek and smiled. She certainly understood why her mother loved it so much.

At the sound of footsteps, she shoved the eagle under her pillow and squeezed her eyes closed. Mama came into her room and sat on the edge of the bed. She felt Mama's hand softly touch her hair. Angelica couldn't stop her eyes from opening, and she gazed up at her beautiful mama. Her long dark hair spilled over her shoulders and her brown almond shaped eyes shone with love.

"Do you still have my lucky eagle?"

"No."

"Are you sure? I can't find it anywhere."

"Yes Mama, I put it back on your clothes." Angelica knew she shouldn't lie, but she just wanted to keep the little eagle a bit longer, to imagine it was watching over her while she slept.

"Love you Angel," Mama said.

Angelica breathed in deep to savor the sweet smell of Grandma's soap on mama's skin as she pressed her lips against Angelica's forehead.

"I love you too Mama," She said. *I'll put it back in the morning,* she thought to herself. She reached under her pillow and felt the smooth jade against her fingertips, found the hard ridges of the wingtips and let her fingernail run down each one.

Maybe I should give it back now, she thought, but Mama closed the door and the thought passed. She drifted off to sleep with the eagle clutched in her palm.

Sometime in the night men's voices awakened Angelica. She slipped out of bed and tiptoed across the floor, opening her door a crack, and peering out. There were two men talking to Mama and Papa, but their voices weren't loud enough to hear. Mama covered her face with her hands and turned to Papa, who put his arms around her, patting her back. After a few minutes Mama turned and saw Angelica peeking out her door. She knelt in front of her, tears on her face.

"I need to go to Grandpa's for a while. He's been hurt by a bear."

"Can I come too?"

"No, you need to stay here and help your grandma like a big girl."

"I wanna go with you." Mama reached out and wiped away the sudden tears from Angelica's cheeks.

"It won't be long. I'll be back before you know it." She hugged Angelica, who clung to her, wrapping her arms around Mama's waist, and locking her fingers in the back.

"Come now, let's get you back to bed," Mama said. "It'll be okay."

Angelica tried to hold on, but Mama gently pried her fingers apart and picked her up, putting her into bed and pulling the covers up to her chin. Angelica sobbed as Mama kissed her forehead and left the room, closing the door behind her.

Angelica pulled her stuffed moose to her chest, letting her tears soak into its soft belly. Eventually her tears slowed, and sleep tugged at her. She let go of the moose and slid her hand under the pillow, finding the eagle, and bringing it out to look at it.

Mama's lucky eagle that watches over her.

What if Mama got lost, thought Angelica? Without her lucky eagle how would she find her way back from Grandpa's cabin? Her chest felt tight at the thought of not seeing her Mama again.

Angelica jumped up and ran to the living room. Papa sat alone on his chair in front of the hearth.

"What are you doing up?"

"I forgot to give mama something. It's important."

"Well, it's too late now, she's left. You'll have to give it to her when she gets back."

"She needs it," Angelica protested.

Papa looked at her with a stern expression. "Angelica, go back to bed."

Angelica's heart sank, and her shoulders sagged, as she trudged back to her room, holding the eagle tightly in her hand. She stopped outside her door and looked back, wondering if she should try one more time. Angelica's chin dropped to her chest as fresh tears sprung from her eyes. She knew it would be useless. Father would only get angry at being disobeyed. She would have to wait until morning and hope Grandma would take her to Grandpa's cabin and give it back to Mama.

TWO DAYS later Angelica finally worked up the courage to approach Grandma. She held out her palm, revealing the little jade eagle.

"I took Mama's lucky eagle, and told her I didn't know where it was," Angelica said. "I have to go to Grandpa's and give it back to her. Without it she'll be lost." Angelica took a deep breath, trying to read the expression on Grandma's face, who barely looked up from the sock she was darning. "Will you take me, please"

Grandma put the sock down and looked up at Angelica. It was a simple enough question, but the look on Grandma's face made Angelica nervous - as though she was trying to think of a reason to say no. Angelica's lip began to tremble.

"Now, now, child, none of that." Grandma smiled sympathetically and pulled Angelica onto her lap. "I'm sure your Mama won't mind if you kept the necklace for now. Just until she comes back." As she spoke, Grandma tied the cord around Angelica's neck.

"But she needs it. Without it she'll get lost," Angelica insisted. Grandma stroked her hair and rocked her gently. Father came in the front door from feeding the dogs.

"What's all this then? Why are you crying?"

"I need to go to Mama. Please, will you take me?" Father's face got hard and his mouth tight. She shouldn't have asked him again. She held her breath and waited for his reaction.

"Your mama is gone. She won't be coming back." He said. The flatness of his voice, and the sharp finality of the words made Angelica's heart hammer in her chest.

She ran to her father and held the necklace out to him.

"She just needs this, then she won't be lost." Her father looked down at her, gazing at the necklace in confusion.

"I'm sorry," Angelica wailed. "I took her lucky eagle and now she's lost. I'm sorry."

Her father turned away from her then, picking up the poker and pushing at the logs in the fire.

"Your mother isn't lost. She chose to leave of her own free will. She has crossed the southern border in search of a figment of an old man's imagination."

"She did what?" Grandma grabbed father's arm and glared

at him. "How could you let her go? Nobody comes back from there."

"Don't you think I tried," Father was shouting now. He yanked his arm from Grandma's grip and strode toward the door.

"When has that woman ever listened to me? When has she ever listened to anybody? She does what she wants without regard to the consequences for the rest of us." Father yanked the door open and it flew against the wall with a crack.

"She's made her choice. We won't speak of her again."

"Anthony," Grandma cried, but he was already gone. Angelica's face burned, and the room seemed too bright. Her head was spinning. She ran to her room, crawling into the closet and curling into a ball. She didn't know whether to cry or scream. Her throat was tight and her whole body was shaking. She put her head between her knees and covered them with her arms, trying to sink into the comfort of the darkness.

Grandma came in, pulling aside the closet curtain and kneeling.

"It's all my fault," Angelica whispered. "I stole her eagle and lied about it, and now Mama's lost and will never find her way home. I'll never get to say, 'I'm sorry.'"

"It'll be okay," Grandma assured her, "we will get a ptarmigan and go to the tabernacle. If you offer a sacrifice for your sins God will forgive you." She wanted to believe her grandma's words, but the look on Grandma's face sent spikes of fear through Angelica's chest. She numbly allowed Grandma to help her from the closet, wash her face, and head to the tabernacle.

As Angelica stood before the altar the next day, and watched the blood come spraying from the bird's neck, a sudden realization hit her.

That should be me.

She couldn't shake the thought from her mind. She was the one who'd done wrong, the one who was guilty, not the ptarmigan. Guilt lay heavy upon her, mixing with the spraying blood, and the smell of burning feathers. It turned her stomach, and its contents spilled out, landing in the dirt at her father's feet. He frowned at her, displeasure in his eyes, and motioned for Grandma to take her away.

Grandma had been wrong - God did not forgive her, and Mama never returned.

Angelica watched and waited as seasons came and went, often going to her secret place on the ridge, and gazing across the landscape where the southern boundary lay. She searched between the trees, her eyes following imaginary paths her mother might have followed. She followed the lines of the streams as they wound their way through the valley, sometimes lined with lush green grasses, sometimes frozen and covered with snow. But her mother never returned.

It didn't matter how many prayers she prayed, or how many times she took a sacrifice to the temple. The blood of countless birds spilled upon the altar for her sins made no difference. God had not forgiven her, and the depth of her sin lay heavy on her heart. Years went by and the memories of her mother faded. What her face looked like, her voice, the scent of her hair, but the ache in Angelica's gut, the hole in her heart, that never faded. She feared it never would, and that nothing short of laying her own self down on the altar would erase what she had done.

THREE

"Here, this will help." Petra's voice startled Angelica, and she jumped.

"Oh, I didn't see you there." She took the canteen from his hand and used it to rinse her mouth.

She avoided his gaze. There was a time when they were kids that Petra was her closest friend. They'd shared everything with each other. Their dreams, their fears, the frustrations of a life where obedience to the law was the most important thing. They would run through the forest together, racing each other to the ridge, before flopping down on their back in the moss, laughing and gazing up at the bright blue sky through branches of aspen and birch. Angelica missed those days and regretted the way things had changed. Their interactions were so awkward now. There was a time when his presence made her feel at ease, but now her heart was hammering in her chest and her palms felt sweaty. He stood there, looking down at her sitting on this log, and she thought he must be as disappointed in her as her father now that he was a priest.

"What are you doing?" she asked through the lump in her throat.

He motioned to the pens. "I work here. Remember?"

She realized then how close they were to the animal pens. How ironic he had the job of caring for the sacrifices. The memory of the young boy who used to help her sneak out at night and free them, made her smile.

"What?" he asked.

"I was just thinking about how we used to open the pens and chase all the animals into the woods, and now here you are, in charge of them."

Petra frowned. "That was another time. I'm grown up now."

She wanted to tell him she didn't want to grow up; she didn't want to marry his brother, that God still hadn't forgiven her.

"Thanks," was all she said, handing the canteen back to him.

"You okay now?"

"Yeah."

"Okay, well, I need to go." he looked at her for several moments as if waiting for her to say something. Did he care that she was promised to his brother? Did he ever think about her? She wished she had the courage to ask him.

He picked up several cages of ptarmigan and, nodding to her, hurried toward the market square.

What a waste. All those birds, destined to die, and for what? Did God ever forgive anyone? Was it just her who was beyond redemption?

Is there even a God at all?

The only good that would come of killing these birds was it would keep people out of the untouchable camp. The untouchable camp was where those who were unclean were forced to live. They were unable to work, or hunt with the rest of the village, unable to offer the sacrifices that would make them clean. These ptarmigans could change their lives, could be the sacrifice those in the camp needed to be declared "clean.".

How long until Petra returned?

There was no time to waste. Angelica grabbed two individual cages and started stuffing ptarmigan into them. She could fit six into each cage. The birds obviously weren't thrilled being piled on top of each other but that couldn't be helped. She picked up the cages, took the nearest trail into the trees, and ran toward the untouchable camp.

FOUR

The untouchable camp was a grouping of sad looking wigwams in a muddy field surrounded by a fence. Empty ptarmigan cages sat forlornly in the mud near many of the homes, and children with hunger in their eyes poked at the ground with sticks. There were few trees to cut for firewood, and behind the back fence lay vast fields of muskeg. Those who ventured onto the muskeg quickly sank into the moss-covered bog. The mushrooms and beaver that lived there provided some food for the untouchables, but getting it was dangerous and difficult. Unable to hunt with the men of the village in the places where game was abundant, their meat caches often remained empty.

To remain ceremonially clean required Angelica to stay outside the gate and give her gifts to the gatekeeper. But what difference did it make? The whole village had always seen her as clean and righteous simply because she was the daughter of the high priest, but she knew it wasn't true. She was no angel, and she certainly wasn't righteous.

How unclean would it really make me to go in? It wouldn't

make any difference at all, she told herself. *Besides, who would know?*

The young man who came to take her gifts stared with wide eyes and an open mouth when she pushed the gate open with her hip and walked right in. A group of men sat on logs around the central fire with drooping backs and bent heads. One of them looked up at her as he passed a pipe to the man beside him. He watched Angelica without expression as she made her way across the mud. It was so unfair. All these people were declared ceremonially unclean simply because they hadn't been able to catch a white ptarmigan. Bad luck doomed them to be outcast and live lives of shame in this rundown camp. Why was there no mercy? Did God really demand such harsh consequences? With a lifted chin and new sense of determination Angelica marched up to the man and handed him a ptarmigan.

"Take this to the temple for the atonement sacrifice. Then you can hunt with the other men and feed your family." She watched as realization crept into his eyes. Wide eyed, he jumped up, and with a grin on his face he took the bird from her. He hurried toward his wigwam, holding the ptarmigan close to his chest so it couldn't escape before putting it into a cage he pulled from the mud. One by one the other men did the same, their faces transforming from downcast to bright and smiling. Several of them came back to hug her after securing their birds.

She kept two of the birds back and made her way to a wigwam at the rear of the camp. She'd watched her gifts being delivered from outside the gate many times and knew just where to go.

A woman with long straight black hair and bronze skin stood outside the wigwam.

"Hello Sarah," Angelica said. "How is she today?"

"The same," Sarah replied.

"Can I see her?"

Sarah nodded and opened the door flap. The dark insides of the tent were lit with an orange glow of sunlight filtered through the Moose hide walls. A small girl lay in the furs, her face pale, and her eyes shiny.

"Hello Eve," said Angelica. "Do you know who I am?"

Eve nodded. "You're an angel who brings me gifts," she said.

The girl's words made Angelica squirm. "Not an angel, just a girl like you," Angelica replied. She reached into her bag and pulled out the doll she'd bought. "I saw this, and it reminded me of you."

The little girl took the doll and gazed at it, smiling, she ran her fingers over the hair and skin. "It looks just like me," she said.

"I thought you would like it," Angelica said.

"Oh I do." Eve hugged the doll close and closed her eyes. Even this little bit of excitement had worn her out.

Angelica turned to Sarah. "Take these ptarmigan and go offer the atonement sacrifice for both of you. Then take Eve to the doctor. He will see her once she's declared clean." She pulled a pouch from her belt. "Take these coins. They will cover the cost of treatment."

"I don't know how I could ever thank you," Sarah said, tears in her eyes.

Angelica hugged Sarah and then made her way back across the muddy field. Most of the men had taken their ptarmigan and left the camp. One straggler held the gate open for her as she left.

"You are a saint sent from God," he proclaimed.

"I'm not," Angelica said. "I'm just a girl,"

"Oh, but you are," he replied, "and we will never forget what you have done for us."

Even as she denied it Angelica couldn't help but think

God had used her to do something good here. She smiled at the memory of the little girl with her new doll, and the sparkle of hope in her mother's eyes. Her heart soared as she remembered the grateful smiles on the faces of the men as they took the ptarmigan from her. The sun shone extra bright, and birdsong drifted in from the nearby forest. The mud seemed to sing of the promise of spring with each squishy step she took, and the ramshackle homes suddenly appeared quaint and homey, losing their sense of hopelessness she'd felt on her arrival. Whatever trouble she might get into for stealing the ptarmigans, it was worth it.

The priests considered these people unclean, but despite what the priests believed, Angelica knew they were just unlucky. It made her heart glad that she was able to bring them all a little luck today.

As Angelica turned onto the path toward home, she heard her dog Chugiak barking. He came zooming down the path at top speed, skidding to a stop before running circles around her, first one way and then the other. His whole behind wiggled with the motion of the large fluffy tail that normally curled over his back.

"Hey boy, how did you get out?" Angelica laughed, scrubbing Chugiak's cheeks with her hands, shaking his head back and forth. His blue eyes in their black mask sparkled with joy as he licked her face, but her joy was short-lived when she heard her father's voice.

"It appears you were correct, Donavon. The dog led us straight to her." Angelica stood still as her father, Donavon, and Petra approached from the direction Chugiak had come. Donavon had a sneer on his face, and Petra's expression was dark and stormy. Angelica's heart sank and her stomach rose toward her throat. Forgotten was the joy she'd felt only moments ago.

Father's expression was unreadable to most people, but she could tell by the hardness in his eyes, and the thin line of his lips that he was angry. "What are you doing here?" He asked.

Angelica wanted to blurt out how unfair it was to banish people for being unable to offer a sacrifice. Ask him what purpose it could possibly serve. Beg him to reconsider the treatment of those who lived there. But she knew it would do no good. Her father was firm and unwavering in his adherence to the law, and he had little patience for shows of emotion, or impassioned pleas. She knew he could see the heat in her cheeks that revealed her guilt, but she wouldn't let him hear the waver in her voice, or see tears in her eyes. She wouldn't let him see how his disapproval filled her insides with dread that bubbled like boiling stew. Clenching her teeth firmly together, and squeezing her hands into fists by her side, Angelica simply lifted her chin, fixed her eyes on the gray curls of her father's beard, and clamped her mouth shut.

"You've been in the untouchable's camp," her father said.

It was a statement, not a question. She looked down at her muddy mukluks.

"AND I DON'T SUPPOSE you know what happened to the dozen ptarmigan that went missing from the temple pens?"

Angelica remained silent, preparing for the lecture about being the high priest's daughter, of more being expected of her, of how she needed to grow up, and soon. Instead, her Father turned to Donavon.

"How will you handle this type of situation, when Angelica is your wife?"

Bile rose in Angelica's throat when she saw Donavon's look of glee. Petra's face was dark red, and his eyes were stormy. Angelica didn't blame him for being angry. Her little stunt could get him in a lot of trouble.

"I regret any trouble I've caused you," she said with her chin up, meeting Petra's gaze full on. Petra shook his head sadly and turned his attention to Donavon. She followed suit, and when her eyes met Donovan's steely gaze, she blurted out "but I am not sorry that I took the birds and distributed them to those in need."

Donavon's mouth turned up into a half sneer, half smile. "I'll tell you what I'll do if she is ever my wife. For her own good, I will declare her unclean." Angelica heard only cruelty in Donavon's voice. She shivered. If she were declared unclean she would either have to present herself for the purification rites or join the untouchables in their camp. Despite the alarm bells ringing out in her gut Angelica met Donavon's gaze with defiant eyes.

"I would prefer living in the untouchable camp to being married to you," He returned her gaze with a hardness that caused her to immediately regret what she'd said.

Angelica looked at her father, holding her breath while waiting for his decision. Her stomach churned and her knees wobbled. His expression wavered, softened just a bit, and Angelica thought she saw sadness there, regret. It was only for a moment though. The glimpse of the man who was her father now turned to stone, and she saw only the High Priest. He was the highest authority there was, second only to God. The set of his jaw spoke of one without weakness. His hard eyes held no mercy.

"I declare you to be unclean," he said. "You will present yourself for the purification rites."

Angelica did her best to hide the trembling that started in her legs and worked its way up into her chest and arms. She pictured herself, naked in the river, being scrubbed clean of her sins, while her father, Donavon, and Petra, waited beside the altar. She tried not to think about what Petra would be thinking at that moment. She'd known what the consequences would be if she was caught, but the weight of it hadn't hit her until this moment. Emotions raged inside her.

It's not fair. Those people needed help. I know that I deserve to be punished, and even though what I did was the right thing to do, I deserve a fate much worse. God should never have made me a priest's daughter. If I'd never been born my mom might still be here. As all these thoughts swirled through her mind, Angelica saw her father approaching and steeled herself. She wasn't sorry for what she'd done, she'd do it again in a heartbeat, but she did her best to hide all the guilt she felt for her many other failures from her father.

She hoped he couldn't see her turmoil. She watched him search her face, for signs of remorse perhaps. She gritted her teeth, determined not to let him see any. He took a deep breath, and just before he turned away, he said. "I suggest you use this week to think hard about what kind of person you wish to be. What kind of marriage will you have if you don't learn respect, and, most importantly, what may become of you if Donavon refuses to marry you?"

Angelica tried to hide the smile that twitched at the corner of her mouth. She loathed the idea of marrying Donavon, and if he refused to marry her, she would consider it a gift.

What would become of her then? Perhaps she and Petra ....

Angelica let the thought fall away. It was better not to hope, not to dream about such things. Then her heart wouldn't be crushed when they didn't happen. If there was anything Angelica didn't need any more of, it was disappointment, and dreams that would never come true. She thought of her mother, the fantasies she'd had of seeing her running to her, catching Angelica up in her arms, and spinning her around. They would laugh and embrace, and Angelica's mom would kiss her again and again. She'd always dreamed it would make everything okay.

It was never going to happen, Angelica knew that now, but still, a part of her refused to give up hope.

The tightness in her throat made it hard to swallow, and tears burned behind her eyes. Even if she were destined to be alone, Angelica would rather live out her days as an old maid in the untouchable camp, than spend one day as Donavon's wife. Hoping that nobody saw the storm raging inside her, she stepped past the men, and walked away toward home. She waited until she was out of sight to take off running, tears streaming down her face, into the forest where the trees spread out their branches to welcome her.

FIVE

The purification altar stood in a clearing on the riverbank. The giant spruce grew on an island in the middle of the river. The island was once a beaver dam long ago abandoned and filled with silt washed down from ancient glaciers. Vegetation sprouted up in the rich soil, and the river, relentless in its journey to the sea, moved around it.

The tree was the marker for the southern boundary. It was forbidden to cross it. The air beyond was believed to have been poisoned long ago during the Great Catastrophe, a time when the world lost its magic. All her life Angelica had listened to the elders telling the stories about it. How all of man's tools worked by magic, and how they just stopped working one day. The magic was gone, and men had to learn to survive without it. Some of the magic had left behind air that was poisoned. There were many tales of those who wandered beyond the boundary, and lost their minds after breathing the poisoned air that lingered there.

The eagle alighting from its nest, tucked high in the branches of The Great Spruce, caught Angelica's eye. In Angelica's mind he was a gatekeeper, watching with wide eyes all who ventured near. However, instead of warning her to stay away, always he beckoned to her, swooping low and turning toward the south as if expecting her to follow, and circling back again, ever patient, when she didn't.

THE EAGLE CIRCLED THE CLEARING, settling on a branch nearby.

Are you happy now? She thought. *I've hit a new low.*

As if in reply to her thoughts, the Eagle's cry pierced the air, bouncing off the mountains and echoing back in waves.

Angelica could hear Chugiak barking, as one of the young priest assistants worked to restrain him at the head of the path. Chugiak was strong and determined, and he wasn't used to being on a lead. The young man had his job cut out for him.

Another priest assistant brought two young ptarmigan forward. Angelica imagined she was the eagle, and that she could just fly away into the sky, and never return. Her father cut the first ptarmigan's throat and drained the blood into a bowl of water.

She would fly south, over the forbidden lands, and find a peaceful place to build a nest.

He dipped the second bird in the blood and water mixture seven times, then set it free.

Go, fly far from here, she thought, but the bird flew only a dozen feet before landing on the ground and waddling under a bush.

Yes, it is always the same with me. Longing to fly, yet frozen, unable to act. She had always been that way, but for what reason, she didn't know.

The eagle cried again, and it was as if the anguish of her soul echoed back to her off the mountains. Angelica tried to stand tall and hold her head up while two old women stripped her of her clothing. She bit her bottom lip to hide it's quivering and blinked away the hot tears that pressed against the back of her eyes. She locked her knees to stop their shaking. This moment would be seared in her memory until she breathed her final breath. The roar of the river drowned out all other sounds. The icy water sliced at her shins, causing gooseflesh to rise. The wind blew against her skin like a thousand tiny razors. The air shone with a strange light, and there was the taste of something metallic on her tongue. *Was this actually_happening?* It was as if she were standing at a distance and watching it all.

She longed to close her eyes and block it all out, but instead, she fixed her gaze on the eagle perched in a tree on the opposite shore. He stared back at her with his all-knowing eye. Her whole body was shaking now, her arms jumping and knocking against her sides despite her effort to pin them there. The eagle watched as she stood naked beside the shore and the women scrubbed her skin raw with their rags and aspen scented soap. Could he see where the rags couldn't reach? Did he know that it was deep inside where the true impurity lie? She lowered her gaze to the river as it moved steadily by. Flashes of light on the waves and the silver fish darting through the milky blue water pulled at her mind. Her mouth began to water as her throat tightened and her stomach threatened to expel its contents.

The scratching of the razor against her scalp barely registered, but the long dark strands of hair were sharp in her mind as they floated on the breeze, before landing gently on the water, and being whisked away downstream. How she longed to let her knees relax, give in to the weight of judgment, and float gently onto the water, sinking into the cloudy blue depths, where the silver fish would dart around her, and the current would carry her away. Angelica felt heat rise into her face, and the world began to spin. Her knees buckled, and she collapsed, landing hard in the cold sand, the icy current pulling at her waist. The two women had their hands under her arms and were tugging at her, trying unsuccessfully to get her back on her feet.

"Let me go!" Angelica imagined her body bobbing on the waves as it was rushed downstream.

The women pulled her from the water, the sand gritty on her bare skin. She could see their faces close to hers, brows furrowed, their lips moving, but no sound coming out. One of them kept tapping her cheek. The whole world was silent and shiny and cold. Then the sound came rushing back in. The roar of the river, the call of a raven, the wind in the trees, and the nasally squawking of the women.

"Angelica, come on, we need to proceed." The woman speaking began snapping her fingers in Angelica's face. After a few moments Angelica swatted her hand away.

"Leave me alone!"

The women continued to pull her up, until at last they had her back on her feet and continued with the shaving and scrubbing. She knew her father, Donavon, and Petra were on the other side of the screen put up to hide her naked body from their view. Could they hear the sobs that shook her as she gave up the pretense of trying to act brave? Knives dug into her gut and the heavy weight she seemed to always carry grew heavier.

These women thought they were purifying her, making her clean, but all they were doing was grinding it deeper in. Her soul was already black with it and her heart pulsed with pain. Angelica envisioned herself building a wall of stones, slapping mud between them to hold it together. She built it taller and taller until she couldn't see her father standing in front of her, looking at her with disappointment. Until she couldn't see the villagers or hear their tongues wagging as they discussed the wayward daughter of the high priest.

Until she couldn't see Donavon's hatred, or the light in Petra's eyes that used to shine for her, flicker out, as he saw her for what she really was. The mud was getting all over her, but it didn't matter, she would build the wall tall enough that nobody would see.

Passover was only weeks away. Then her father, in his role as High Priest, would venture into the most holy place, moving backwards through the veil with his incense. The smoke would fill the room and hide him from God's wrathful gaze just long enough to sprinkle the sacrificial blood on the mercy seat. The blood would hide the law from God's sight for one more year, sparing them all from judgment.

How she longed to burst into that room where it was said the Spirit of God dwelled, and beg him to tell her why he refused to absolve her of her guilt, why must he reject her over and over, why there was no mercy for her sins, but she knew it would do no good. If He really dwelt there, He would strike her dead for daring to enter the most holy place defiled.

Perhaps nothing at all would happen. She was starting to wonder if He were even there at all, did He even exist. Or was this all just some big elaborate hoax, a lie, carried with them from a world so full of lies that its very foundations crumbled in the Great Catastrophe they'd heard so many stories about.

By the time the women pulled a rough muslin gown over her head and declared her purified, her tears had dried, the knives in her gut had turned to heavy stones. Her heart was numb, cold like the river. She stared straight into her father's face when they removed the screen. His recitations fell on deaf ears and her face remained devoid of emotion. She watched him shake his head and turn away, walking back toward the village with his hands clasped behind his back. Donavon followed in the same manner. Petra looked at her for a long moment, sadness in his eyes, before he too turned and followed his fellow priests. Her things were handed back to her and Chugiak came tearing into the clearing, running ecstatic circles around her and yelping with delight.

She immediately put the jade eagle on its cord back on. This was the first time it had left her neck since the day after her mother left. She grasped it tightly, relieved to have it back where it belonged. Her other hand rose absentmindedly to brush her hair back over her ear, only to find bare scalp. She ran her hand over the smooth skin, her cold fingers raising goose flesh.

"C'mon boy," Angelica said, absentmindedly ignoring his attempts to kiss her and walking out of the clearing toward the ridge. "Time to make camp."

SIX

Angelica sat on a log, put her elbows on her knees, and rubbed her hands over her bare scalp. The wind blowing against her damp clothes caused her teeth to chatter.

"Better build a fire," she said aloud. At the word, "fire," Chugiak ran dutifully into the trees, and Angelica smiled, knowing he'd begun a thorough search for sticks. She peeled a handful of the papery white bark from the trunk of a nearby birch, then gathered some twigs and sticks from the forest floor. Chugiak appeared again, dragging a dead tree. Angelica smiled. "You silly dog. Who can stay gloomy with you around?"

She pulled the axe from her pack and soon had Chugiak's harvest cut into logs. It wasn't much wood and would likely burn up before the night was out, but at least it would help get her dry. As this was a spot Angelica frequented, that was about all it took to set up camp.

After a hot meal and another trip into the trees for more firewood, Angelica sat in front of the fire with a cup of hot tea in her hands. Chugiak lay beside her, gnawing on a bone. The aurora borealis danced above them, twisting and spinning in a green-blue river of light. She should be happy and content here in her favorite place, with the tall spruce trees surrounding her, their branches creating a protective canopy. The smell of earth and water and spruce was a balm to her aching heart, and the sounds of the forest calmed her spirit. It seemed funny that a hurt in one's heart, a hurt that was invisible, spiritual, could also make her feel physical pain. The hurting down deep in her heart was why her head throbbed and her eyes stung from tears.

I'm a failure.

Keeping a hopeless old man from being cheated had only earned her Donavon's wrath. Helping a sick child had only caused humiliation, banishment, and the death of more innocent creatures.

What is the point?

Perhaps she should break camp in the morning and head south.

Like Mama.

What would her father think?

She remembered what he'd been like after her mother had gone. Angelica had only been a child, but she'd recognized his pain. Once she'd found her father sitting on the edge of his bed, head hung down, giant tears dripping onto the floor. She'd run over to hug him, her own tears bursting from her eyes at the sight of his.

He'd pushed her aside, yelling at her, "get out!" He'd shut the door firmly behind her. He'd shut her not just out of his room that day, but also out of his heart. She'd been trying to get back in ever since.

The problem is, I'm too sentimental.

Hadn't Father always said so? She couldn't see a creature in need, be it human or animal, and do nothing to help. Even if it meant breaking all the rules.

The rules. Always, I break the stupid rules. What is wrong with me?

Chugiak looked up at her, his head cocked, as if he could read her thoughts. She rubbed his ears and smiled. "I'm okay boy, chew your bone." He dutifully returned to his task. Even picking Chugiak was breaking the rules, she thought. Of all the pups she could have chosen, she fell in love with the runt. He had been the literal underdog, his brothers and sisters climbing on top of him to steal all the attention, and almost all his mother's rich milk. Angelica had pushed all the other squirming, whimpering show-offs all aside and picked up the little guy, rubbing his tummy and laughing when he sneezed in response. It was love at first sight, for the both of them.

"Guess you're the exception to the rule, old boy," the one instance of her rule-breaking she could be happy about. Angelica sighed. This is who I am, she thought, a runt-picking, bird-freeing, unclean failure. How could I ever believe I could be anything else? She fell into her furs that night under a heavy weight - beyond hope, beyond redemption. No matter how many animals were slaughtered, no matter how many times they scrubbed her flesh raw in the icy, purifying water of the river, it would never be enough to wash away her guilt.

"I'm sorry Mama," she said through tears, fingering the figure of the jade eagle that hung around her neck. "I tried; I really did."

Then she drifted off to sleep.

SEVEN

Angelica awakened in the gray light of dawn. She heard the snap of a twig, the faint sound of footsteps in the dirt, then the crackling of the fire. Somebody was outside her tent, and they were stoking the fire. *Why hadn't Chugiak barked? Was it someone he knew? Who would risk becoming unclean by visiting her?*

She threw open the flap to find Petra leaning over the fire, carefully balancing the kettle over the flames.

"Ah good, you're up," he said. She was glad he'd spoken first. She'd intentionally not thought about what it would be like to see him for the first time after the ritual, when she had been forced to stand shamed before him. She climbed from the tent, pulling on her parka, and flipping the hood up to cover her bare scalp.

"Where's Chugiak? Off somewhere with Denali I assume," Angelica said.

As if they'd heard the question the two dogs bounded into the campsite and flopped down by the fire, their tails wagging in unison.

"What's up?" she asked Petra. "they will declare you

unclean if you have contact with me before I'm declared purified." Petra continued to stoke the fire but looked up at her. The worry lines above his eyes alarmed her, and she realized this visit was not just a social call.

"What is it?" she asked.

"Your Grandpa," he replied. "He's terribly ill. They found him this morning beside the river, wet and freezing. We believe he may have been there all night."

"Grandpa!?"

Angelica's heart leapt into her throat. The air took on a shimmery quality and seemed to swim before her eyes.

"Sit down," Petra said, moving to assist her as she sat shakily on a log.

Memories of her grandfather flooded Angelica's mind. He'd taught her and Petra to make drums from moose hide, how to build good strong sleds, and to carve skis. He'd helped them train their dogs when they were just pups. First to obey, and eventually to pull a sled. Grandpa's house was the place where she and Petra had grown up together. They went there every chance they could, learning the lessons that children did in life. Eventually becoming inseparable. It had always been a refuge for Angelica, a place she could be herself. Grandpa had been there through all the times she'd messed up. Never once had she seen disappointment in his eyes, even when he corrected her, his eyes only shone with love. She knew that Grandpa was like a father to her, as he was to Petra. She couldn't lose him, she just couldn't.

Would God be so cruel? Was he so angry with her that he would take Grandpa from her, just as he had taken her mother?

"I need to go to him," Angelica said, throwing her tea into the fire and heading to tear down her tent.

"You can't. The purification rite...," Petra protested.

Angelica ignored him, pulling the moose hide off the tent framework and folding it up to fit back into her pack.

"Angelica!"

"I have to go to him Petra. You've delivered your news, so just go."

Petra sighed. "Nobody can ever stop you once you set your mind to something." He grabbed one of the furs and began rolling it up. "Don't be surprised if you end up in the untouchable camp."

"As long as Grandpa is okay, it won't matter," Angelica said.

They worked in silence then, packing up the camp and dousing the fire. When they were done Angelica hoisted her pack onto her back and called to Chugiak.

"You better go," she said to Petra. "Before somebody discovers you in my presence."

Petra nodded and headed for the trail home, Denali falling in beside him. At the edge of the clearing he turned back.

"I think Donavon is going to refuse to marry you," he said.

"Good," Angelica replied. Petra met her eyes then, with an expression she couldn't read, but it made her stomach flip, the way it tended to do whenever his eyes met hers. She couldn't understand it and knew only that she loved and hated it at the same time.

Then he and Denali were gone, and she and Chugiak made their way to Grandpa's cabin.

EIGHT

Angelica paused at the edge of Grandpa's yard. His two-room cabin sat in a small clearing on the outskirts of the village. Moose Creek ran alongside the property. The tables near the dock where Grandpa could always be found, working with hides and sinew to make sleds, horseshoes, and drums, sat empty. The yard seemed unnaturally quiet. Even the dogs lay silent in the openings of their houses, only lifting their heads in curiosity when Angelica entered the yard, some of them thumping their tails on the ground.

The familiar sound of furs, lashed to their drying frames, and flapping in the breeze, calmed the ripples in Angelica's stomach. The door of the cabin opened and Miriam, the village healer, stepped out, tossing a bowl of water onto the grass, and hanging a wet rag over the railing. She saw Angelica, and a frown creased her forehead.

Angelica hesitated. Miriam could very well turn her in for breaking her exile. Ignoring the warning thought, she hesitated only a moment before striding purposefully across the yard and entering the cabin.

Grandpa lay shivering under his furs. The redness in his

cheeks concerned Angelica. She placed the back of her hand against it. It burned with fever. His lips moved with incoherent words. Miriam came back into the cabin; her bowl filled with fresh water.

"How long has he been this way?" Angelica asked.

There was no answer. Miriam stared at her, her mouth hung open, shaking her head as if she couldn't believe what she was seeing.

"It's just hair," Angelica muttered, running her hand over the stubble, and turning away to hide the heat flooding her cheeks.

"Oh, I'm not shocked, don't be ashamed child, it's just that, well, you look so much like your mother, with your hair shorn closely like that. When Hannah was young, she was always running off on some crusade to help the less fortunate; going into the untouchable camp and such." Miriam worked while she talked, rewetting and wiping Grandpa's head with the cloth and straightening his blankets. There was a pot of bone broth bubbling on the woodstove and it filled the cabin with its tantalizing aroma.

"Of course, when she married Levi she had to settle down, and that was the end of all those wild escapades. Or so we thought." Miriam stopped talking and looked quickly at Angelica, as if suddenly remembering who she was talking to. She wagged the spoon she'd been stirring the broth with at Angelica.

"Now, you visit with your grandpa for a bit and then you need to go. You're not supposed to be here, and I've got this well in hand." With that, Miriam picked up a pile of dirty linens and headed out the door. Angelica watched through the window as Miriam made her way to the creek with the laundry. Then she sat on grandpa's bed and took his old wizened hand in hers. His skin was hot and dry. He awoke momentarily and looked at her with glassy eyes.

"Hannah," he groaned, gripping Angelica's hand tightly. "Take the journal." He pointed a long shaking finger before letting his hand drop to the bed.

"No Grandpa, it's me Angelica," she said. His eyes closed again, and his head turned in such a way that it highlighted the two long scars that ran down the right side of his face from brow to chin. The evidence of an encounter with a bear from long ago.

Angelica loved her Grandpa's scarred face. It gave him character; tough but gentle, brave but compassionate. It showed that he had lived a life beyond this quiet village and the idea filled her head with dreams of adventure. Especially when he told stories of his journeys into the forest. Those scars were part of what made him who he was.

Angelica thought about the time she had gone into the village with him and a group of children had run away, screaming, when they saw those fearsome scars. Grandpa had played along, growling, and chasing them around the square. The children soon laughed as they ran, and finally trusted the old man enough to accept the treats hidden in his pocket. Grandpa chuckled at them and shook his head with a smile as they took their treats and ran away again, wanting to continue the game, but he simply waved at them before continuing on his way.

Now this same gentle man, confused with fever and convinced Angelica was his beloved daughter, was pleading with her to do something.

How can I say no?

She looked in the direction he'd pointed. Next to his old spruce rocking chair was his memory box. It was covered with a moose hide, and his pipe and tobacco pouch lay on top of it. The journal he'd mentioned must be in there. What did he mean by saying she needed to take it with her?

No, not me. He doesn't know he's talking to me. He thinks I'm my mother.

Grandpa's hot fingers wrapped around Angelica's forearm with a sudden urgency. He tried to sit up, struggling, and agitated.

"Get the journal Hannah. It's imperative you take it with you."

"Take it with me where?" Angelica asked, her voice almost as frantic as that of the delusional old man. "Why is it so important."

Grandpa's eyes cleared a moment and she saw the realization dawn in them just before they fell closed again. It was several moments before he spoke again.

"What have you done, Angelica?" he whispered.

Angelica reached up and touched her bare scalp before dropping her gaze to the floor.

"I went into the untouchable's camp," she said.

"Foolish child." The effort of speaking seemed to drain him, and he closed his eyes again, soft snores escaping his lips.

NINE

Angelica stood and made her way across the room to the memory box. She removed the pipe and tobacco pouch, pausing a moment to breathe in the scent of his tobacco. It smelled like cedar and fruit, a smell she associated with her grandpa, and the aroma brought a smile to her lips. She pulled the hide off the rough hewn cottonwood box. The lid was secured with a leather thong. Angelica loosened this and lifted the top of the trunk.

The first item inside was a pair of tiny moccasins decorated with beads and shells. Angelica wondered if they were hers or her mom's. Probably her mom's, judging by the design of the beading. Angelica carefully set them aside and lifted out a priest's robe. Grandpa hadn't worked in the temple for a long time, not since before Angelica was born. She held the robe to her nose, breathing in the smell of the soft leather and the musky scent of Grandpa. Setting this aside as well, she pulled out a book.

This must be the journal.

Its brown leather cover was old and worn. Inside, the paper was yellowed with age, but it was thick and glossy, and the script was well preserved. Angelica turned to the first entry:

May 12, 2468

It has been nearly 200 years since our people first came to Lake Clark and the rift between the factions has become irreparable. We've decided that those who believe in The Law will travel north and find a new place to settle. We have no idea what awaits us in the wilderness, but we will put our trust in God's promise to reward those who obey him. I will keep this record of our journey for future generations. We leave in the morning.

Angelica couldn't believe it. The entry was over 200 years old. Her heart burned within her. Where had Grandpa found this book, and why did he think her mom needed it? She glanced skeptically at the feverish form in the bed. Did he even understand what he was saying? She chewed her lip as she considered. Obviously, this was something important to Grandpa, and important to her mother. She had to get to the bottom of it. She sat down on Grandpa's rocker and continued reading.

May 13, 2468

We have not made as much progress as I'd hoped. Just getting across the lake with all our supplies has been a tedious process. There was some argument about taking the canoes up the system of rivers that feeds into the lake from the north, but there aren't enough canoes for everyone, and I am reluctant to split us up. I have decided that we will walk. It will take longer but whatever challenges await us we will face together. Those who disagree grumble and whisper, but they do not argue with my final decision. We camp tonight on the north shore and move on at first light.

ANGELICA TRIED to imagine what it would be like to pack up and leave your village and travel through the wilderness to an unknown destination. She thought about how she would feel if she had to leave this little village, nestled in the valley beside the Turquoise river. It would be exciting to be embarking on a brand-new adventure, but the thought also terrified her.

What evil lurks out there in the wilderness?

Where had that thought come from? She knew about the toxic air beyond the southern boundary. All her life she'd listened to stories about those who wandered away, never to return. Where had all those people gone?

Where has my mother gone?

No, Angelica didn't see how she could leave her village the way these people in the journal had done. What if her mother returned and found Angelica gone?

Assuming she does come back.

Was that Angelica's lot in life? To never answer the voice that called to her when she stood on the ridge? To never have any of the adventures she imagined in the moments before falling asleep? All to wait for an event that may never happen.

SHOULD she stay and wait so she didn't miss her mom's return, or answer the voice calling her into the wilderness and follow the Eagle when he circled away toward the south, silently beckoning her to follow?

Angelica sighed. She suspected the question would haunt her forever. Stay and wait so she didn't miss her mom's return, or answer the voice calling to her. She supposed she would just have to be satisfied with the life she was given. For now, it was enough to hear about somebody else's adventure. Angelica turned the page and continued reading.

May 15th, 2468

After Two days of walking in the drizzling rain, as well as several run-ins with the local wildlife, our people were weary and begging to stop, when we found ourselves on the edge of a ravine. On the other side were the most beautiful green fields. It appeared to be the perfect place to pitch camp for a couple days. After some time devising a way to get across the ravine, we made it to the fields. One step onto the lush green moss revealed our mistake. Underneath of muskeg. We had to decide whether to move everybody back across the ravine, or move forward, along a narrow path of dry ground, until we found a suitable camping spot.

We chose the latter, and it was late into the night before we found a suitable spot. The people were tired, sore, and grumpy. Some fresh meat or fish would help fill their bellies and calm them, but the hunters are too weary, and the rain keeps falling, so they do not go out. We will hunker down for the night and decide what to do in the morning.

"Angelica."

Angelica snapped back into reality at the sound of her name. Grandpa was sitting up in bed, doing battle with the blankets to remove the covers that were tangled around his legs. Had she overstepped by prying into Grandpa's things? Hoping he hadn't noticed her reading the journal, she slipped it under a fur and went to his side.

"You need to stay in bed Grandpa, you're sick."

"Bring it here," he said.

"Bring what here, Grandpa?" Angelica said, trying to sound innocent.

Grandpa lifted a hand and pointed a slim finger in the direction where the journal lay hidden.

"Bring it here, Angelica."

"There is some delicious bone broth here," Angelica tried, but she recognized the determined expression on her Grandfather's face. This was no feverish request, this was serious.

Guilt flooded Angelica. She'd gone through Grandpa's things and touched what belonged to him. Would she ever learn? She retrieved the journal and handed it to him with her head hung down, hoping he would forgive her.

Her grandfather did not speak right away. Instead, he took his time exploring the book with his hands, running his fingers over the soft leather spine. As his hands worked, his eyes closed and an expression of delight as beautiful as an Alaskan sunrise, blossomed across the old man's face,

Angelica did not know what to think. Her Grandfather obviously felt something very strongly about the journal in his hands.

"Grandpa?" She finally whispered, in a voice as thin and papery as the old man's skin.

His eyes opened briefly, but it was enough to reassure Angelica that he would speak when he was ready. After another few moments of silent reflection, he began his tale.

"I took this journal from the temple many years ago," his voice was surprisingly strong, his words spoken clearly as he once again ran his fingers over the soft leather spine. "It contains information vital for a journey south. Your mother didn't know about the journal and went beyond the boundary without it."

Angelica looked up at Grandpa's face. His eyes were sad, and his brow furrowed. He knew where her mother went. Hot tears stung Angelica's eyes. Why didn't he tell her?

. . .

"YOUR MOTHER DIDN'T KNOW about the journal..."

"Your mother...went beyond the boundary..."

TEARS FILLED ANGELICA'S EYES. How could her grandfather, the one person she trusted to treat her with love and kindness, keep information like this from her? How could he keep Angelica's mother from her?

"Grandpa, what are you saying?"

But the old man ignored the question. His agitation had returned, and he was more insistent than ever that the journal was a subject of terrific importance. "You must take it with you," Grandpa was saying. "Put it in your pack, quickly, before Miriam returns."

Angelica started to protest but Grandpa held up his hand and repeated, "Do it. In your pack, quickly, before she comes back."

With her heart hammering, Angelica took the journal and put it in her pack. How wonderful it will be, she thought, to sit at the campfire, sipping tea, and read about the adventures of these wanderers.

Wanderers like Mama.

The journal safely in her pack, she approached her Grandpa's bed. She closed her eyes for a moment and took a deep breath, quieting her racing thoughts and emotions, then took Grandpa's hand in hers and asked,

"You've known all this time where my mother went, and you never told me." It was a statement, almost an accusation, and a question, all rolled into one. Angelica realized she was holding her breath as she waited for his answer. She forced herself to breathe. It wasn't until she looked up and met his gaze, his eyes sad yet resolute, that he answered her.

"I could not tell you."

Angelica waited for an explanation, but he didn't offer one. She opened her mouth to ask, but he patted her hand and said, "I know you don't understand, but one day you will."

The old man leaned wearily back against his pillows. "I have longed to tell you, but also dreaded the day when I would."

"That makes no sense," Angelica said, shaking her head in confusion. "You longed to tell me, you couldn't tell me, you dreaded the day you would tell me. Why are you speaking in such riddles? Is your fever back?" Angelica went to put her hand on his forehead, but he reached out and gripped her wrist in his, his eyes searching hers with a worried frown.

"I was foolish. I tried to spare you. I knew that it was you God was calling to go. You, Angelica. But I couldn't bear the thought. You were just a small girl, so pure and sweet. I took it upon myself to go in your place, but all I accomplished was getting mauled by a bear."

Angelica allowed her fingers to trace the scar on her grandfather's face as he loosened the grip on her wrist.

"Because of me?" She whispered.

She sank down hard on the bed, her eyes on the scars running down his face. He'd never really told her how it happened, "You only ever said you got in between a mama and her cub and paid the price for it." Grandpa waved his hand in the air. "It is of no consequence, what is done is done. We must move forward now to accomplish the mission."

"I don't understand Grandpa, where am I supposed to go? And Why?"

Grandpa sighed and closed his eyes. "I have dreaded this day," he said, reaching for her again, caressing her small hand in his large, leathery one. "I've been afraid, because I knew that once I told you, you would go, and I was afraid you may never return. I hope you'll be able to forgive me. I realize now that there is no denying God's plan, and since it is His plan, it is the best plan. I can see that the path you're on now cannot end well. It is time to set things right."

Angelica couldn't think of anything to say. She simply gazed at the man who had taught her to mush and to care for dogs, the man who always told her how beautiful she looked when she put on her special garments for the celebrations of the feast days, the man who had taught her to hunt and to fish, and how to survive in the woods. He was more of a father to her than a grandfather and she loved him with all her heart. All this time he had been trying to protect her by not telling her the one thing she longed to know. Her whirling emotions threatened to rise to the surface, so she closed her eyes, breathing deeply until they sunk back again behind the wall she'd erected against them.

AFTER A FEW MOMENTS, Grandfather continued. "The Bible is incomplete," he said. "It was torn and there is another half out there somewhere."

What was he talking about? Surely, Grandfather's fever had returned, and he was once again delirious. She moved to get the cool rag for his forehead, but he stopped her, holding her fast with his grip on her wrist.

"There is a page kept secret in our Holy Book that is in the temple. It is the last page and it is of a new section titled "The New Testament". It starts with a book called Matthew, and the first line says, 'The genealogy of Jesus the Messiah, the son of David, the son of Abraham'"

"The messiah?" Angelica said. "But we've been waiting for him for centuries."

"400 years to be exact," Grandpa said. "The same number

of years the Israelites were slaves in Egypt."

"All this time, and he already came? What does it mean?"

"It means there is another half of The Holy Book out there, somewhere in the south, and it's up to you to find it and bring it back."

"Me? Why me?" Angelica pulled her arm free. "You are feverish and saying things that make no sense. The Bible is torn? I am chosen to go find the other half? The Messiah we've waited for has already come? Those things can't be true Grandpa, they just can't."

A gasp from behind her caused Angelica to turn. Miriam stood in the doorway, her hands over her mouth, staring at them with wide eyes. Angelica didn't know what to say. She sat frozen in place while Miriam gathered her things, giving them both a long harsh look before exiting the cabin with a snap of her head, and marching away down the path.

"She will tell your father," Grandpa said. "You must go now. Take the sled from behind the house, the small one. Chugiak should have no trouble pulling it alone. There are supplies already prepared in the shed. Go, before they come."

This whole thing was crazy. How could she just go, just like that? It was an insane idea. But Grandpa was right about one thing, Miriam would tell, and soon her father and his priests would come; and she wasn't supposed to be here.

Angelica grabbed her pack, then went to his bedside and took his hand in hers.

"I'll leave Grandpa, if you promise you'll stay in bed and get better."

Grandpa gave a weak nod. "I'll be praying for you, my child," he said, closing his eyes in exhaustion.

"I love you Grandpa," Angelica whispered as she kissed his forehead.

Angelica slipped out of the cabin then, called Chugiak, and made her way back to her campsite.

Just as she got the fire going, and was sitting down to wait for her kettle to boil, Petra came running into the campsite, breathless and flushed.

"They'll be coming," he panted. "Miriam told them you broke the purification rite, and that your Grandpa was speaking heresy. You need to go."

"Go where?"

Angelica asked, standing quickly to her feet.

"Doesn't matter," he said. "Somewhere they can't find you. Buy some time, come back when your week is up. It'll give all this time to die down, give you a chance maybe."

"Why is everyone trying to send me away?" She asked, starting to dampen the fire. She'd meant her whining tone to come off playful and light, but there was nothing playful in Petra's intense stare as he placed a hand on her shoulder and met her gaze. "Leave it. I'll take care of it. Just go. Now."

Her stomach flipped in the usual way at his touch, bringing back to mind the time when they were close. Her heart swelled. She turned away from him before he could see her eyes mist over with tears. She made a show of adjusting her pack, pulling at the straps, and rolling her shoulders against the weight. She murmured her thanks to Petra, being careful not to meet his gaze, and called to Chugiak, who reluctantly left off the happy reunion he was having with Denali to follow her.

Angelica and Chugiak took off down the path, she wasn't sure where she should go. Grandpa wanted her to go south, but that meant crossing the southern boundary. There was evil there, and the air was poisonous.

It makes you go crazy.

That's what they said. Was that true?

Mama went that way. Grandpa said so.

. . .

WHEN THEY REACHED THE RIVER, Angelica looked toward the south and the giant spruce that marked the southern boundary. The eagle alighted from its nest, circled around Angelica, and looked down on her with its all-knowing eye. Then he headed north, riding an air current until the trees hid him from view.

Angelica turned toward the north, following where the eagle led. A million thoughts whirled through her mind as she walked. With the thoughts came emotions, fear, confusion, anger, and pain. It was all too much, and she stopped and looked up into the sky. It was blue like a forget-me-not, with fluffy white clouds floating through. The dark tops of spruce trees framed it in, and the eagle glided across, the feathers of its wingtips spread like fingers against the blue sky. She focused on the eagle as it circled, breathing deeply until her thoughts and emotions faded back to where they'd come from.

Angelica continued north, reveling in the crisp spruce scented air, and the sounds of forest creatures, but slowly her thoughts crept back into her mind.

Angelica tried not to think about her conversation with Grandpa. According to him she should be going south, but how could she? It was forbidden to cross the southern border and she was in enough trouble already. Each time the thought she should be going south nagged at her mind she countered with another reason she shouldn't. Besides, hadn't she just been reminded of all the terrible stories people told about the air being toxic south of the boundary, poisoned by the Great Calamity?

Finally, her mind rested on the biggest objection of all.

Why would God choose me?

He wouldn't, Angelica decided. She wasn't worthy. In all

these years nothing she'd done to earn God's forgiveness had been good enough, so he definitely wouldn't choose her for such an important task. God would need someone good for such a mission. Someone loyal and obedient.

Maybe someone like Petra.

Just then, Chugiak let out a jubilant bark and made a half-hearted attempt to pounce on a disappearing gopher.

Angelica laughed as the dog first stood blinking in surprise at the hole down which his quarry had sprinted, and then padded over to her side. "You're such a good boy," she said. crouching to access his ears more easily, she pressed her face into his soft fur. "Maybe God should have chosen you."

But chosen Chugiak for what, exactly? A trip over the southern boundary to face toxic air and other unknown dangers? Then a new thought occurred to Angelica - what if this was some kind of penance? What if finding the missing part of the Bible would finally earn her the freedom from guilt she'd always longed for?

She stopped on the path and looked up at the eagle soaring across the sky, at the same time fingering the jade pendant she still wore under her tunic. Maybe she should turn back, head south. Even Chugiak seemed to agree. He'd been trudging along behind her, but now that she stopped, he perked up, wagging his tail, and looking back toward the south in anticipation.

"Not you, too?" she said.

Chugiak only wagged his tail harder and "woo wooed" at her.

"I can't," she said. Though who she was saying it to, Chugiak, God, or herself, she wasn't sure.

"If I'm supposed to go, there will be a sign, an obvious sign that I can't ignore. Until then, we go to fish camp." She started off, and Chugiak whined several times before falling in behind her once again.

TEN

Angelica stood on the bluff above the Kuskokwim River. The midday sun hung high in the cornflower sky. A bead of sweat trickled down her temple. Below her, the river ran like a giant silver snake out of the northeast, twisting and winding southwest toward the Bering Sea. Angelica had never seen the sea, but the story tellers spoke of it as an endless lake with no shore where a man could get lost and never be seen again.

From where she stood, Angelica could see the fish camps lining the southern bank all along the river. She recognized the wigwams and fire pit that were Matanga's camp. The familiar sight warmed her heart. Here, she could take her place at the cutting tables, and be one of the family. Here, there were no expectations, only love.

"Well boy, if we leave now, we should get there by dinner."

She scrubbed the big dog's head lovingly. Chugiak licked her face, his fluffy curled tail whipping furiously through the air.

Chugiak raced down the trail ahead of her, his apprehension at going north apparently forgotten in the anticipation of being at fish camp. Angelica smiled at her memories of him running in the sand with her and the other children and lying next to her by the fire at night. This place was just as much a part of his history as it was for Angelica.

The sky was void of clouds and a slight breeze blew in from the east, cooling the sweat on the back of Angelica's neck. The air smelled of spruce trees and dirt and spring-time. The feeling of her leg muscles stretching and contracting as she moved surefooted down the trail filled Angelica with a sense of power, and she almost forgot her worries for a while. Fish camp was a place where she belonged. She fit there in a way she never had at home. She had a feeling that once she got to fish camp everything would be fine, no matter how far fetched that seemed. If only she could silence the voice nagging at the back of her mind, reminding her that she was meant to be going in the other direction.

The sun was just kissing the horizon, filling the sky with streaks of soft pink and purple when Angelica and Chugiak arrived at Matanga's camp. The children saw them first and ran to greet them, leaving little footprints in the wet sand. One of the boys lifted the pack from Angelica's back, while the girls grabbed Chugiak's saddle bags. The smaller children ran across the beach, giggling and shrieking while Chugiak chased them.

"Did you have a good journey?" Asked Matanga's son Joe, hoisting her pack onto his shoulder.

"Yes, thank you and how is the Hooligan run this year?"

"More abundant than ever, we could walk across the river on their backs, they are so thick."

"That's wonderful. There will be plenty of oil for our lamps this winter. God has blessed us."

None of the children asked about her hair, although she saw them glancing at it with curious looks. Matanga's wife,

Kali'ma, looked up from where she squatted before the fire, roasting Hooligan on a hot stone in its center. A warm smile lit up her face and she rose, rushing to envelop Angelica in a warm hug.

"Angelica, I am so glad to see you."

After a dinner of hooligan, tundra potatoes and hot tea, Angelica sat in the glow of the fire, half dozing. Matanga's mom, Catherine, began to tell a story. The firelight lit her face with an eerie orange glow and danced in her black eyes. Her weathered brown hands moved through the air before her as if it were they who were telling the story, and her long gray braid lay in her lap. It brushed against the moose-hide of her parka when she moved, making a soft shuffling sound.

"Long ago in the time when giant shining birds flew above the earth there was a boy. That boy lived in a village with wigwams so high the birds had to fly around them to avoid hitting them, and so crowded that there was no room for the spruce tree or the aspen to grow."

Angelica had often wondered about this world with towering wigwams and a land with no trees. Most of the stories of the old world started this way. Angelica had always thought of them as fables, full of half-truths and myths, but now, after hearing her Grandfather's story, and reading the journal, she was beginning to doubt everything she believed. Could this land of giant shining birds and towering wigwams possibly be real?

Catherine's tale continued.

"The boy lived with his mother and father high up in one of those wigwams. They worshiped the One True God but had to do so in secret, because the rulers of the village were evil and forbade it. One day some soldiers in that village did terrible things to the boy's mom and she died. So, the father decided to take his son and flee to the wilderness where the villages weren't so tall and there was plenty of space for the spruce tree and the aspen to grow."

Catherine's eyes were far away as if she were seeing the story as it happened. Her hands wove pictures in the air, pulling up from the ground to demonstrate the enormity of the wigwams. The children sat at her feet, leaning forward, not wanting to miss a word.

"He took with him a copy of the Holy Book that he kept hidden in a secret place, but the soldiers chased them into the wilderness. The father and his son managed to find passage across the big waters on a fishing boat, but the little fishing boat was no match for the giant iron boat that spit fire and death. Before they could reach shore, the soldiers caught up to them. The father gave the Holy Book to his son and told him to hide it, but a soldier found where the boy was hiding, and he had no choice but to jump into the ice-cold waters."

Catherine paused and looked at the children with wide eyes. They all stared back at her, with their mouths hanging open.

"What happened to him?" one of the children blurted out.

As if this were the invitation to speak she'd been waiting for, the old woman continued with her tale.

"Some of our people were waiting on the shore and saw the boy jump into the water. They leapt into their kayaks and paddled out into the tempest, pulling the boy from the freezing water. But sadly, they were too late. The cold of the icy water took him."

Here Catherine paused again, as though to give a moment's silence for the soul of the departed child. When she continued speaking, it was with excitement and renewed energy.

"But the boy still clutched the holy book in his frozen

fingers. Those men carried the book across the mountains and brought it here - into the wilderness - and it sits in a special place in our temple to this very day."

"Oh," all the children seemed to sigh at once. Angelica remembered being a child and having the same fascination with the familiar story. It was a part of who she was, part of who her people were, and now she heard it with new ears. It almost seemed as if it were her own story being told, the one Grandpa was trying so desperately to get her to believe. How long ago had the truth been lost? Where was the other half of the book that sat in the temple? The pull in her heart to go find out hit her with a new urgency. Angelica felt like all the air had been suddenly expelled from her body. As soon as she could speak, she excused herself and headed to her wigwam, not wanting to hear the rest of the story.

As she pulled back the door flap she turned to look back toward the fire. Ma'tonga was looking at his mother with one eyebrow raised. Catherine shook her head and then looked straight at Angelica. She felt as if the old woman was looking into her soul.

There was no way she could know about the call. Could she?

The call? Was that what this was, a calling from God? Was she, like the little boy of the tall wigwam tale, meant to do a great deed for God? Angelica ducked inside and shut the flap, hoping to shut out the calling in her heart along with the knowing in the old woman's eyes. It was no use however, and she spent the night tossing and turning in her furs.

ELEVEN

Levi stood in his temple chambers with his hands clasped behind his back. Flashes of anger betrayed the serenity on his face. Eli, a lesser temple priest, stood before him, breathless, and stammering.

"Your daughter's gone sir. She left her Grandfather's cabin yesterday. He's been ill and claims he doesn't remember her visit; but the healer Miriam confirmed she was there.

"Did you check her campsite outside the village, to be sure she hasn't returned there? Levi asked, pinching the bridge of his nose.

"We did sir. It appears she must have broken camp right after visiting her Grandpa."

Rage bloomed in Levi's heart. He took a slow deep breath to control himself.

"And my mother? What did she say?"

"She hasn't seen Angelica either. Angelica never came to your cabin."

"Tell Donavon and his brother to find her; and bring her back here, she can't have gone far. Tell them to go to the fish camps first," Levi ordered.

"Yes sir." Eli bowed before hurrying from the courtyard.

Levi paced, a deep scowl on his face. He wanted to go after the girl himself, but duty confined him to the tabernacle in preparation for the Passover week.

Leave it to Angelica to defy me once again. She couldn't even comply when she was being punished.

He'd lead her to repentance, he vowed to himself. She'd taste the wrath due those who disobeyed, the consequence of having shamed him once again. He'd assure her punishment would prevent her pulling such a stunt ever again.

Donavon had already refused her as his bride. He'd come by earlier that morning, apologetic and full of regret, saying he couldn't marry a girl who wasn't pure. Levi heard the accusation in his words, accusing her of a far greater sin than willingly entering the untouchable camp, accusing him of being an inadequate father who couldn't control his own. He had failed to keep a firm hand with Angelica's mother, and now his daughter. He didn't intend to make any such mistakes again.

Levi pounded his fist against the high wooden table, causing the scrolls lying upon it to roll onto the floor and the ink to spill across its surface. He stormed from the room, shouting for someone to clean up the mess, as he made his way down into the cells below the tabernacle.

TWELVE

The next morning everybody was up early, drinking mugs of hot tea and eating fry bread with berries. Angelica put on her caribou skin breeches and boots, which were treated with animal fat to make them waterproof. She made her way to the river to join Ma'tonga and his family. Everybody had a job to do. Mom and Dad used the dip nets to scoop up the great piles of fish and put them into a pool the kids had dug in the sand. From there they took them to the tables for cleaning and separating into those they would eat, and those which would be used for oil.

Ma'tonga handed Angelica a net on a long pole. She waded out a little way into the water, being careful not to step on the slippery fish. There were so many of them they seemed to take up all the water in the river. Scooping out a net full of fish made an empty pool, which quickly filled again.

Angelica worked hard until lunch time, feeling the ache in her arms and back with each scoop. Her legs protested when she walked to the pool and dumped the slithery silver creatures in. After a quick lunch. Angelica was glad to be moved to the fish cleaning station. Fish guts didn't bother her, and it was nice to use some different muscles for a while. Ma'tonga's mom sat by the fire, stirring a giant pot, rendering the fat into oil. A multitude of empty clay jars stood behind her on the beach, waiting for the oil to fill them. There would be a great feast after Passover, and each family would receive their portion of the oil and dried fish to carry back with them to the village.

The smells from the smoke house were making Angelica's stomach growl as the sun began its descent. It wasn't long until the bell rang, and it was time for dinner. Once again, they feasted on the hooligan, tundra potatoes, leftover fry bread and berries, and mugs of hot tea. Nobody complained about the meals being the same. A meal of fresh fish was just what they craved after a long winter of eating dried or smoked meats and preserved fruits and vegetables.

After the meal, once again Ma'tonga's mom began to tell a story. This one was about a man named Joe. He journeyed deep into the mountain passes in search of food for his family, but he got lost and could not find his way out. Sure that even God would never find him, he built a fire, and determined to eat his last meal and die in despair. However, God sent an ermine to him, who led him out of the forest to his home. "Why did you despair?" asked the ermine. "Don't you know that even if you went to the edge of the world, God is there?"

As Catherine finished the famous last line of the story, she clapped her hands together for emphasis.

Angelica jumped at the sound and looked up to find Catherine's eyes on hers. Catherine gave her a nod, as if she and Angelica had just agreed to something. Then Catherine stood and hobbled toward her wigwam with Ma'tonga holding her elbow.

"Tomorrow Angelica will work with me," she heard the

old woman say. Just before she slipped through the flap of her wigwam, she looked back at Angelica and gave her a grin and a wave. Angelica felt heat flood her face. She didn't know what the old woman was up to. She just hoped it had nothing to do with the nagging feeling she was being called south by God.

The heat from the fire added to the burning in her face. Her full belly felt heavy and so did her eyelids. They drooped and her head pitched forward several times while the family continued to talk and tell stories around the circle. Finally, Angelica stumbled to her tent and climbed into her furs. Asleep almost immediately, she found herself once again within a dream.

ANGELICA STOOD on the beach with an ulu in her hand, cutting through the slippery silvery fish and pulling out the guts with her fingers. The work was easy and repetitive. She gazed at the southern horizon. The mountains that lined the Turquoise valley stood high against the bright blue sky; their tops still covered with winter snow that hadn't melted yet. Angelica knew that the turquoise river started in the crevices of those mountains, the glacial runoff feeding it on its journey south, the glacial silt it carried creating the green blue color of the water.

As she continued to cut the fish and pull out the insides, her fingers sticky with it, she found her eyes pulled again to the south, this time to the ridge that looked down on the beach where she stood. As she looked, she saw a man standing on it, beckoning to her. Her heart burned within her and she ran across the wet sand bar toward the man, her feet barely touching the ground.

Chugiak ran ahead of her, the wind whipping his fur as he raced up the incline. He reached the man first, who knelt and grabbed the big dog by the jowls, rubbing them and shaking the dogs head in a friendly fashion. A fallen tree blocked Angelica's path, and she looked down as she leapt over it. When she looked back up the man was gone. Chugiak stood facing south and looking back at Angelica.

"C'mon let's go. It's time." Said Chugiak in the voice of a man.

ANGELICA SAT STRAIGHT UP in her bed, suddenly awake. The morning light shone like a shaft into her wigwam, illuminating the furs that covered Angelica's legs.

"C'mon let's go. It's time for breakfast." Ma'tonga was saying from outside her tent. "Don't make me send the kids in there to wake you."

"I'm coming," muttered Angelica, throwing off the furs and pulling on her waterproof pants and moccasins.

As she made her way to the fire for breakfast the muscles in her back and arms burned. As she chewed the delicious tasting fry bread smothered in sweet blueberries, Ma'tonga's mom tapped her on the shoulder.

"You there?" she asked.

"Oh, sorry," said Angelica. "Did you say something?

"Yes dear," replied the old woman. "I said you will work with me at the fire today. Finish your breakfast, then come help me over there."

Angelica popped the last bite into her mouth and hurried to the fire as fast as her sore muscles would allow.

"What are you doing here?" asked the old woman.

Angelica hesitated. Hadn't the old woman just asked her to come over here?

"I'm helping with the Hooligan," she said. "You asked me to help you today."

"That is not what I meant," said the old woman. She stirred the pot with her giant wooden spoon and looked at Angelica intently, as though waiting for a different answer.

"I'm not sure what you mean," said Angelica.

"The Lord has called you to something else has he not? Yet here you are instead."

"How do you know about that," asked Angelica.

"Don't ask an old woman how she knows things, just accept that my many years in this land have given me wisdom that many will never know.

"Well, how can you be so sure that God has called me when I am not even sure myself."

"Has your heart not been burning within you? Have you not struggled to banish the idea from your mind?"

"Well, yes, but..."

"There is no 'but'," declared the old woman. "If the Lord has called you to go, you must go."

"If only there were a way to be sure," Angelica said.

"Let me tell you a story."

The old woman struggled to her feet and moved near Angelica, as close as she could get while still stirring the pot.

"Let me do that so you can have a rest, ma'am." Said Angelica, simultaneously taking the spoon and standing to relinquish the wooden stool she'd been perched upon.

"Please, call me Catherine," said the old woman, eagerly relinquishing the spoon to Angelica before settling in.

"There is a story in The Holy Book," she began, "of a prophet named Jonah..."

Angelica had heard the story many times before, but she remained silent while Catherine told the tale, moving her arms in wide gestures as she spoke. Angelica listened with respect as Catherine repeated the familiar tale of the prophet, who tried to run from God. It didn't work, and he ended up swallowed by a great fish, only to be spat out again once he'd agreed to go where God had asked him to go in the first place.

The lesson was not lost on Angelica. Catherine chose to

drive it home anyway, lifting a finger toward her as she spoke.

"So you see Angelica, running from God will do you no good. If you do not go, you will only end up in the belly of a fish, instead of with a belly full of fish." She poked that finger gently into Angelica's abdomen to punctuate her last few words.

"I mean no disrespect," Angelica replied, trying to sound as convincing as possible, "but if God really wanted me to go on some quest, wouldn't he have done a better job of making sure I knew it was his will? I mean, for sure, beyond all doubt?"

"Indeed, he will confirm it. In your heart, and in your mind, and from the mouths of weathered old women who tell stories by the fire, he will confirm it. Child, you must learn to recognize when he is speaking."

With that, Catherine pulled herself to her feet, leaning heavily on her walking stick, and made her way back down the beach, hanging heavily on her walking stick as she lumbered along to where her wigwam sat amongst the others. It was the last Angelica saw of her until dinnertime, when Catherine reappeared from her wigwam, joining Ma'tonga and his family for the meal and another evening of storytelling.

Angelica excused herself right after dinner, walking with Chugiak down the beach. The river lapped lazily on the shore, and Chugiak ran over the sand, his nose to the ground.

In the place where the river curved, driftwood had washed ashore, piling up into a tangled mess on the beach, Bleached gray by the sun, it made a kind of sculpture at the edge of the water. Angelica picked out a suitable place and sat down, staring out at the current. It seemed to move gently, rolling along at a leisurely pace, but Angelica knew that out near the middle, the current beneath the calm surface was strong and swift, and could easily carry a man away.

A beaver popped its head out of the water several feet away from where Angelica sat, watching her with a curious expression, before disappearing again beneath the surface. Angelica was just wondering where Chugiak was, when he came running back down the beach. She prepared for him to jump on her, greeting her with a wagging tail and wet tongue, but he ran right on past her.

Curious, Angelica turned to see where he was headed.

Ma'tonga was walking up the beach towards them. Chugiak ran circles around him before taking off again in Angelica's direction. When he reached her he skidded to a stop, standing close enough so she could rub his back, his tail wagging in greeting as Ma'tonga approached.

"If only there were a way to get him in the river with a dip net," laughed Ma'tonga. I bet then he wouldn't be so energetic after dinner."

"No, he'd probably crawl into the wigwam and be snoring before the sun set," said Angelica.

"Beautiful night for a walk," said Ma'tonga.

Angelica only nodded, looking out at the river and the mountains in the distance, purple against the crimson sky.

"You seem troubled," Ma'tonga continued. "I think it is time you told me what it is that's troubling you."

"Didn't old Catherine tell you?"

"No. She did not. But I can tell by her eyes that she knows something she is not saying. I thought it would be best to ask you directly. Perhaps there is something I can do."

"I doubt it," mumbled Angelica. "Unless you can see into the past and tell me what happened in another place centuries before we came here." Angelica moved her hand to indicate the land all around them.

"That I cannot do."

"Well then perhaps you can tell me how to know for sure if God is speaking to you, or if a "calling" is an actual thing or if it's just a fanciful whim."

"Now that is a question I may be able to help you with," said Ma'tonga. "What is it that you think God is saying to you?"

Angelica hesitated. How could she tell Ma'tonga the secret revealed to her by her Grandfather? It would be betraying his trust.

"I can't tell you everything," Angelica finally said. "Only that he wants me to do something that most people would say is crazy."

"I see," said Ma'tonga.

"Maybe I have lost my mind. Would God really tell me to do something crazy, possibly even reckless?"

"Well actually," began Ma'tonga, "God often does exactly that. There are many stories in The Holy Book where he asks His people to do 'crazy' things."

"Like Joshua and the walls of Jericho?"

"Yes, and Noah and the ark. Certainly, people mocked Noah and called him crazy."

Angelica mulled over all the stories she had heard of when God asked incredible things of His people.

"Asking Abraham to sacrifice Isaac," she added to the list.

"Exactly," replied Ma'tonga. "I would be so bold as to say, the crazier the thing you think he's asking of you, the more likely it is to be Him doing the asking."

Angelica knew that what Ma'tonga was saying made sense.

"Even if it means defying my father?" she asked in almost a whisper, afraid to say the words too loud. "Even if it will make him very angry?"

Ma'tonga sighed. "I cannot answer that for you child. All

I can tell you is that God's authority is higher than your father's, and if he is really asking you to do something, you must do it. Pray to him. Ask him to confirm it with another person. Ask him to give you conviction in your heart. Ask him to give you the courage to do as he asks. If it is Him who wants you to do this thing, He will be sure you know it."

"I'm not sure."

"Well, I'm going to leave you alone with Him," Ma'tonga said, standing from the log. "You spend some time talking to Him. I am sure he will answer you."

"Thanks Ma'tonga."

"No problem child, you know that I think of you like one of my own daughters. If you need to talk..."

"I know. You and your family have been particularly good to me. I love you all."

Ma'tonga placed his hand on Angelica's shoulder, giving it a gentle squeeze. Then he walked back down the beach toward the camp.

"What do you think, Chugiak?" Angelica asked the big dog who had settled in at her feet. "Do you think we are supposed to go on this crazy quest?"

"Woo-! Woo!" barked Chugiak with his nose in the air. Then he jumped to his feet and ran forward a few yards. He turned to look back as if to ask, 'What are you waiting for?'

"I'm glad you're so confident about it," Angelica laughed. She stood from the log, brushed the sand from her behind, and started down the beach after her dog. "I wish I could be."

That night, the dream from the night before was back, waking her sometime before dawn with her heart racing away inside her chest. Chugiak lifted his head, looking at her with an expression of concern. She rolled over and pulled the furs over her head. The lonesome sound of a wolf howling somewhere far away echoed through the night. She heard

Chugiak push the tent flap aside and slip out into the dark. Then she heard nothing.

The next few days went by in a blur. Angelica worked hard during the day, filled her belly at dinner, and then walked with Chugiak up the beach to the pile of driftwood to pray and think. She still didn't know the answers to her questions, and Catherine kept giving her knowing looks. Angelica avoided her.

One night, as she sat beside the river, Angelica closed her eyes and said.

"Lord, if you really want me to do this, please take away my doubts. Please give me the courage to do what you say, and please send another person to confirm it, so I can be sure."

When Angelica and Chugiak arrived back at the fire, most of the others had gone to bed. Only Ma'tonga's daughter, Panika, was still sitting by the fire whittling a stick with a bone knife.

"You're up late," said Angelica, pouring the last of the tea from the pot into her mug and sitting down.

"I was waiting for you," said Panika.

"For me?"

"Yes. God wants me to tell you something. It is strange. It makes no sense to me, but I won't sleep unless I do it."

Angelica's heart began to race as the girl spoke.

"It's a story I heard once," she said to Angelica. "My grandfather told it to me."

Angelica sipped her tea, trying to control the shaking of her hands. The hair on her arms began to stand on end.

"THERE WAS a man who took his Kayak out on the big water," said Panika, her long black hair reflecting the fire light and her dark eyes full and wide.

"And when he was out on the big water his kayak capsized and sank. So there he was, in the cold water where the icebergs live. 'Save me Lord', cried the man to God. "

Panika looked up at Angelica, meeting her eyes. They were full of love and Angelica sensed no judgment in them.

"God sent a whale who said to the man, 'Climb in my mouth and I will carry you to shore'. 'No,' said the man to the whale. 'God is going to save me.' So, the whale swam away. Then God sent a family of otters. 'Take our hands," said the otters to the man. "We will pull you to shore." "No," said the man again. "God is going to save me." So the otters swam away.

"Finally, God sent a great ship from a land far away, with men of a strange tribe in it. 'Get in our ship,' said the men. 'We will take you to shore.' 'Go away,' said the man. 'God is going to save me.' So the men sailed their ship away over the horizon. But the man was very tired, and so he drowned.

"When the man reached the heavens and stood before God, he asked Him, 'why didn't you save me?' God threw up his hands and said. 'What do you mean? I sent you a whale, a family of otters, and a great ship all the way from a faraway land, and you refused them all.'"

ANGELICA COULDN'T SPEAK, she only stared at Panika, who looked back with a smile in her eyes.

"That's all," said Panika "That's what he wanted me to tell you." Then she rose from the furs, nodded to Angelica, and went off to bed.

Angelica stayed by the fire long into the night, thinking about the story Panika had told her, Catherine's stories, and her own dreams. Still, she couldn't accept it. She just couldn't believe.

You don't want to believe.

Her throat tightened at the thought of crossing the southern boundary. "I am afraid," she whispered as she gazed up into the sky. The auroras were dancing tonight, and their bright colors reached down to her with fingers that seemed to beckon her, pulling her southward. Exhaustion finally got the best of her, and she stumbled to her tent, only to be haunted once again by dreams like the nights before.

The man was standing on the bluff and beckoning to her. Chugiak stood beside him, watching Angelica expectantly. She tried to turn away, but her body was frozen.

Suddenly, three figures appeared at the tree line and stood beside the man. At first, they were only silhouettes, barely distinguishable as people, but slowly they began to take the shape of a stooped over old woman, a young girl, and a man. As they moved alongside the man, Angelica recognized them. It was Ma'tonga, Catherine, and Panika. They all beckoned to her now. Calmly at first, but then more urgently, until they all appeared to be yelling at her, as if there was something behind her she should flee from.

She turned to look, only to see a giant whale closing in on her, it's mouth open, ready to devour her. She ran toward the bluff. As she got closer, the figures of Ma'tonga and his family appeared to melt, and then changed into three different creatures altogether - a whale with human legs and arms; an otter leaning on a cane; and a ship with legs that danced along the dry ground while wind whipped at its sails.

Just as suddenly they changed back into their three familiar figures before disappearing completely, like the popping of a soap bubble. The man alone remained, and he smiled at Angelica as she ran toward him. When she was only yards away, his smile changed and, morphing together with his pointed nose, became the hooked beak of an Eagle. The man's arms became wings, and then he took off, flying high above her, circling her as he slowly moved toward the south.

ANGELICA SAT STRAIGHT UP inside her wigwam. It was dark, but a full moon illuminated the furs, allowing her to see Chugiak looking up at her from his spot by the door.

"I wish you could talk. I wish I could make you understand. Everything we've known is about to change."

Chugiak cocked his head at her as she talked. Then he moved next to her, licking her face, his tail flapping against the moose-hide wall of the tent. Angelica wrapped her arms around his neck and buried her face in the fluffy fur of his neck. He waited patiently while she held him. Eventually the fear in her heart grew silent and she was able to let go.

"It'll be OK. We'll trust God to guide us through what he's called us to do."

With a few more flaps of his tail, Chugiak lay his head on Angelica's chest. Angelica tried to sleep, but the thoughts swirling in her mind and the mosquito hordes buzzing in her middle kept her awake. At last the sun peeked above the horizon, and the sounds of the morning fire being kindled signaled it was time to rise and face the new day.

Angelica ate her breakfast in nervous silence. Old Catherine kept glancing at her, a grin on her face. Ma'tonga studied her with concern, but the love she knew he had for her shone from his eyes, and his daughter Panika gave her a shy apologetic smile. She knew she had to tell them about her decision, but she wasn't sure how to say it. She chewed her fry bread so quickly that it got stuck in her throat when she tried to swallow. Someone handed her a mug of tea and whacked her on the back

"Thanks," she mumbled when she'd stopped coughing and could breathe again. She put the rest of her fry bread to the side and nursed her tea for the rest of breakfast, her stomach threatening to revolt against even that.

Old Catherine shuffled off to her wigwam with seemingly new energy, and quickly appeared again with a bundle in her hand. She sat beside Angelica, breathing heavily.

"You are going to need this," she said to Angelica. "And I want you to know that my constant prayers, and those of our family, will cover you no matter what you may encounter in the days or weeks to come."

"How did you..." Angelica began, but the Old woman rose, shaking her head.

"I told you, don't question the wisdom of an old woman. Come, we will anoint you for your journey before you go."

Angelica knelt near the fire and the family surrounded her. Catherine placed both of her hands on the top of Angelica's head and chanted in a sing-song voice.

"You shall walk, you shall run, with strength that is renewed; for like the Eagle you shall mount up. You shall mount up like Eagles wings, and the Lord Himself shall renew your strength."

Angelica had heard the chant many times before. It was sung each time the men were sent out to hunt, or on other journeys. She had heard that it had also been used in a time when warriors were still needed, but there had been no need for warriors in Angelica's lifetime, or for a long time before that.

Then the chanting gave way to prayer. Even though Angelica's head was bowed and eyes closed, she could see in her mind's eye the image of Catherine, with her hands on Angelica's head, and her face lifted toward the sky, illuminated by the sun as she prayed.

"Give her spiritual gifts according to your will, to aid her on her journey."

As Catherine spoke the words, a strange buzzing started

in Angelica's toes, and traveled up into her belly and down her arms. Her head swam, and her heart pounded in her chest. Air buffeted her face and she opened her eyes. Behind the family that surrounded her were seven glowing creatures. They appeared to be puffs of cloud, until she looked closely. They had forms and features like that of a man. Their bodies shone like the sun and fire burned in their eyes. They stood twice as tall as a man and held flaming swords in their hands. Their giant wings moved in unison, creating the air currents that buffeted her face. These could only be the angels spoken of in the Holy Book. Behind them black storm clouds swirled and swelled.

As Catherine continued to pray, more angels appeared and sped off toward the storm clouds, which separated into individual creatures not unlike the white ones, only they were black as night. These dark creatures fled in front of the angels. Cold spread through Angelica's veins at the sight and she froze, unable to move. Her heart hammered against her ribs, and the words Catherine was speaking seemed to be coming from far away.

"Don't be afraid," said a voice. It was deep and powerful, yet soft and kind at the same time. Was it real or only in her head? She looked around, but the others didn't seem to notice what was happening all around them. Angelica squeezed her eyes closed, and when she opened them again the world was back to normal. She breathed a sigh of relief, but she couldn't help but wonder what exactly she had gotten herself into.

THIRTEEN

"Angelica doesn't give her father a moment's peace," Donavon said as they packed. "She defies him at every turn."

Petra said nothing. He and Angelica had been close once. Her mom had left around the same time Petra's mom had died. He'd seen his own pain reflected in her eyes. How often they had sat side by side on the ridge, tears streaming down their cheeks. No words needed to be spoken, they'd simply sit and hold onto each other's hand, their fingers entwined. Together they'd grieved their losses when nobody else seemed to understand. Something about it had bonded them together, and though they'd grown distant from each other in recent days, the connection they'd forged still burned in his heart.

"You have a soft spot for her," Donavon said. "Do you know what I think?"

"Please, tell me," mumbled Petra

"She resembles her mother a little too much for comfort," declared Donavon.

Petra felt the muscles in his jaw grow tight and he gritted his teeth.

"She's never where she needs to be. She's always disappearing into the forest. Then there's that dog of hers. She is far too attached to that animal if you ask me. I heard he even sleeps on her bed.

"If that's how you feel, I'm surprised you'd even want to marry her." The words flew out before Petra could stop them, but once they were said, Petra was not sorry. He met his brother's arrogant gaze across the room. For a few moments, the tension in the air hung uncomfortably thick. Then a small smile broke across Donovan's face.

"I assure you, brother, if I intended to make Angelica my wife, once we were married things would be different. That mangy animal would live out in the yard where he belongs for one thing. Not only that, there would be no more running around in the woods. She would be a proper wife, or she would reap the consequences."

Petra continued his preparations in silence, though his actions were jerky and abrupt. He hadn't missed the language Donavon had used. 'If I intended', and 'she would'. Did Donavon intend to refuse to marry her? Part of him thrilled at the idea, but another felt frightened for Angelica. What would her father do if Donavon shamed him like that? Petra so desperately wanted to ball up his fist and drive it straight through the smug expression on Donavon's face, but he refused to give him the satisfaction. It never changed for Angelica, he realized, or for any of them. They were called to either obey, or suffer punishment, and God forbid there should be any mercy or fairness in any of it.

Is God so hard and unmoving that he feels no compassion for the pain his children suffer? Petra understood Angelica. He knew about trying to be strong, when you only wanted to crawl into your furs and cry. He understood the pressure to obey at all costs, and how the pressure to be perfect can have the opposite of the intended effect on a person. But Petra also knew saying any of this to Donavon was pointless. He was a true disciple of the High Priest, and was just as unmoving with matters of the Law as Levi. Petra believed in his heart that God was far more merciful than He was portrayed by those with the power on earth to deny absolution. However, he also knew better than to say so when he was at the mercy of those without it.

He wished things could be different, not just for himself, but for Angelica. To live under the threat of condemnation was difficult for him, and he wasn't a child of the High Priest. How difficult it must be for her. He said a quick prayer for her as he packed his things.

"You ready?" Donavon asked, his pack on his back, a walking stick in his hand.

"I am," replied Petra.

"Good, let's get her home where she belongs."

The two men set off along the river trail in silence, headed north to the fish camps. The storm had passed, and the sun shone, sparkling on the river. Melting snow dripped off the ends of the spruce branches. Two bald eagles circled high above, looking for a meal. The sights and smells of the forest were home to Petra. His body was strong and conditioned to walking, and the air smelled clean and fresh. He put his thoughts aside, and revelled in the familiar comfort that being in the forest brought him.

The sun touched the horizon when they topped a rise. The entire valley was spread out before them. They could see the smoke from the fires of the fishermen and their families.

"They are several hours away. We'll camp here." said Donavon.

Donavon crawled into his furs shortly after dinner. His snores soon drifted over the campsite. Petra lay awake late into the night, thinking of Angelica, and watching the bands of color paint the sky with the Aurora's light.

FOURTEEN

Angelica skirted around the outside of the village, stopping at the edge of her own yard. She squatted behind a bush and looked for signs of anyone being around. Thick gray smoke rose from the chimney. Grandma must be using the stove. Angelica settled in to wait, sitting cross legged on a patch of squishy moss. Chugiak took off through the trees chasing scents. The dogs in the yard looked her way with curious expressions. Their ears stood at attention, but they didn't bark.

Many times before, Angelica had come out here to sit on this spot, sometimes to be alone, but most often to avoid her father. Would this be the last time she would sit here, looking at the cabin from the outside, while life went on in the inside? It always seemed the right place to be, out here on her own looking in. Even when she was inside, she still felt like she was on the outside anyway.

Eventually the smoke from the fireplace thinned to a tendril, and a few minutes later her Grandma hurried from the yard, carrying a woven basket covered by a patchwork cloth.

She must be bringing food to one of her friends.

Once Grandma disappeared around the bend in the trail, Angelica slipped out of her hiding place, hurried across the yard, and entered the cabin.

On the table was a plate of leftover fry bread, dried fish, and some caribou jerky. Baskets of root vegetables sat nearby. *Thanks, Grandma,* thought Angelica as she grabbed the plate and emptied it into a sack, along with some of the vegetables. Then she went into the pantry and took out several handfuls of pemmican and added them to the sack also. When she was done in the kitchen she went to her room and repacked her pack. She expertly fit everything she needed in with just a small amount of space to spare.

The pack she'd made with her Grandpa several years ago was still in relatively good shape, and she was sure it would last well on the journey. As she stood at the front door, she looked around the house she'd lived in her whole life. There was the main room with the fireplace where Father would sit reading long into the night, and the kitchen where Grandma and she would prepare the meals or sit and talk over hot cups of tea in the dark winters. Angelica and her father were often like fire and ice, but she loved him, and there were fond memories in this cabin. She took a picture in her mind that she hoped would see her through whatever lay ahead.

ONCE SHE WAS DONE inside the house, Angelica headed to the storage shed. She filled Chugiak's saddle bags with dog food, several pairs of mittens for his paws, his jacket for subzero weather, and some lines and harnesses. She put the saddle bag back on Chugiak, and then they slipped into the woods, skirting the village once again, and making their way to Grandpa's cabin. She needed to talk to him about the angels she'd seen. Plus, she had some questions for him about the journal entries, things she needed to understand more clearly before she went off on her quest.

Grandpa was in the yard, scraping a moose hide with a long bladed knife. He looked up when he heard Angelica and Chugiak coming down the path. Then he hurried to his cabin, went inside, and quickly reemerged with a package wrapped in moose hide.

"I have made this ready for you," Grandpa said, handing it to Angelica.

"What is it?"

"Just a few supplies."

Grandpa looked up at the sky, and turned to peer at the eastern horizon.

"A snowstorm is coming," he said. "I have also prepared a pair of skis for you to use.

"The sun is shining," Angelica protested.

"Yes, for now, but trust me, it is going to snow soon, and God himself will cover your tracks from those who would wish to stop you going on this journey." Grandpa put the skis and poles next to Angelica's pack by the back gate.

"Come inside and have a meal with me. When the first snowflakes fly it will be time for you to leave."

ANGELICA SAT across from her Grandpa with her belly full of moose stew, and a mug of hot tea in her hands. Angelica told him of her dreams, and the vision she'd had during Catherine's prayer. Grandpa spoke many words to her, answering her questions, and offering wisdom for the journey. It was all so overwhelming, and when she looked out the window, trying to absorb it all, she saw that the sunny blue sky had slowly filled with gray clouds that got steadily darker by the minute.

Grandpa warned her to be cautious of wild animals and

brought different parts of the journal to her attention to help guide her. The nervousness in her stomach kept her from being able to focus fully on what he was saying, though she tried her best to listen attentively.

"Angelica? Are you listening," her grandfather asked in exasperation?

"What? I'm Sorry Grandpa, I'm just so nervous."

"Well listen to me carefully now. You must not miss this." He turned to the last pages of the journal, on which a rudimentary map was drawn.

"The journal writer made a map!" Angelica exclaimed.

"No," Grandpa said. "That was me. I tried to visualize the journey through the journal entries. I prayed while I was doing it, that the map would be accurate, but I cannot guarantee it."

Grandpa pulled at his beard for several moments. Finally, he placed the journal in Angelica's hands and said. "Follow the map, but always compare it with the journal entries and what you see around you. If all else fails pray for God to send a guide. I believe the scripture promises God will send a guide to His people. If I am right, and it's already happened, then I have to believe that guide is also available to us."

"What kind of guide? How will I know it is the one from God?" asked Angelica.

"You will need to have faith," said Grandpa. "And stay in constant communication with Him. Perhaps the angels you saw will guide you, or perhaps it is the eagle in your vision. Don't forget, I will be here praying for you every second you are gone." He kissed Angelica on the top of her head. A single snowflake drifted down from the sky and landed on the porch railing outside the window.

"It is time," Grandpa said.

Angelica held tight to her Grandpa as they hugged their good-byes by the back gate. Would she ever return to this village? Would she ever see this precious old man again? She wasn't sure so she held him extra-long, committing to memory the feel of his beard on her cheek, and the smell of woodsmoke mixed with leather and pipe tobacco. She soaked in the feel of his arms around her and the rhythm of his breathing.

"I love you Grandpa," she whispered.

"I love you too Granddaughter," he replied, and a single tear slid down the scarred side of his face.

A BANGING from the front of Grandpa's cabin stopped Angelica in her tracks. Grandpa motioned for her to go and turned to hurry toward the sound. As he rounded the corner of the cabin, she heard a voice call loudly, "You are accused of blasphemy and will stand trial on the day after Pentecost." Angelica rushed back into the yard, going around the far side of the cabin.

"Search his cabin." It was Donavon's voice. Angelica stopped, pressing her back against the wall. "The healer said the journal was in a box near the hearth."

Angelica tried to breathe evenly, but panic set in. It stole the breath from her body and doubled her over. She sucked in deep gulps of air until the tightness in her chest eased, and she caught her breath. She tried to decide what to do next. There had to be some way to help her Grandpa.

Loud voices carried from the front yard. Angelica snuck over and peered around the edge of the cabin. Donavon had pulled her grandfather's crate out of the cabin and was dumping its contents onto the ground. The little moccasins lay topside down in a puddle, and one of the guards stepped on them on his way back inside, grinding them into the mud. Angelica clenched her fists. She wanted to go out there and scream at them all to leave her Grandpa be, to stop touching his things, but she knew that would do no good. If Donavon saw her, there was no telling what he would do. He might even go looking for her pack and search it for the journal. She needed to get herself, and the journal, away from here. She would go to the ridge and then decide what to do. She turned to sneak back around the cabin.

"Oh," she gasped as she collided with a Caribou skin clad chest. She lifted her head to find Petra looking down at her with concern in his eyes. She tugged her hat down further over her missing hair and ducked her head to hide the heat in her face.

"Angelica, I'm sorry. I didn't mean to startle you." He hesitated a moment before continuing. "You should go from here."

"It's not right Petra." She whispered. "I am going to go talk to my father. He has to see that this isn't right." Angelica felt so helpless. She wanted to shout, but she was afraid of being heard by the others.

"Angelica please," said Petra. "I know you think you need to fight everyone else's battles, but just this once, think of yourself. Go home and stay out of this one for your own sake."

"What has happened to you," Angelica snapped. "What happened to the boy who used to sneak into the temple pens to free the ptarmigan and moose calves? Where is the boy who believed in justice as strongly as I did?"

Petra reached out and put his hands on Angelica's arms. "He grew up Angelica, and I pray for your sake, that you will do the same."

Angelica yanked her arms away and stalked by Petra without saying a word. She picked up her pack, called to Chugiak and strode into the woods.

"Grow up!" She spat when they were out of hearing

distance. "Can you believe he said that? Grow up! Why would I want to do that, and turn into a stick in the mud like him?"

Chugiak lifted his eyebrows at Angelica, his tongue hanging from his mouth as he trotted along beside her. After stomping through the woods for some ways, Angelica began to calm down. By the time she reached the ridge, she was clear headed enough to sit down and think about what in the world she was going to do now.

FIFTEEN

The clouds hung low in the sky and snow drifted lazily to the ground. Angelica's stomach twisted within her as she paced back and forth along the ridge.

The snow is what Grandpa had been counting on to cover her tracks.

Grandpa.

She pictured him alone in a room below the tabernacle. In her mind's eye, he was shivering, huddled in a dark corner, still weak from his illness. How could she just leave him? There had to be something that she could do. But what?

This is all just a big mistake.

Grandpa wasn't spreading heresies; he was trying to get people to see the truth. If she went to her father with what she knew about the other half of the Bible, and Angelica's calling to retrieve it, would he help her grandfather? Perhaps if she showed him the journal, and explained the things grandpa had found in the scriptures, her Father might persuade the high council to let Grandpa go. He was the high priest, if anybody should be able to understand what was written in the scriptures, it was him.

Angelica left her pack and Chugiak at the ridge. She hurried through the snow toward the temple in search of her father. Nobody paid any attention to Angelica, assuming she was just another person scrambling to get last minute preparations in place for the sabbath.

I'll check at the temple first, thought Angelica, hurrying around a bend that led into the back of the square. As she approached the front corner of the temple, Angelica heard her father's voice.

"Did you search the yard and his storage shed," her father said.

"Yes sir." It was Donavon's voice. "I hesitate to suggest it sir, but Angelica was there before we arrived. The old man thought it was her knocking, and asked why we were back so soon. He used her name"

"And you think she may have the journal?"

"I'm sorry sir, but I think it is a definite possibility."

"Find her. Bring her to the temple. Search her bags. Search her room."

"Sir, she could face the same fate as her Grandfather, if we find she has it."

"Do it. The Law and our people are my first responsibility. I will not allow sentimentality to interfere. Now, Go."

Angelica pressed her back up against the wall. She lifted her eyes and watched the tops of the trees swaying against the perfect blue sky. The familiar sound of the river roared in the background. She couldn't think, she couldn't breathe, something heavy wrapped itself around her chest, and she clamped her hand over her mouth to muffle the sob that pushed to be let out.

Angelica had always known that her father was a hard man, a serious man who rarely laughed or smiled, but this, this was something she'd never imagined. Did he really not care if she lived or died? Did his duties to the tabernacle really matter to him more than her? She'd just heard the evidence with her own ears, and yet her whole being wanted to reject it. How could a father be so unfeeling toward his own child? She heard the heavy door close indicating her father had gone back into the tabernacle.

What am I going to do now?

She longed to speak to her Grandfather. He would know what she should do. But how? An idea popped into her head and she hurried toward the animal pen, where Petra sat with a moose calf in his lap.

~

THE CALF in Petra's lap bellowed for his mother. Petra offered a skin of milk, trying unfruitfully to satisfy him.

"C'mon boy," he coaxed, but the calf only bellowed louder. Petra sighed. What was the point? The poor creature's life would be over tomorrow. He pushed the calf away and stood. He was determined not to think about the fate of the little guy, nor that of the other animals he was assigned to care for. It would do no good to get attached, only to deliver them over for the sacrificial altar. Petra brushed the dirt from his breeches and moved to leave.

The Moose cow's voice, calling back to her calf, echoed through the trees. Petra stopped, and looked down again at the pitiful calf. His mama wasn't far away, and she wouldn't stay away with her baby putting up such a fuss. Petra knew she would do whatever it took to get him back, most likely destroying the pen in the process.

The calf jumped up on gangly legs and wobbled toward the fence, wailing all the louder. Petra picked him up. He kicked and squirmed, but Petra held him firmly as he made his way out the gate and into the forest. It was almost sunset, and everybody was in their homes preparing for the Sabbath. There was little chance of being seen, but Petra hurried anyway.

The calf cried louder as the sounds of his mom got closer. Then, there she was, standing in the path, head down, snorting, and kicking at the ground. Petra quickly put the calf down and backed away. The calf ran to his mom and scrambled beneath her back legs in search of his dinner. The cow continued to snort and stomp, a warning that needed no translation.

Petra backed away a good distance, and then turned and hurried back. As he walked out of the woods, Angelica was there, leaning on the pen rail with her arms crossed. Petra tried to ignore the victorious grin on her face, but he knew he was busted.

"Grew up, did he?" Angelica said.

"What are you doing here Angelica?" Petra asked, trying not to look at her. He picked up the skin of milk and tucked it into his belt. He could feel the heat on his face and hoped it was too dark for Angelica to notice. Her grin said otherwise, but it must have also made her forget her missing hair for a moment, because she pulled the hat from her head. Getting busted was worth it, just to see Angelica's guard down, if only for a moment.

"If you want to pretend you didn't just set that calf free, I'll play along." Angelica approached, put her face close to his and whispered. "I promise I won't tell anybody, but I need you to do something for me."

"What?" Petra's knees were suddenly just as wobbly as those of that baby moose calf, and he was not sure if it was because she was mere inches from him, or if it was because he wondered what crazy things she would require of him.

There was no way he could set the other animals free. It would never go unnoticed. He knew his answer would disappoint Angelica, so he steeled himself, and waited for the question.

"I need you to take this message to my Grandpa for me," she said.

That was not the question he'd expected. He stared at her for a long awkward moment before he realized she was trying to hand him something.

Petra took the rolled-up piece of birch bark from her hand.

"I can bring it to him with his breakfast in the morning," Petra said, relieved at the relatively easy task.

Her smile turned to a frown. She twisted her cap in her hands. "It can't wait till morning. I need an answer tonight."

"I can't Angelica. It's almost the Sabbath, and if I don't leave now, I won't make it home in time." Petra hated telling her no, and even as the words left his mouth, his mind worked to figure out some way to do what she asked, but it was impossible.

ANGELICA KNEW she'd asked the impossible, but she'd had to ask anyway. Petra was right, there was no time. She needed to decide right now what she would do.

She couldn't go home, and she couldn't even stay in the village. It was only a matter of time before the temple guards found her, and if that happened, she wouldn't be able to help her grandpa. The only hope she had of proving his innocence was to finish the quest.

"Tell my grandpa I won't let him down." She didn't meet Petra's eyes. She just turned and ran into the woods before he could reply. As she took the path out of the village, she heard Petra calling her name. She didn't look back. The snow was falling thick and fast, and by the time she'd made it to the ridge, it had already covered her tracks.

SIXTEEN

The low hanging clouds obscured the normally beautiful view from the ridge. When Angelica closed her eyes, she saw it the way it looked on a clear day. She could see the mountains standing tall, their peaks topped with white; the blue tinted glaciers tucked into their crevices. The glacial runoff was the source of the Turquoise river that snaked through the valley, which glowed milky blue in the sunlight. She saw the deep green spruce trees, and white barked aspen, and the wildflowers that painted a pop of color against the green among the scattered ponds and streams.

She could see the giant spruce on the island that marked the southern boundary, and the eagle that lived in its branches, flying with its wings spread wide against the sky. The feathers, like fingers at the tips, fluttering in the wind.

Angelica pulled up the hood of her parka and tucked in her scarf. She adjusted her fur mittens for what seemed like the hundredth time, and swallowed the lump in her throat. After adjusting the heavy pack on her shoulders, she peered at the eastern sky where dark clouds billowed and rolled.

Chugiak stood in his harness, his curled tail wagging furiously. He yipped and barked while he waited for her to attach herself to the traces. He couldn't understand they may never come back to this valley. Otherwise, perhaps he too, would hesitate and wonder like Angelica, if leaving was the right decision.

Chugiak looked back at her, his blue eyes bright in their black mask, waiting for her command. Angelica pulled her mittens off and wiped her hands on her parka. She fumbled with the lines, trying to get her trembling fingers to cooperate. Chugiak lifted his nose to the sky and howled in impatient protest.

"Sorry boy, I'm almost ready," said Angelica.

Angelica closed her eyes and took a deep breath. Then she straightened her skis and called out. "Hike!"

Angelica's skis swished against the slushy snow. Her leg muscles ached as she pushed through the thick soupy mixture. Though the wind swirled around them in icy gusts, Angelica was counting on the snow to cover their tracks.

They reached the river in good time despite the slush. The milky turquoise water tumbled over rocks and fallen trees. Chunks of ice from the spring thaw raced south with the current, pausing only when they got stuck in the eddies. There they would spin until being sucked back into the current again. The familiar rushing of the water, the briny smell of it, and the silence of the winterfall, eased the churning in Angelica's stomach.

When they reached the giant spruce, she stopped and looked back. Normally, thin columns of smoke could be seen rising into the sky from each individual chimney, and one bigger one from the sacrificial fire inside the Tabernacle. But today it was impossible to see beyond a few dozen yards.

Angelica imagined her father inside the Holy Place, carrying out his duties as high priest, holding the scrolls containing the Law of Moses in his hands, not knowing his only child was, at this moment, crossing the southern boundary. She would do so in direct disobedience to the directives handed down by the high council since the first settlers arrived here 400 years ago. Would her father care if she never returned, or would it be a relief to him to have her gone? Would he be glad to be rid of the constant disappointment, not to need to deal any longer with the shame she brought upon him? Based on the conversation she'd overheard; she couldn't help but think he would be.

How often she had failed to be the daughter he expected her to be.

Yes, Angelica decided, once he got over his anger, her disappearance would be a relief to him. She shuddered to think of how angry he would become. Shaking the thought from her mind, she turned to face her destiny. A destiny that would take her through a wilderness that terrified her, to complete a task that seemed impossible. No matter what she had to endure, she would do so for a chance to save her grandpa and restore the Holy Book.

She imagined the eagle alighting from his nest and soaring across the sky toward the south, leading her into her uncertain future. She looked up to find him watching her from a nearby branch. He almost seemed to be waiting for her.

"Okay, let's go," she said.

At her words, the majestic bird spread his wings and took off into the sky, disappearing into the snow and clouds.

SEVENTEEN

"I am sorry to disturb you sir." Eli bowed, waiting for the High Priest to respond.

"Yes, what is it?" Levi waved him into the room. The scroll of the Law was unrolled on the table, and a candle sputtered next to it, doing little to dispel the gloom. Levi looked expectantly at Eli.

"The men have returned from the north."

"Good, bring my daughter to the gate. I will speak to her there." Levi returned to his scroll.

Eli looked down at his feet, shuffling.

"What is it?" Levi scowled.

"I'm sorry sir, but they didn't find Angelica."

Levi clenched his fists and his eyes flashed. He stared at the priest. He was stooped and gray. His robes hung limply on his thin frame. but he stood stoically under Levi's scrutiny.

"Tell them to question her grandfather more thoroughly."

Eli turned to go.

"No! Wait! Bring the old man to me," Levi said suddenly.

"Sir?"

"Just do it," said Levi. "He was once a priest, put him through the cleansing ritual and put him in a priest's cell. Notify me when it's done."

Levi paced the room. The old man, Christopher, irritated him like no other. He knew he should have respect for his father-in-law, but he still blamed him for Hannah leaving. If he was responsible for Angelica leaving also...

Levi continued to pace, teeth gritted, and fists clenched. When Eli finally returned, Levi flew from his chamber and through the halls. He barged into Christopher's room and glared down at the old man. Christopher knelt beside the bed with his head bowed in prayer.

"Where is my daughter," demanded Levi.

Christopher lifted his head and gazed at Levi for several moments. "Why do you ask me? Is she not your daughter?"

"Do not play games with me old man. Answer my question!" boomed Levi.

"Perhaps you should inquire of the Lord, you are the high priest after all. God speaks to you directly, does he not?"

Levi grabbed him by the collar, pulling him to his feet, and staring into his eyes. "You tell me where my daughter is right now, old man, or you will live to regret it!" hissed Levi.

"If I know where she is, and I tell you, who then will live to regret it?"

Levi threw the old man onto the bed, causing his head to hit the wall with a loud crack. This arrogant fool who had sent his own daughter across the southern boundary - this man who was likely sending Angelica off to a similar fate, he was to blame for everything. Enraged, Levi pounced on him, grabbing him and smacking his head against the wall several more times before pulling him back to his feet.

Taking a deep breath, he straightened Christopher's robe and smoothed out the wrinkles.

"Where is she?" Levi asked again, his voice softer this

time, but the old man didn't answer, he just looked at Levi, swaying slightly.

Levi clenched his teeth. The old fool had no intention of telling him anything. Levi was sure if he beat the man to a pulp he still wouldn't tell. He closed his eyes and took several deep breaths. A war raged within him, but he refused to give quarter to that part of him that was tempted to be grief stricken over the loss of his wife, and afraid of the subsequent loss of his daughter. Anger was easier, so he fed it with the idea that Christopher had wronged him.

Rage won the battle. Levi hauled back and punched Christopher hard in the face. The man's head flew back as if in slow motion. His teeth clamped down and he fell back onto the bed, hitting his head again. Blood dribbled from the corner of his mouth and his eye was already swelling. Levi took several deep breaths as he watched Christopher try to refocus his gaze, then he bent low until his face was only inches from the old man's.

I could kill him, Levi realized, and felt his grip grow stronger on the neckline of the prisoner's tunic.

"If you have filled her head with your ridiculous tales and sent her to her death like you did my wife..." Spittle flew from his lips spraying Christopher in the face. Then Levi straightened and turned toward the door, looking back as he opened it.

"You will remain here until I find my daughter," he said in a low growl. "And if I find out you sent her on some crazy quest, alone, in that wilderness, you can be assured that I will not rest until your dead body lay under a heap of stones!" Levi strode from the room.

"Lock him in," he ordered the priest standing guard. Then he stormed back down the hall.

"Eli!" He shouted. "Eli, to my chamber. Now!" His voice

echoed through the tabernacle and soon Eli appeared in the doorway, a concerned look on his face.

"Fetch Petra and his brother once more. They must mount another search for my daughter, this time to the south!"

Eli's mouth fell open, but he quickly shut it again. He paused, peering at Levi with a questioning look.

"Well, what are you waiting for?" Levi snapped.

Frowning, Eli nodded, and slipped from the room.

Levi threw himself into a chair. He wasn't aware of the dark shapes that swirled around him, but he felt their effects in his gut. A tornado of emotion made it impossible to sit still, or focus on the scrolls he should be studying. He stood up again, pacing around the table, over to the door, then back to the chair. Only to stand up again and pace once more, like a stallion anxious to escape its corral.

A niggling thought from somewhere deep inside told him he needed to do something, but what could he do? He was trapped here in his duties, his responsibilities as High Priest. Ever since he was a youth, he'd been ambitious and longed to be the High Priest, studying harder than the other boys, spending his time at the tabernacle instead of playing. Disciplining himself to obey all the laws. Now that he was High Priest, he found it a hollow victory. He had all the power he'd ever dreamed of, but in exercising it, he'd lost the respect of his own household. The bitterness of all he'd lost and could never grasp had taken root in his heart long ago, and it continued to grow with each new day. He didn't know what more he could achieve but he knew he wanted it. If only the people around him would stop making things so difficult. He thought then about Angelica.

He'd never really been able to connect with the child. She was so much like her mom; looked so much like her mom. His insides twisted. He ran his fingers roughly through his hair. Anger boiled within him, and frustration beat relentlessly upon his mind. The emotion grew within him, pressing down on him, until he let out a roar to rival one of a grizzly. He let everything building up inside him out with the sound, but as he did, the emotions only grew larger and sharper in his mind.

The dark shapes swirled around him, unseen, whispering things only heard by the soul. Their speed and numbers grew stronger, increasing each time their victim hearkened to their voice.

"Sir." Eli stood in the doorway.

How long had he been there?

"Petra and Donavon are at the gate," Eli said.

Levi didn't like the look on the man's face. It made him feel like a child who'd disappointed his father.

No respect, even among those in my own household.

"Thank you Eli," Levi grumbled.

“Eli," he said just before the old priest reached the door. "With my daughter being missing, I'm finding it hard to concentrate. Perhaps you could..." he gestured toward the scrolls still open on the table.

"Of course sir. I'll take care of them," the man replied with a sympathetic smile.

EIGHTEEN

At mid-day two days into their journey, the sun was high in the sky and Angelica was sweating. She removed her parka and stuffed it into her pack. The cool breeze moved over her skin like tiny fingers of ice. She removed her hat and revelled in the feel of it blowing against her scalp and damp neck.

Signs of spring were popping through all the places where the snow had melted. Iris blooms blanketed the meadows and hills. The blue carpet was interspersed with the pink pop of salmonberry blossoms. Small mounds of snow still hid in places, snug under the shade of the pines, but everywhere else the green of new grass and early blueberry shrubs colored the landscape and filled the air with the fresh smell of new life.

It was a time of new beginnings for the animals too. Bears had already emerged from their dens, cubs in tow, to feast on fish and ripening berries.

Angelica had come across a Cow moose with a calf earlier that day. The baby had hobbled down the path toward them on gangly legs. The cow began to stamp her hooves and snort, her head low in warning. Angelica backed down the path, only turning once she was sure they were a safe distance from the angry mama. They'd have to wait her out or take another path. Choosing the latter cost them a couple of hours, but with no way of knowing how long she'd have to wait, Angelica decided she'd take the risk.

Just as dusk began to settle, an outcropping of rock presented itself, and they stopped for the night under the shelter of the two giant aspens which grew there.

"That's the last of the dried fish," Angelica informed Chugiak after dinner. "And there's just enough pemmican for our breakfast in the morning. From now on we hunt for our food." Chugiak cocked his head at her, his tongue hanging from the side of his mouth.

Angelica laughed, "Quit trying to be cute and go chew your stick. I have some reading to do."

Angelica sat at the fire and thumbed through the journal until she found a description that resembled the area they were currently traveling through.

We have been following the cliff that borders a river with water that glows a peculiar blue. It has been two days since we've been able to access the river. Our canteens are almost empty. I only pray we can find a way down to the river, or get a rainfall, before the water runs out.

Angelica flipped the page.

At last the landscape has changed and we are on the same level as the riverbank. As if to say "Oh ye of little faith," God has also sent a driving rain to fill the low places in our path and drench us to the skin. I am sure the joke will be funnier in hindsight.

"THREE DAYS," she informed Chugiak. "They followed this ravine for three days and they were traveling with many people. We are only two and we have plenty of water in our canteens. I predict that by nightfall tomorrow we will be back beside the river, our canteens will be full of water, and our bellies will be full of hooligan."

Chugiak smiled at Angelica before returning his attention to the stick he was shredding.

THE SUN TOUCHED the mountain peaks, and streaks of purple and crimson colored the sky. A wolf howled at the rising moon that shared the sky with the midnight sun. An answering call sounded from the other side of the ravine.

The call of wolves had always filled Angelica with a feeling of longing to join them, but here, in the unknown, the sounds made her heart race and the hairs on the back of her neck stand up.

Angelica shivered and pulled Chugiak close. The warmth of his body and softness of his fur made her feel better. Angelica climbed into her wigwam and pulled the furs over her head to block out the light. She thought about her Grandpa, asleep in his cell. Did he have enough blankets to keep him warm? What about her father? Did he miss her, or did he lay his head on the pillow at night with no thought of the daughter who had run off into the forbidden wilderness?

Finally, she thought of Petra. Was he lying under his furs thinking of her also? Were he and the search party close, or had they turned back? Did Petra think her dead, or was he hoping to find her again? A tear slid from her eye, traveling across her cheek, and dripping onto her furs. She hoped he would find her, but at the same time the thought of it was terrifying to her. Would he try and drag her home, or would he understand why she needed to go on this journey?

Despite the thoughts swirling through her mind, Angelica soon fell fast asleep and slept the way of an exhausted traveler, dreaming she was walking along the trail. Chugiak took his place at the door flap, resting, but alert for danger while his master slept.

NINETEEN

Petra stood with Donavon and the three men accompanying them. Of the three, Samuel and Joshua were priests like himself, although their job descriptions had less to do with the worship of God, and more to do with security and policing. Ma'tonga was a tracker like his father and grandfather before him. Descended from the Athabaskan tribe, who were the original inhabitants of this land, Ma'tonga was the best tracker they had. He was also a good man. His wife had been kind to Petra when he was a boy, and the family had always welcomed him into their home. Their house felt like more of a home to him than his own had in the years after his mom died.

Petra was glad Ma'tonga was with the party. They had pulled him away from the fish camp and his family for this mission, and for that Petra felt bad. Still, Petra trusted him, and he had seen his own misgivings about this whole mission reflected in the older man's eyes. Perhaps they would have a chance to sit and talk at some point along the journey. Petra knew that Ma'tonga was wise and he valued his opinions.

The sun was just peeking above the eastern mountains and the men's breath made clouds in the chilly morning air. When they were informed that they must journey south of the boundary a look of shock came over the men's faces, but they were assured that the stories about the dangers of crossing the boundary were only myths created to keep the people from wandering beyond it. Petra understood the deception of the people was believed to be for their own good, but was it not still deception? The Law was clear, 'Thou shalt not bear false witness'. Did the law only apply to the people and not to the priests? Should it not apply even more to the priests, whose job it was to represent The Most High God to the people?

Petra kept his misgivings to himself while they made their way along the river. As they prepared to move south past the great spruce standing upon its island, they stopped. The men exchanged furtive glances, but Donavan forged ahead, leaving them watching as he pressed deeper into the forbidden land. When he realized he was not being followed, he turned.

"You are Priests of God and have nothing to fear. Let's go," he barked. The men followed reluctantly.

After an hour on the trail the group stopped while Ma'tonga examined the path before them.

"She was here," he said. "These are her tracks, intermingled with those of her dog."

"Very good," replied Donavon. "Let's follow them."

"It will be difficult, and progress may be slow. There are very few signs due to the snowstorm, but at least we know that we are headed in the right direction."

"Yes, of course," replied Donavon. "But she is a young girl with a runt of a dog. We should easily overtake them. Then we will return her to her father where she belongs and be done with this crazy mission.

The men all nodded, adjusting their packs, and moving out to follow the tracker along the trail. Their eyes darted to and fro, half expecting some mythical monster to appear out of the trees at any moment, but they all kept their fears to themselves.

TWENTY

Dawn came, gray and damp. The clouds spit a halfhearted drizzle down on the world, and the logs in the fire pit steamed and foamed with boiling sap. A cup of hot tea, and some leftover fire roasted rabbit, filled Angelica's belly when she broke camp. The water clinging to the leaves as they brushed by the trees, soon had Angelica's arms soaked, and her spirits seemed determined to match the weather's mood. She couldn't shake the sorrow that had taken hold the evening before when she'd thought of Petra, her grandfather, and even her father. A voice inside kept whispering to her, "You will only fail. This journey is a waste of time, and it will only end with you dying alone in the wilderness."

"We can do this," said Angelica. "It's just a bit of rain."

Chugiak looked back at her and wagged his tail.

"Woo Woo," he answered.

"A little further and we'll stop for a break," she told him, as if he were the one begging to stop.

Angelica thought nothing of it when the trail twisted to the left. It often left the ravine's edge to circumvent one obstacle or another. That was, until they rounded a curve and before them stood a great wall.

It was made of stone, and stood several feet higher than a grown man. Angelica pushed on it only to find it solid and unmovable. She looked to the right and to the left, but the wall seemed to go on unending in both directions. The tree line stopped several feet from the wall creating a tunnel of sorts, but the path continued toward the east, away from the river.

Chugiak caught a smell and headed up the path, nose to the ground. Angelica followed him, promising herself that if they got too far from the river they would turn back. After walking for a good while, they came to a clearing. Trees lined the perimeter in an almost perfect circle stopping at the wall, where there stood a gate.

The thick black bars of the gate were as tall as the wall and there was a great chain wrapped around the middle bars, orange with rust, but holding it fast.

Chugiak sniffed all around the base before sticking his nose between the bars to sniff the air on the other side.

Angelica put her hand on the hard black material the gate was made of. She'd never seen anything like it. The lock that held the chain in place was shiny and silver with only a few spots of rust where the moving parts came together.

Angelica was positive there was nothing in the journal about a wall. She had read through it again only the night before. Perhaps that meant the others had traveled around it somehow without seeing it. Angelica peered to the east. The wall went on for miles disappearing into the trees that camouflaged the base of the mountains.

If there was a way around in that direction it would take a week or longer to find it, and she would have to climb part way up the mountain to do it. She turned toward the west and headed back the way they came. Chugiak took one last sniff around the gate before following her, eventually running ahead. Angelica had disconnected his tether and harness and it was obvious the dog was loving the freedom to roam. He ran from bush to tree and back to Angelica again, his tail wagging furiously, his tongue lolling out of the side of his mouth and he had what could only be described as a huge grin on his face.

When they reached the end of the path, Angelica continued into the tunnel between the trees and the wall. It was just wide enough for her to walk through, although she had to push aside branches from time to time, or duck to avoid being whipped in the face.

As she looked up into the trees above, she realized she could easily get over the wall by climbing a tree, scooting out along one of the many branches, and dropping down on the other side. If she didn't have Chugiak along, she would do just that, but there was no way she would leave him behind, so she merely continued on toward the increasing roar of the river, hoping when they reached it there would be a way around the enormous wall.

The river was deafening now, and Angelica could see the gap up ahead where the edge of the cliff dropped down into the ravine. The wall went right up to its edge. They would have to turn back and climb up the mountain to get around.

Lost in her thoughts and thinking her journey may be over already, her grandpa doomed to his fate; Angelica almost tripped over Chugiak who was digging at the base of the wall.

"Are you going to dig our way under?" She asked. Then she realized there was already a hole there, and Chugiak was simply digging out the dirt and leaves that had been washed into it. Chugiak dug with enthusiasm, throwing moist dark clumps of pungent earth behind him, his tail swatting pieces of it to the side as he went.

"Good boy," Angelica said, her heart swelling as she watched her beloved companion reveal the hole beneath the wall.

Soon the hole was big enough for Chugiak to slip through. Angelica could see light coming from the other side. If Chugiak could fit, she would have no problem. She tied a rope to their packs and scooted through the opening on her belly. The damp moldy smell of earth was strong in her nose. For several seconds, the earth pressed in close...almost too close, but then she climbed out the other side, dirty but relieved. Chugiak jumped on her and licked her face.

"Good boy, you got us through."

He sat down and grinned at her.

"Try not to let it go to your head," Angelica laughed, rubbing his face and ears, before climbing to her feet and brushing the dirt off her clothes. She pulled at the rope around her waist until their packs appeared in the hole and then popped out this side of the wall. As she untied the rope, she considered refilling the hole, but all the dirt was on the other side, and besides, she would need to use it again on the way back.

After some swallows from the canteen for her, and a small bowl of water for Chugiak, they continued on their journey along a well-worn path that ran alongside the ravine.

TWENTY-ONE

Ma'tonga knelt beside the remains of a fire pit, his palm flat on the ashes.

"It's been at least 24 hours, maybe more, since they were here." Donavon watched him with narrowed eyes. Ma'tonga would have to be extremely cautious. "The trail will be easier to follow now that the snow is melted," he said.

They moved out again, picking up the pace a bit. Angelica was following a well-used game trail and making good time, but Ma'tonga held back a bit, not anxious to actually catch up to her. He stopped at regular intervals, pretending to be searching for signs, careful not to make it obvious that he was trying to delay the group.

Donovan had arrived at fish camp three days earlier and insisted that Ma'tonga leave his nets and help with this ridiculous chase. As the days wore on it became more and more clear to him that Donavon would stop at nothing less than Angelica's capture, and the southern boundary lurked behind them on the horizon, reminding them of the folly of crossing it.

. . .

THE SUN WARMED the spring air. Walking through the forest was pleasant this time of year, before the mosquitoes hatched, and Ma'tonga wished he could enjoy it. This whole thing sat wrong with him. The dishonesty of the High Council gave him a sour taste in his stomach. He had always been loyal, always obedient, believing it to be right to honor and trust the High Council. Now he found himself questioning everything.

What had Angelica done wrong, exactly? Why were they chasing her down? Ma'tonga knew Angelica had not left lightly. He had seen her wrestling with the decision during the hooligan run. But one question weighed most heavily on his mind, so heavy it felt almost like a physical weight on his shoulders.

Should I tell what I know about her belief God was sending her on a mission?

To chase down this girl and bring her back arbitrarily didn't seem fair. Perhaps she had a good reason to leave. Ma'tonga pushed the thought away as he had done innumerable times in the past few days. The girl could defend herself, after all. It seemed reasonable to Ma'tonga that the search party would ask her, when they found her, what the purpose of this journey was. At least ask where she was going and why.

But much as he tried to deny the fact, Ma'tonga doubted Donavon would act so honorably. The High Priest had ordered them to bring his daughter back and Donovan, their leader, wouldn't stop to question it - he would simply obey.

Ma'tonga stopped, crouching down to study the trail.

"What's the problem? Why are we stopping so often?" asked Donavon

"They stopped here, and then turned back," said Ma'tonga. "I'm trying to determine why." Motioning for the others to stay where they were, he stood and walked about a dozen yards up the trail.

"Moose," he called back, "cow and calf."

Not needing to explain what that meant to a group of men raised in these woods. Ma'tonga began to backtrack, going slowly to be sure he didn't miss any side trails.

"Here," he said, and they turned onto a lesser used path.

"That is out of our way," complained Donavon. "We should stay on the main trail."

"We could do that, but if they didn't get back on the trail... it could set us back," Ma'tonga replied. Donavon looked at Ma'tonga, his eyes boring into him. Ma'tonga concentrated on keeping his breathing even and his expression neutral. Finally, Donavon nodded and motioned for Ma'tonga to continue. Ma'tonga followed the path where Angelica and Chugiak had gone. It was an easy trail for him to follow, but to the untrained, broken branches close to the ground, a patch of grass that looked 'not quite right,' would be easily missed. Ma'tonga took his time, stopping to study broken branches and footprints in the dirt.

"Bear and two cubs," he said at one point, pointing out the tracks to the others. "Be on your guard."

It was obvious to Ma'tonga the bears had come through after Angelica, so he wasn't worried for her safety, but that didn't mean there weren't other animals in the forest that posed a threat. She had Chugiak with her. He was a faithful friend and would protect her at all costs, but that didn't mean he could hold his own against an angry mama protecting her babies. Ma'tonga hoped if there was trouble the dog would at least afford Angelica the chance to get away. But would she take it and leave her beloved friend behind? Ma'tonga prayed she would.

The trail was getting steadily further from the river's

bank. Ma'tonga continued on, pausing now and then to make a show of concern.

"Where could she be going?" Petra asked. He had been silent up until now. but Ma'tonga saw in his eyes that he was as unsettled about the idea of chasing Angelica down as he was.

"Doesn't matter where she thinks she's going," said Donovan "We'll have her shortly, she won't be able to go much further."

"It is a vast wilderness," Petra replied.

Donavon smiled, his mouth twisted and his eyes flashing.

"Have faith little brother," was all he said.

Petra picked up his pace until he was walking side by side with Ma'tonga.

"What do you think? Do you share Donavon's confidence that we will overtake her soon?"

"I do not," Ma'tonga said, in a voice too low for the others to hear. "She is at least two days ahead, and obviously knows not only what she is doing, but where she is going."

"Two days," exclaimed Petra. His eyes flicked instinctively to Donovan, who had not seemed to hear his outburst. "I thought you said one day."

"Keep your voice down," Ma'tonga whispered. "Donavon is watching me like a hawk."

"Where do you think she is going?" whispered Petra, peering nervously over his shoulder at his brother.

"I have never traveled this far south before," replied Ma'tonga, "but I can tell from the terrain that this valley narrows and presumably comes to an end several days to the south. She seems to be following the river. Unless she encounters unknown obstacles, we will not catch her."

"Obstacles? Like another ravine or a cliff?" asked Petra

"Exactly," replied Ma'tonga.

"Donavon seems pretty sure we'll catch her," muttered

Petra, his eyes downcast. Ma'tonga wondered what the boy was thinking. Was it a boyhood crush that had him doubting their mission, or something deeper?

When Ma'tonga didn't reply Petra looked over at him, searching his eyes.

"Is there something else? What aren't you saying?" asked Petra.

"No, there are only personal feelings that are better kept to myself," said Ma'tonga.

Petra nodded and the two continued on in a companionable silence. Ma'tonga's suspicions that Petra's feelings closely matched his own seemed to be confirmed, and when they broke company later, the nods they gave each other spoke volumes, more than words ever could.

TWENTY-TWO

The evening sun dipped below the mountain peaks, causing what little heat it had been providing to disappear. Angelica looked for a place to stop for the night, but there were no trees anywhere to provide a clearing to camp in. The cliff overlooking the river was to the right, and the muskeg was on the left. Streams of water from the over saturated muskeg crossed over the path in the low spots, tumbling over the cliff to the river below. She was cold and wet, and Angelica began to understand the feelings of the settlers she'd read about in the journal. If she didn't know how far she'd have to travel in these conditions, she might give in to despair also. Even Chugiak trudged along the path, his ears flat on his head and his tail drooping.

Angelica finally stopped to make camp on a relatively dry rise of ground. They were exposed on all sides and Angelica struggled to fall asleep. Even Chugiak seemed nervous, frequently lifting his head, and cocking it to one side, listening to the sounds in the night. It took forever for morning to come. Angelica lay in her furs, shivering, and her muscles aching. She forced herself to wait until the sun was high enough to warm the air a bit before finally rising. After a quick breakfast that did little to satisfy, they hit the trail again, cold, sore, and their spirits dragging.

Angelica had thought this part of the journey would be easier. Slogging through this bog for the second day sapped her energy and every little thing irritated her. The feel of slightly damp cloth against her skin, the rubbing of her boots, even the sound of Chugiak's panting made her want to lash out. She pulled her hat down over her ears to muffle the sound. Eventually her low spirits had her numbly staring down at the path in front of her, dreaming of warm days picking berries on the hillsides. At some point she realized the path had widened and was lined on either side by trees. Relieved to be out of the bog and back into the forest Angelica's spirits lifted, but a vague sense that she was being watched dogged her. She stopped often to peer into the trees, looking for signs of somebody or something. She worried Donavon and his crew had caught up with her, and were lurking out there somewhere, waiting for the right moment to pounce.

A twig snapped with a loud crack behind her. She whipped around and stared into the shadows. She knew she hadn't imagined it.

"Who's there?" she called.

As if in response to her query, a bull moose lumbered out of the trees. A branch hung from the corner of his mouth, bouncing as he chewed.

"What a relief," she said to Chugiak. He cocked his head and gave her a quizzical look. She kept her eye on the bull until she was far enough away to be sure he wasn't going to charge at her.

As they followed the trail near the edge of the ravine, she continued to feel as if she were being watched. It wasn't the wildlife. Something was out there, something sinister, something that made the hairs on her neck stand on end and caused her arms to break out in goose flesh.

Angelica crested a ridge and looked out across the landscape in front of her. The forest was multiple shades of green blanketing the valley floor, and the purple mountains stood against a pale blue sky. The Turquoise river snaked through the middle of it all, sparkling as it reflected the sun's rays. It was absolutely beautiful, and yet something evil was out there, lurking. She could sense it, even if she couldn't see it.

Maybe it's just the leftover memories of old stories told to scare children?

No, this was real, she knew it for certain.

"Lord, show me the danger if it's out there," she whispered, half afraid God would answer her, and not sure if she really wanted to know.

It started as a wisp of smoke rising through the trees, twisting, and swirling as if blown by the wind. Yet there was no wind, the day was as still as the glass surface of a pond. The plumes grew thicker and spun themselves into a circular shape before racing across the sky in all directions. She looked up as a line of it crossed directly over her head, and a face, with empty black eyes looked back out at her from within.

TWENTY-THREE

A wall loomed in front of them. The men gave Donavon questioning s, waiting for some instructions on how to proceed. Ma'tonga stared up at the barrier, shaking his head in wonder.

Donavon stood with his arms crossed and a victorious grin on his face. He looked at Petra, and the "I told you so" spark in his eyes was unmistakable.

"You knew this was here," Petra said.

Donavon ignored Petra and strode forward. He smacked the wall affectionately with his palm.

"We have her now!" He declared. Then to the men he said, "Come, the gate is this way. She won't have made it through, and we will soon be heading home with the little runaway in our grasp." Ma'tonga opened his mouth to speak but Donavon passed him by and headed up the trail without a word. All the other men, except for Ma'tonga and Petra, followed Donovan unquestioningly. Ma'tonga held back, waiting for Petra to move alongside him.

"She did go that way, but the tracks show that she back-tracked and then went to the right, there is no trail per Se, but there is a passageway of sorts between the trees and the wall there. I see no signs of them having come back this way again."

Petra thought it over for a few minutes. Should they keep silent and follow Donavon like the others, or should they take off on their own, and follow Ma'tonga's instincts? After several moments he made up his mind.

"You follow the others," Petra said to Ma'tonga. "Try to delay telling them they've gone the wrong direction though. Even so. Donavon is so sure of himself he probably won't listen to you until he realizes for himself he has lost her. I will go to the right. If I can catch up to her first, maybe I can convince her to come home willingly, or at the very least find out what in the world she's doing out here."

Ma'tonga agreed and they parted ways. Ma'tonga went to the left after the others, and Petra through the tunnel made by the trees and the wall to the right.

Petra was an above average tracker himself, but it was difficult to see in the dark narrow space between the trees and the wall. He stopped frequently to search the dirt until he saw the tracks he was looking for. He peered up at the trees occasionally, seeing branches that would make climbing over the wall quite easy, for a person anyway. Chugiak was a big dog even for a runt. There was no way Angelica could lift him over the wall even if she had rope and a harness. He dismissed the option and continued forward.

His decision to separate from the others was confirmed each time he found a new foot or paw print in the dirt. As he got further into the tunnel of trees the sound of the river grew louder. The ravine was at least 30 feet deep and there were no banks at the bottom. The only options were to cross the ravine somehow, or to turn back. The Alder bushes were thick in this part of the forest, and the clearings were filled with the giant spade shaped leaves of Devil's Club. From a distance they looked like rhubarb, but when you touched them the instant burning would reveal your mistake. It wasn't impossible to travel through them, but it would be a last resort. Soon Petra could see the gap across the ravine and smell the brine of the water. A fine mist hung in the air, evidence of a waterfall or spray of water over rocks. He was so focused on what was ahead he failed to where he was going. He didn't notice the mound of fresh dirt until it tripped him up, and he landed on his chest, nose in the dark rich earth. He got to his knees and began brushing the dirt off. That's when he saw the tunnel under the wall.

He looked back the way he'd come, then took off his pack, pushing it in front of him, and slithered through the tunnel. It was a tight fit and at one point he wasn't sure whether he would make it or not, but he wiggled free and at last was out on the other side.

The terrain on this side of the wall was quite different. The trees were sparser, and the fields were filled with tundra moss and salmon-berries. The single trail was either hard packed dirt or stone. It would be difficult to find any tracks going forward, however with only a single trail, and the knowledge that Angelica's plan was to follow the river, there could be no doubt which direction she'd traveled.

HE CONSIDERED GOING BACK to get the others. Donavon would be angry when he realized the wall hadn't stopped Angelica. All his blustering about how they would catch her with no problem was nothing but a puff of smoke whisked away by the wind. Donovan would be more upset then ever when they finally did catch up to Angelica. No, it was best that Petra proceed on his own. The best chance of catching up to her first was for him to continue alone. Petra began to fill the hole with dirt and anything else he could find, pushing it through with his feet until he was satisfied he'd filled it the best he possibly could. Ready to continue after Angelica, he looked across the landscape before him and sighed.

What have you gotten me into now girl?

Angelica had done a lot of impulsive things in the years he'd known her, and he'd joined her in some of them - freeing the sacrifices from their pens, running through the forest when they were supposed to be in school, and sitting on the ridge gazing at the southern horizon and dreaming of being explorers and going to another world. Thinking of the ridge got him thinking about the one kiss they'd shared. His heartbeat quickened at the memory, but the shame, the constant companion of that particular memory, quickly followed. Angelica was promised to his brother and was not his to kiss. Still, no matter how hard he tried, the memory refused to let him go.

The way she looked at him had set his heart racing. Something had clicked between them at that moment. An intimacy he'd never known before, a feeling of belonging, a perfect fit with another person. His heart swelled and his throat tightened as moisture filled his eyes. It was the fulfillment of a longing he'd carried deep inside all his life. He leaned down and kissed her without reservation, without thinking, and that moment had been perfect, right up to the point where he'd remembered she was promised to Donavon.

Petra quickened his pace, determined to put the memories out of his mind and concentrate on the task at hand. The path meandered in strange directions, so Petra decided to stick to the edge of the ravine. He would follow the river and save time. Turned out the plan was not as straightforward as it first appeared. What at first glance looked to be just another patch of tundra moss covering the rock beneath, turned out to be a patch of tundra moss floating on a bog. Before he knew what was happening, Petra was hip deep in the cold brackish water.

After finding his way back onto the trail, he moved more cautiously, being careful not to veer from the path. By the time the sun started to sink in the sky, he was shivering from the cold wind. Early spring in South Central Alaska often got very cold at night, and it wasn't unusual to wake to the ground being covered with frost. He needed to build a fire. Petra made his way slowly to a copse of trees, sure there would be solid ground beneath them.

Dusk had set in by the time he made it. He quickly gathered sticks and spruce needles, and coaxed a fire out of them. He took off his wet clothes and hung them from a line he rigged between two tree branches. His canteen was only half full, so he decided it best to fore-go hot tea and ate a dinner of pemmican washed down with what little water he felt he could spare. Ironic, he thought to himself, to be surrounded by water and still be thirsty. He had no desire to take his chances on what myriad diseases might be lurking in the murky bog water, so he choked down his dinner and settled in for a cold, uncomfortable night in the middle of the hellish landscape. The only blessing was it was still too early in the year for mosquitoes and other insects that thrived in such places. It was a small blessing, but for it, Petra was grateful.

TWENTY-FOUR

After another restless night, and well into another dreary day, Angelica stood at the top of a cliff, looking down at the Turquoise River as it slithered off toward the horizon. She looked behind her, half expecting Donavon and his men to be standing there, waiting to drag her home. Thoughts of Donovan were enough to send a shiver up her spine. She was afraid to even think about the creatures in the smoke she'd envisioned. She decided she must have been imagining things. She hadn't been getting much sleep, and she'd heard lack of sleep could cause a person to see things that weren't there. Still, she continued to peer at the tree line, expecting to see something among the aspens, waving at her as the wind blew through their branches.

Pulling off her pack, she squatted down and felt through the contents, hoping to find one last piece of pemmican or dried fish that may have fallen from its wrapping. In the river there was plenty of fish for the taking, as well as the tender shoots of grasses and weeds that were edible growing along its banks. But up here, nothing but moss covered the rocky ground. She needed to find a way down to the river.

Chugiak whined, nudging her hand with his nose.

"Sorry boy," she said. "The sooner we find a way down, the sooner we eat."

Chugiak barked and took off in the ravine's direction as if he'd understood every word.

Angelica followed. She'd learned a long time ago to trust Chugiak's instincts - they had gotten her out of tight spots before. Like one time when she was a kid. They'd been out in the forest and she lost track of time. It had gotten dark, and Angelica had lost her bearings. Chugiak led her out of the dark woods, and right up to where her father stood, hands on hips and a scowl on his face. She imagined that was the look he'd have when he saw her again. If he saw her again.

A couple hours into the days' journey she thought she caught a flash of movement. Was there someone hiding there among the trees? She kept perfectly still and waited, watching the place she'd detected movement, but whatever may have been there did not show itself again. It was the time of year bears were emerging from hibernation, hungry and desperate for a meal. To be more cautious, Angelica sang loudly as she walked.

The sound of Chugiak barking ahead made Angelica break into a jog, and when she came through the trees, in a little clearing, was a large log across the ravine. It's position over the river wasn't an accident, it had been placed there purposely. It was secured in place by posts pounded into the ground. Chugiak ran across, tail wagging, and began to explore, sniffing the ground excitedly on the other side. Angelica looked down at the river. There were no rapids in this part of the ravine, but the rolling current looked fast and powerful. There were many things hiding beneath the surface of the water that could break the body of a person who might fall onto them. She took a deep breath, stealing her nerves. It wasn't heights she was afraid of; it was falling.

That was what she used to tell Petra when they were kids and she wouldn't quite go to the edge of the ridge.

"This is your safe place?" He'd say. "Shouldn't a safe place be somewhere that doesn't scare you?"

"It's not the place that scares me," she'd protest. "It's the edge, and I see no reason why I need to go to the edge anyway."

"Angelica?"

She smiled. Funny how a memory can make you feel like the person is right there with you.

"Angelica?" Angelica spun around. Petra approached, his hand out.

"Come on Angelica. It's time to go home."

"I'm not going home."

Angelica stepped onto the log.

"Stop her!" It was Donavon's voice. Angelica quickly took three steps, throwing her arms out wide when she wobbled.

"If you're not going after her, get out of my way." She heard Donavon say.

"These posts are dry rotted; I don't think the log will hold with two people." Petra replied.

"Just move," Donavon shouted.

The sounds of a scuffle broke out behind her. Angelica quickly took a few more steps. The cracking of wood echoed in the air, and the log moved. Angelica's feet slipped. She thought she heard Petra screaming her name, or was it just the roar of the river in her ears?

Then she was falling. The shock of the icy water knocked the air out of her. She surfaced, then gasped as she pulled at her parka, managing to get it off before it pulled her back under. The river's current rushed her downstream as she struggled to swim. If she could get closer to shore, she may be able to grab an overhanging branch or fallen tree. A warming sensation replaced the cold, as if the water were a gentle flame.

There was no time to think. She funneled every ounce of strength into her limbs as they struggled to move her across the current, inch by inch, closer to the shore. She could barely feel her arms and legs now. She only had a few minutes to get out of the icy water before the cold overtook her.

As the current whisked her around a bend, she spotted a fallen tree. She renewed her efforts, pulling against the pain and stiffness to swim to it. She wrapped her arms around it, its rough bark rubbing against her cold wet cheek. The current pushed her torso against the tree, making it hard to move, but slowly she managed to drag herself toward the shore.

The tree's roots were still in the ground, holding it fast. She would have to grab hold of them and pull herself the two feet up to the shore. Dirt crumbled away and plopped into the river, quickly disappearing downstream as she pulled herself up, but her arms were so weak, her fingers were cold and began to slip. She pulled. From somewhere deep inside, a deep guttural yell escaped her lips as if from someone else. Her fingers felt raw, her arm muscles screamed at her. Her legs felt like jelly.

Lord, help me.

Somehow, she got her chest up over the overhang, then her torso, and finally her legs. She lay on the ground and looked up at the gray sky, pregnant with threatening clouds. A single snowflake drifted down. It twisted and turned before landing gently on Angelica's forehead. She began to sob, her shoulders shaking. It was a silent crying, yet, as if the clouds heard her, they let loose their contents in solidarity and snow began to fall, the flakes mingling with her tears as they ran down her cheeks.

She was bound to fail, she always did. Always missed the mark no matter how hard she tried. Now she would die here, frozen to death alone, in a vast wilderness.

Did Mama die this way?

She thought of Chugiak and her heart ached with sorrow. What would happen to him? Would he sit by her body and howl in grief at the full moon?

Would he find his way back to the village, or would he turn feral and join the wolf packs that roamed the valleys and mountains?

Her whole body was shaking now, not just with her sobbing but with the cold as well.

"Are you there?" she called up to the sky. "Did you call me away from home just to let me die all alone in the cold forest?"

As if in reply, an icy wind blew through the trees, raising the hairs on her already damp skin, leaving a thousand tiny pricks of pain.

Then the sound of faint barking broke the silence of the snowfall.

Chugiak!

He was coming for her. Everything would be okay.

Angelica forced herself to sit up even though her muscles screamed in agony. She looked around. There was an aspen tree with a bed of dry needles beneath it, and a fallen tree nearby. She forced her stiff muscles to move through the excruciating pain, and went to work, snapping branches from the dead tree, and building them into a teepee before striking the flint she'd fortunately put into her pocket instead of her pack.

Chugiak bounded into the clearing just as the spark found the dry pine needles and roared to life. He jumped on Angelica, licking her face, his tail pumping furiously. He calmed then, sniffing her, and whined, moving his body so he was lying against her back, as if he knew he must help her stay warm.

The night seemed to go on forever. Angelica forced herself to stay awake and keep the fire going. The convulsive shivering that wracked her body subsided as the warmth of the fire dried her clothes and warmed her skin. Chugiak's warmth against her back helped immensely. She pulled her arms inside her tunic, holding them against her torso and rubbing her palms against her upper arms. When the first rays of sunshine blinked in over the mountains, Angelica rose, and began to walk back upriver.

Chugiak had run across the log bridge ahead of her, and Angelica had exited the river on that same side. If it had happened any other way, they would have been separated, with no way to reach each other across the river.

Was it only fortune, or was it by design?

If it was by design, why had she gone into the river at all? Even as her mind pondered these questions, Angelica kept moving - the walking helped warm her - and kept her eyes on the bank. Her pack was heavy, and had probably sunk to the bottom, but there was a chance the parka may have floated downstream.

Chugiak trotted to the bank to get a drink. It was a rare spot where the beach was level with the river. The water gathered there in a relatively still pool, thanks to several dead trees lying just below the surface, their roots still embedded in the permafrost that held them fast. And there, in the bottom of that still pool, lay her pack. It looked like it was unharmed and intact.

Before she could bring herself to reenter the icy water, Chugiak jumped in, grabbing the pack and pulling it onto the beach. Grateful at not having to go back into the river, Angelica sat on the ground and pulled her pack toward her. She couldn't believe it was back in her hands, and it took her several moments to gain her wits from the shock. Water ran off the moose hide exterior and poured from the openings, making a puddle on the ground. But the contents would dry with time and a little sun. Maybe she would have a chance after all, but hope seemed like something it would take too great an effort to achieve.

Was her mind so frozen from being overwhelmed or was it...hypothermia. Angelica began to go through the list of symptoms in her head, but lost track after only three. She needed to get out of these damp clothes. There was no time to find the perfect spot, so she began to gather sticks and pile them up right there on the riverbank.

TWENTY-FIVE

Angelica pulled on the breeches she'd warmed over the fire, reveling in the feel of them against her cold skin. She'd been lucky to find her pack, and even though everything was wet from being submerged in the river, it was easy enough to dry it all out again. It just took time.

Time.

How much do I have?

If Petra and the others had found a way across the ravine, they could catch up to her at any time.

Petra.

Angelica couldn't silence the echo of her name, cried aloud in Petra's voice, following her as she plummeted from the log and into the raging water below. Was the obvious fear she'd heard in his voice proof he still cared for her? The thought of him being her enemy made her heart ache. They'd been a team at one time. Always together, sharing their deepest thoughts and fears

A dog sled race to redemption creek when they were ten had sealed their bond. One of the other racers was gravely injured. Petra and Angelica had worked together to get the girl to safety in a blinding blizzard that had blown in unexpectedly. After that, the two had been inseparable.

Angelica missed their friendship. Over the years Petra's duties in the tabernacle had increased; they'd drifted apart, like rings of smoke or an errant eagle's feather floating on a cross-current...

The sun shone on Angelica's blankets, tunics, socks, and underthings, which hung from every available branch, some on makeshift poles she'd set up near the fire. Steam rose from the blankets. Though the sun was shining, it would be dark soon, and with it would come the cold. She would need a dry blanket and tent if she didn't want to spend another night awake, shivering in front of the fire.

She sat on a log and watched the flames jumping and dancing around the logs. It was hard not to wonder if she would die out here in this wilderness, never to be heard from again, her family never sure what had happened to her.

Is that what happened Mama?

Angelica imagined her mom wandering the forest, alone and lost, before finally succumbing to the elements. A tear slipped down her cheek.

She didn't have her eagle.

Angelica's hand reached for the jade figure that hung from her neck, rubbing the smooth stone. The feel of the cool jade against her skin was oddly comforting. She forced her thoughts away from her mother, and thought instead of Petra. Where was he right now? Had he and Donavon found a way across the ravine? Or had they turned around and gone back, giving her up for dead?

It was a miracle she wasn't dead. Her fall into the river could have gone badly. She could have hit a rock. The log bridge could have landed on her when it fell. She could have hit her head and drowned. A few more minutes in the river and the cold would have killed her. The dried pine needles had been right there for fuel, and her Flint was in her pocket and not in the river's bottom somewhere. Angelica could no longer deny the strong possibility that God had his hand in it all.

But, if that's true, the persistent nagging voice in Angelica's head asked once again, why did I have to fall into the river in the first place?

Angelica's hands flew to her head as if to still the thoughts that swirled within. She was tired of running, tired of this relentless nagging question that had chased her out of her village, beyond the boundary, and into this wilderness. She became, as much as she was able to become, still.

It was then that the answer, like the Borealis that appeared with a certain regularity and predictability over the Alaskan tundra, became obvious.

So those who are pursuing me cannot not follow.

TWENTY-SIX

All the next day Angelica couldn't shake the feeling of being pursued. As she continued south, the trees began to thin out, and eventually disappeared.

Thoughts of Petra kept her company as she trudged along. His smile always did something to Angelica's insides. She was strong, and she could harden her heart against almost anyone, including her father, but when Petra was near it was different. He could melt her resolve like fat in a hot pan. Turn her fiery defiance into dust blown away by the wind. It had killed her to say no to him when he'd asked her to come home, his hand held out for her at the end of that log.

The sky was gray, and a drizzle of rain began to fall as Angelica plodded along. The river meandered around several bends and ended in a small waterfall.

Before her stood a vast muskeg. The bog filled the valley from side to side and went on beyond the horizon. Three separate paths meandered their way through the swamp. Angelica sighed. It would be a long trip to get through it. She scrambled down the rocks onto the sandbar and stood contemplating which path to take, distracted by questions that plagued her mind.

Was Petra angry with her, or disappointed perhaps? Did he even love her at all, or had that kiss been nothing more than the impetuous urge of a man who finds himself too close to an attractive woman? Was he still chasing her, along with his brother, determined to bring her home to face her father?

Chugiak ran forward down the center path and she followed him.

Would Petra stand silently while they put her Grandfather to death? Would he smile and congratulate her after they forced her to marry his brother, or would he stand up and declare his love for her instead?

Angelica had no answers to her questions, and so they continued to swirl through her mind. The weight of them lay heavy on her heart and made her journey through the muskeg slow and cumbersome.

It was late the next afternoon before Angelica finally saw the tree line ahead that signaled the end of the muskeg. The river had reformed a while back and she was grateful Chugiak had chosen the path that ran beside it. She'd spent a restless night on the sandy bank, fighting off gnats and sand fleas. Poor Chugiak was miserable, chewing at the places the fleas bit him and snapping at the gnats. In the morning he'd found a still pool and lay down in it, a smile on his face for the momentary reprieve from the itching.

Angelica wished she could do the same, but she couldn't dry off anywhere near as well as he could. Indulging in a soak would only leave her cold and miserable, and she'd had enough of that on this trip already. The exhaustion, itching, and the incessant buzzing of insects in her ears made each step seem like an eternity. It was a great relief to see that tree line and Angelica quickened her pace.

A glance to her right stopped her in her tracks. The

muskeg was on fire. Tendrils of smoke rose from the bog, getting thicker and increasing in volume with each passing moment. *How was that possible?* She approached the edge, her heart hammering in her chest, searching the plumes for eerie faces looking out. The urge to run began to build inside her. The marshy grasses, which would grow to be taller than her by midsummer, were only a foot high. As Angelica got closer, she saw them - mosquitoes, hatching and escaping their watery womb to take to the air by the thousands.

Angelica backed away until she was on the edge of the river. The tree line was close but not close enough. She checked the netting that hung from the brim of the hat she'd put on when the first swarms of gnats had appeared - a shabby affair, fit only for keeping them from getting into her eyes and mouth - and tucked its edges deeper into her neck-line. She pulled her sleeves down. They covered only half her hands. She fished her gloves from her pack and tucked her sleeves into them. Her pants were tucked into her boots. Hopefully, she hadn't missed any openings that mosquitoes could get in. They were surrounded as the buzzing blood suckers caught up to them.

Chugiak found a patch of mud, and rolled in it for several minutes before catching up to Angelica as she made her way toward the tree line. She kept her head bowed against the bombarding insects. Though still vulnerable to the blood-thirsty stings, the fresh layer of mud that caked Chugiak's fur would help protect him.

The swarms of insects darkened the sky, and it was getting darker. The billions of airborne creatures seemed to move in a swirling motion, as though dancing. They moved across the bog toward the trees on either side, searching for a meal. The darkness of the swarm increased, until it filled the entire valley like dark smoke. Then a face appeared in the swarm, then another, then hundreds, with empty black eyes and sharp rows of teeth in their mouths that twisted into sinister smiles.

Angelica ran. With all the strength left within her she pushed her body to move faster, her lungs to breathe deeper, praying as she went that God would keep the evil creatures from catching her.

She made it to the tree line, but she just kept running. Chugiak raced ahead. *Could he see the creatures too?* She leapt over fallen trees and rocks. Shrubs and tree branches scratched her skin and grabbed at her hair. After running for what seemed like hours, nearly at the point of exhaustion, she slowed her pace. Holding her breath, she dared a quick glance behind her. The smoke, the faces, and the mosquito hoard were gone.

Her whole body ached, and her cheek stung where a branch had scratched her.

Even though there was no sign of the creatures, she still felt their presence, invisible, all around her. Her stomach twisted and the urge to run gained strength again. She moved south and east through the trees in a controlled yet purposeful stride until she once again found herself on the riverbank, staring out at the river. It rolled ever onward like a giant leviathan, swelling over boulders, and foaming white where the bigger rocks broke the surface. Sometimes sticks or vegetation sped by on the current, sometimes there were whole trees. The water pooled in eddies in places and the water was slower in those spots.

Angelica chose one of them to splash water on her face and fill her canteen. The ice-cold liquid soothed her aching head. She sat on a piece of driftwood to catch her breath. According to the journal, she needed to follow the river south for two more days. The river would turn toward the west, but she would continue south into a valley marked by a rock that resembled the face of an eagle.

It was getting late in the day but there was still a good hour of light for traveling. She pulled her pack onto her sore shoulders and moved forward on aching feet, one painful step at a time. An hour later they made camp in a copse of spruce several dozen feet from the river's edge. Angelica was asleep moments after she crawled wearily into her furs. Chugiak settled by the shelter's entrance, keeping guard over his master.

Angelica continued south along the river the next day. She could see that the landscape below the cliff differed from above. It was full of meandering streams and ponds filled with all manner of life. A brisk wind was blowing, and Angelica was grateful for the relief it provided from the mosquitoes.

TWENTY-SEVEN

The morning mists were still clinging to the ground in the clearings, and the leaves of bushes that grew among the trees were lined with dew. Angelica had been awake for some time, having woken up cold and shivering. She built a fire and boiled water for tea then settled in to thumb through the journal.

"After we finally got our whole company across the lake, we set out north through the forest. In the early evening we encountered another obstacle. A small river running through the bottom of a ravine. The ravine wasn't very deep but still presented the problem of how to cross it. We will camp here for the night and discuss our options in the morning.

I am quite sure this isn't the last obstacle we will face, and will most likely not be the worst of them. The landscape is exceedingly beautiful, and the mountain peaks give one the feeling of being watched over by God, to whom I am exceedingly grateful."

. . .

ANGELICA SET the journal down on the log beside her and rose to her feet. She stretched her arms out above her head, rolling her neck as she did so. Her muscles were slightly stiff and achy, but nothing like they had been in the beginning of this journey. If the journal was correct, she wasn't far from the lake it spoke of. She didn't know how she'd cross it once she got there, she might have to walk around, but she was beginning to learn that she didn't need to know the answers in advance. God would guide her if she ran into trouble.

"NATURE CALLS," she announced to Chugiak, who looked up from the stick he was chewing momentarily as she made her way into the trees.

SHE WAS on her way back, enjoying the morning sun shining in streaks through the trees, lighting up the forest floor in patches, when the sound of Chugiak barking echoed through the trees. She began to run. She stopped just short of the clearing when she saw Petra standing by the fire with the journal in his hands, reading it.

ANGELICA CLAMPED her hand against her mouth to disguise her gasp. A feeling somewhere between panic and elation filled her. She loved the way his blond hair hung over one eye, and the muscles in his jaw moved as he clenched and unclenched his teeth, something he'd always done when reading.

The smile that was blooming on Angelica's face was wiped away when Donavon burst into the clearing.

"Is that the Journal? Why are you reading it? Give it to me." Donavon's face was twisted, and his eyes had a wild look in them. Angelica moved further behind the tree, squatting down, and peeking around to see what was happening, and hoping it would hide her from them. Angelica wondered if the expression on Donavon's face was due to the influence of the dark creatures. They were swirling around him like smoke, their fingers like talons wrapped around his arms and legs. They swirled around Petra, but didn't touch him, although it seemed like they wanted to.

"Yes, it's the journal, but I am puzzled at what it's value is. It is simply an account of our ancestors' journey to the village centuries ago."

"That is not your concern," said Donavon, reaching his hand out for the journal. "That our High Priest says it is valuable is enough. Now give it to me."

Petra stepped back from Donavon, his finger on the page he was reading.

"It says right here they had a disagreement with those at the original settlement, over the other half of the Holy Book. It seems the old man may not be a crazy heretic after all."

"Watch your tongue little brother." Donavon's voice had changed, the words coming out in a hiss, accompanied by spittle. "You wouldn't want to be accused of heresy yourself, and join the old man in his fate."

Petra took another step back. "But if he's not guilty..."

Petra's words were cut off when Donavon lunged at him. Petra backed away, holding the journal out of Donavon's reach, and pushing him back with the other hand.

"Give it to me," Donavon hissed.

Chugiak continued barking at the men, his hackles up and his teeth bared. Petra backed up again. He was dangerously close to the edge of the ravine. Some of the dirt broke loose and his foot slipped.

"Petra!" Angelica screamed. Petra looked up and met her

eyes. Donavon lunged again for the book. Chugiak jumped at Donavon, sinking his teeth into his thigh.

As if the world had slowed down, Angelica watched Petra fall backwards with Donavon on top of him, both of their hands clinging to the journal. A chunk of breeches and flesh tore from Donavon's leg, still clenched in Chugiak's teeth as the men fell from view. Chugiak dropped it and went to the edge, barking at whatever he saw below a few times before turning and coming to where Angelica stood, frozen, unable to believe what had just happened. He licked her hand, whining.

Angelica looked down into the large brown eyes of her furry protector, then took in a deep gasp of air. She hadn't even realized she'd been holding her breath until that moment. Angelica rushed to the edge of the ravine, looking down to see the men's bodies sprawled below on the rocks. The journal had fallen from their hands and was teetering on the edge of a rock. Angelica watched as the waves lapping against it pushed it over, and it fell into the river, where it was whisked away downstream.

The angry voices of men turned her attention to several of Donavon's men, who had entered the clearing. Some of them began to search for a way to scramble down to the rocks below, and two of them approached Angelica. Chugiak moved between her and them, snarling and snapping. The black smoke creatures surrounded them; their gruesome teeth twisted into wicked grins.

"Run."

Angelica wasn't sure if someone had spoken aloud, or if the voice was in her head, but she didn't question. She ran. As she sped through the trees the path through them seemed to be lighted, and she could see two angels ahead, beckoning to her to follow. Chugiak caught up and ran ahead of Angelica after the angels. It felt as if she were flying herself, her feet barely touching the ground. The journal was gone. Her pack and all her supplies were gone. But Angelica didn't care. All she could think about was the sight of Petra, lying broken against the rocks, with one hand outstretched toward the journal which bobbed in the river's current.

AS ANGELICA'S feet flew over the ground, tears coursed down her cheeks. A memory of Petra as a young man filled her mind, running ahead of her through the trees, his hair flying out behind him as he turned to call back to her.

"C'mon Angelica, catch up. My Grandma could run faster than you."

Then he took off again and she pushed herself to catch up, until they reached the ridge and they'd both collapsed, lungs burning and ribs aching.

Petra had rolled onto his side, his elbow in the dirt and his head on his hand, looking down on her. Something about the way he looked at her made Angelica's inside feel like boiling water. He reached over and moved a strand of hair from her eyes, and the next thing she knew his lips were pressed to hers. For one blissful moment her whole body thrummed, and her heart beat in wild ecstasy, but he drew back, staring down at her with a look that said he was as shocked as she was about what had just happened.

"I'm sorry," he stuttered. She knew what he wasn't saying. Their fathers had an agreement that when they came of age Angelica and Donavon would be married. For Petra to kiss her, or even have feelings for her, was like a betrayal. To return those feelings would also be a betrayal on her part, but Angelica didn't care. She'd already done the unforgivable, why should she worry about something so small as a kiss. She put her hand on the back of Petra's head and kissed him back, pouring all the feeling her soul contained into it, and he responded in kind, right up until the moment he jumped up and stood looking down on her, an expres-

sion on his face she couldn't read. Her heart began to pound even faster.

"Petra?"

"I can't," he said, and then he was gone, disappearing into the trees.

That was the last time they ran together through the forest. There were no more heart to heart talks after that, no more working side by side on some hair-brained scheme, no more practical jokes, and worst of all, no more laughter.

Angelica collapsed to her knees as the sobs shook her body. She'd told herself that one day she'd clear the air with Petra, tell him it had been a mistake, and try to see if they could be friends again. Now that would never happen.

When she looked up, she realized she was on the lakeshore, and directly in front of her, bobbing on the waves, was a kayak.

TWENTY-EIGHT

When the kayak finally touched bottom on the opposite shore, there were no clouds of demons, no feeling of being watched. All of nature seemed more at ease. Angelica's heart ached for Petra, but underneath that, there was a sense of peace, a confidence that everything would be okay. It made no sense, but there it was.

Angelica tied the kayak to a piece of driftwood and walked along the tree line until she found an old fire pit, probably used by fishermen. It didn't take long to get a fire going, and set up a lean-to of pine boughs lashed to a fallen log. There were only a couple hours until dawn and Angelica was exhausted. She fell asleep within moments of laying her head down and dreamed of Petra.

They ran through the creek behind Grandpa's cabin, water splashing outward from their bare feet, wetting the bottom of their caribou skin breeches. Angelica had a bow in her hand, arrows slung across her back, and Petra ran ahead of her, a spear balanced on his shoulder, ready to be thrown.

Suddenly Petra dropped to a crouch and twisted around to mouth a message to Angelica. 'Bear', he said silently, his lips exag-

gerating the word. Angelica nodded. They crept forward, trying to be as silent as possible, and hid behind some tall weeds. The sounds of the foraging bear came from the other side of the weeds. They held their breath.

Then the weeds parted, and a strange man stood there. He wore a beaded coat, and a headband decorated with raven feathers. There was a thick walking stick in his hand.

"Wake up," he said.

Angelica turned to look at Petra, but his image faded into the landscape.

Wake up," the man repeated.

Angelica sat straight up. Her vision focused, and the man from her dream stood outside her lean-to. She rubbed her eyes, unable to believe what she was seeing, and looked again. There he was, the man from her dream, with the same beaded coat and headband decorated with raven feathers. He leaned on his walking stick. Chugiak sat beside him, his tail thumping the ground, as the man rubbed his ears with his free hand.

"Who are you?" asked Angelica.

"I would ask you the same thing," the old man replied.

"My name is Angelica."

"I am Joseph. What brings you to our shore, and why have you stolen our kayak?"

That's when Angelica noticed the kayak was being paddled back across the lake.

"I was being chased."

The old man's face registered alarm. He let out a loud whistle like the call of a hawk. The girl in the kayak looked over her shoulder at him. The old man motioned to her, and she turned around, paddling back toward shore.

"Who was chasing you?" the old man asked.

Angelica wondered what to tell him. If she told the truth, would he even believe her?

"My father's men," she replied. "And..." She hesitated.

"And?"

"And something else, something evil, something you would have to see to believe."

"Demons?!" Angelica couldn't tell if his exclamation was a statement or a question.

He put his hands to his lips and cried out the call of a Raven. Men began to pour out of the trees, pulling kayaks between them in pairs. Joseph spoke to them in hushed tones. He gestured across the lake. The concern on their faces was obvious. When Joseph was done speaking the men jumped in their kayaks and took off across the lake. The girl made it back to the beach as the men were leaving.

"What's going on Grandpa?" The old man took the girl by the elbow and led her away. Once again Angelica couldn't hear what he was saying. He gestured toward Angelica, and the girl stared at her with wide eyes. The old man headed off down the beach, leaving the girl and Angelica on their own.

She approached Angelica and said, "I'm Mary. Grandpa needs to pray. I'll take you to the village." The girl began to kick sand over the fire.

"I just built that," protested Angelica.

"I'm sorry, you probably haven't eaten. The village isn't far, my mom will make you something."

The girl led Angelica through the trees on a well-worn path. Before Angelica knew it, they were walking through a wide gate. Its logs were gray from exposure, and blue wild-flowers grew along its base. The A-framed cabins of the village weren't much different from the ones back home. Soon they approached a house set back in the trees. Flower boxes on the front porch bloomed with salmonberry blossoms and the smell of cured meat frying wafted through the air. Angelica's stomach growled. A woman came out on the porch, wiping her hands on an apron embroidered with an eagle.

"You're here just in time for breakfast," the woman said with a smile. "Who is your friend, and what have you done with your Grandfather?"

"This is Angelica. Grandpa put her in my care and went off to pray."

"Of course he did," the woman replied. "Well, come on inside then."

It was warm inside, and the smell of fry bread made Angelica's mouth water. Mary sat at the cozy round table and began to pile food on her plate. The woman gestured for Angelica to do the same and grabbed the coffee pot off the stove to fill their cups.

"Where are you from Angelica?" she asked as she poured. When Angelica hesitated, Mary said.

"She is from across the northern boundary and she brought the hordes of hell with her."

"Mary!" Her mom exclaimed.

"What?" The girl looked at her mom with shrugged shoulders, her cheeks puffed out with food.

"I'm sorry," the woman said to Angelica. "My name is Elizabeth, and I apologize for my daughter's bluntness."

"It's okay," Angelica said between bites. "I am from across the boundary and there do seem to be demons chasing me."

"Well," Elizabeth turned to the stove and stirred the bubbling pot in silence.

Angelica wished she could sink into the chair she was in and disappear. Was it possible she'd brought evil to these people? She had just assumed it was already here. In her visions they were coming from the south. What if the visions were just fancies of her imagination? Angelica had lost her appetite. She pushed her food around on her plate. What could she do but leave this place?

If you do you will never find what you are searching for.

"You gonna eat that?" Mary pointed to Angelica's plate. Angelica pushed the plate toward Mary, who scraped the food onto her own, hunching over and shoving it in her mouth as if she were starving.

"Mary!" exclaimed Elizabeth.

"What?" Mary said through half chewed fry bread. "I'm hungry."

"Best be getting to your chores," said Elizabeth, giving her one of those looks only a mother could pull off. Mary sighed, but pushed back from the table and headed for the door.

"C'mon, you can help," Mary said to Angelica, leading her behind the cabin to where the dogs were each tied to its own house. When they saw the girls, they barked and wagged their tails excitedly. Chugiak ran to Angelica and greeted her as if she'd been gone for ages.

"You can tie him to that house there," Mary said, "It's empty."

"I don't tie Chugiak," Angelica said.

"Seriously? How do you keep him from running off?"

"Ever since he was a pup, he's stayed close to me. If he wanders off to explore, he doesn't stay gone long."

"Huh. Well if these dogs get loose, they run right off into the woods. Most of them join the wild packs, the packs used to be only wolves but now they've mixed so much with our dogs, it's hard to tell them apart."

"Are there a lot of them around here then?"

"Oh yeah, and they're none too friendly either."

Angelica repeated the phrase over in her mind, trying to decide whether Mary was saying they were, or weren't, friendly. The strange way Mary had of speaking made Angelica want to giggle. This last thing she couldn't quite decipher.

"So, you have to be careful then I suppose," Angelica said.

"Well, yeah, but not more so than you'd be careful of bears, or Moose even. Just make a lot of noise. They tend to steer clear."

Angelica helped Mary feed the dogs, change out their straw, and fill their water. Then they went into a shed and collected eggs from the strange looking birds Mary called chickens. After she scattered their feed, the girls took the eggs into the house.

Later, in the barn, Angelica met two of the ugliest looking creatures she had ever seen, standing side by side in a pen. They were shorter than a moose by half, and white with large black patches, or were they black with large white patches, Angelica wasn't sure. They had huge milk sacks hanging between their back legs, which they kicked out when Mary gently coaxed their milk from them into silver pails. "You can get that one," Mary said, pointing to the second animal.

"That's okay, I think I'll just watch," Angelica said, backing away as she spoke.

"You act like you ain't never seen a cow before," Mary said. "She won't hurt you."

Angelica shook her head again and took another step back.

"Fine, grab that pitchfork and muck the stalls then."

Mary pointed to the stalls, and Angelica realized she was meant to clean them. She grabbed the pitchfork and began to throw the dirty straw out onto a pile. What a strange place, thought Angelica, so much that was the same as back home, but it was like an entirely different world. Cows, and chickens, and their strange way of talking. Then there was the way they just accepted that there were demons chasing Angelica as if it weren't strange at all. It was all a bit overwhelming, but exciting at the same time. She wanted to ask a million questions, but time was something Angelica couldn't afford to waste. She decided she must ask them about the book the moment she got the chance. There was no time for getting better acquainted. The thought of her Grandpa in a cell, waiting for a death sentence made her shudder, and she doubled her efforts to finish the chores so she could get on with more important things.

Back inside the cottage, Mary's Grandpa, Joseph, was sitting at the table with several other men, each with a mug of steaming coffee in their hands. Elizabeth leaned against a kneading table with a worried look on her face. When she saw the girls, she grabbed a basket covered with cloth and headed toward the door.

"We have some visiting to do. C'mon along with me Mary."

"But Mom," Mary started to protest, but Elizabeth grabbed her arm and pulled her out the door, closing it firmly behind them.

"Why do you always treat me like a baby?" Angelica heard Mary saying before their voices faded away down the trail.

"Please, have a seat," Joseph said, indicating an empty chair. Angelica sat. Joseph's long hair was dark gray, and his brown skin looked like leather. Angelica figured the feathered headband he wore meant he was some kind of leader. The other men were much younger. They all dressed in similar animal skin shirts and breeches with moccasins on their feet. Their hair was long and black, which some of them tied back with leather thongs. They all had serious expressions except one, who smiled warmly at Angelica, winking at her when she met his gaze.

She quickly looked away, a pang of guilt quickly turning to alarm. Petra's smile always made her feel special, and safe. This guy's smile was different, sinister somehow. If she were Chugiak, it would raise her hackles. She decided to avoid this man in the future, especially any kind of eye contact.

One man handed Angelica some coffee, which she took willingly, wrapping her cold fingers around the warm mug, and relishing the heat of the bitter liquid as it ran down her throat: one of those familiar things from home. Joseph motioned to the men, and they all filed out the door.

"I have many questions," began Joseph, "but first I must ask, are you related to a woman called Hannah?"

"My mom's name is Hannah," Angelica cried. "Do you know where she is?"

TWENTY-NINE

"We haven't seen Hannah in many years," said Joseph. "She came to us injured. She'd had a run in with a bear. She barely survived, and it took months for her to get back on her feet. We became quite close in that time and spoke about many things. She often talked of you and how much she missed you."

A single tear escaped Angelica's eye. She'd longed for answers for so long, now she just wanted to cover her ears with her hands to block out what was coming next.

"The last time I spoke to her she was heading home to you, and by your question I'm guessing she didn't make it." Joseph said, shaking his head. "I'm deeply sorry. It's such a shame."

"Had she found what she was looking for? Was she bringing it home?" asked Angelica in a choked voice.

"Unfortunately, no," said Joseph. "The last clue she found led to Anchorage, and when faced with the decision to carry on or go home, she went home. She felt she'd been gone too long already."

"What do you think happened to her," whispered

Angelica.

"There are many dangers out there," Joseph replied.

They sat in silence. Visions of her mom being torn apart by a bear, stomped by a moose, lying broken upon the rocks at the base of a cliff, and a million other terrible outcomes whirled through Angelica's mind. Tears coursed down her cheeks. She'd waited all those years for her mother to return, when all along she'd been lying dead somewhere in the wilderness. Now she'd lost Petra too, and if she didn't find the rest of the Holy Book, she would lose her Grandpa as well.

Get it together Angelica. Your Father was right - it is time to grow up.

She swiped at her eyes and steeled herself, looking Joseph squarely in the eyes.

"What is the clue she would have followed to Anchorage. I don't have much time. I need to finish what she started."

Joseph stood. "Come," he said. "I will take you to the one who has the answers you seek." Angelica followed him out the door and down the path away from the little house in the trees. A momentary pang of regret at leaving the idyllic scene was soon dismissed, and she hardened her resolve, following determinedly behind Joseph to a little village that lay along the shore of an unfamiliar river.

Joseph led her to a large teepee across from a wooden pier with smoke billowing from its peak.

"Please remove your moccasins." He said, holding the flap open for her to duck inside. Chugiak tried to enter with her, but Angelica shooed him back. He sat next to Joseph then, his tail thumping the ground and his eyes full of pleading. Angelica patted his head and planted a kiss between his eyes before entering the teepee.

When they were seated, Angelica realized it wasn't smoke billowing from the top of the structure, but steam. An old woman poured water onto a pile of hot rocks in the center of the room, causing new clouds to rise. Angelica sat watching the old woman as she rocked back and forth, head back, eyes closed, her mouth moving with unheard words. Occasionally she poured water onto the stones.

Then the woman stood and ducked outside, Angelica followed. The woman ran to the end of the pier and jumped into the river. The current wasn't strong, and she floated on her back, a big smile on her face. Angelica ran after her and only hesitated a moment before jumping into the cold water. It felt so good she didn't care that her clothes were drenched.

Chugiak chased Angelica to the edge of the pier and jumped in after her, paddling in a circle around her before heading toward shore.

After a few minutes, the old woman and Angelica left the river, standing on the pebbly beach while the water dripped in puddles around their feet.

Joseph approached them.

"Leah, this is Angelica," he said.

Leah smiled, taking Angelica's hands into hers and holding them.

"Angelica, I am so glad to meet you. You want to know about your mother."

"How did you know? Did you see it in a vision, back in that sweat house, while you prayed?" asked Angelica.

Leah's laughter rang like bells.

"I did not have any visions," she replied. "I was not praying but singing a song that my mother taught me as a child." She winked at Angelica. "The steam is good for my aching joints. There is no magic other than that."

"So how did you know about my mother?" Angelica asked.

"Just look at you child," Leah said. "Anybody who knew Hannah would know who you are. That is, unless you found the fountain of youth and haven't aged in the last 12 years. Come, let's find somewhere warm and dry where we can talk."

Leah took Angelica to a cozy looking little cabin near the center of the village. Chugiak tried to follow but Joseph held him back. Chugiak rewarded him by choosing that moment to shake the water from his fur, spraying Joseph in the process.

"We'll be waiting," Joseph assured her. After a command from Angelica, Chugiak stayed with Joseph, but he whined as she walked away.

By the time they arrived at the cabin, Angelica was shaking with cold. Thankfully, a fire burned in the hearth and the front room was warm.

"Here, take off your wet things," said Leah, throwing Angelica a tunic, before stripping and slipping into her own. The rabbit fur garment felt soft against Angelica's skin, and she was grateful for the added warmth it provided. Leah pulled out a round contraption made of sticks which she set near the fire, then hung their wet clothes from it.

"These should dry nicely here," she said, before disappearing into another room. She came back with a pile of blankets, two of which she gave to Angelica. Then she filled a pot with water and hung it above the fire to heat.

"Some nice hot tea ought to do the trick," she said.

After Leah settled into her seat with blankets pulled up over her lap, she asked, "What is it you want to know?"

"My mom was here a long time ago," said Angelica. "Just before she left this place, she'd been talking about going to Anchorage."

"Yes." said Leah. "I will tell you what I told her. There is a legend that has been passed down through our family for generations. I am not sure how accurate or important it is, but your mother seemed to think it was significant."

Angelica's heart beat faster and her mouth went dry. She leaned forward in her chair, holding her breath as she listened to the old woman tell her story.

"Long ago there was a man and his son. The man was a cousin to my father's great grandfather. He was fleeing from the government who sought to take from him the last printed copy of the Holy Book."

Angelica slumped in her chair. It was the same old story she'd heard a thousand times growing up. What could she possibly learn from it that she didn't already know? She opened her mouth to tell Leah to stop, but Leah continued on.

"The little boat they were on was overtaken by a government warship and sunk, and in the process the man and his son were both lost, and the Holy book was torn in two."

Angelica's eyes went wide at Leah's words. This is what Grandpa had been saying - that the book had been torn.

"You mean it's true?" Leah did not seem to hear the question. She had her eyes closed and swayed as she recounted the rest of the story to Angelica.

"The son went into the water with his half of the book clutched to his chest, which the men waiting on shore for them recovered. It was the front half, the old testament that those men brought back with them. The second half, containing a new testament, remained in the clutches of the captain of that warship, which headed to Anchorage."

Angelica's head spun. It seemed incredible that this information had been so close for so long, and yet nobody in her own village knew about it. Then it hit her - somebody had built a wall, and set a boundary, and made a law against crossing it. Could this be the reason? But why? Why would anyone want to keep this truth from reaching her village? It was too much to wrap her head around.

"Two days later, while the warship sat in the Anchorage

harbor, the great catastrophe happened. My family has many tales of that day, the fire that rained from the sky, the suffering of the people, the starvation of the children," Leah shuddered, then met Angelica's gaze and continued. "That warship never left the harbor again, but still sits, a ghostly shell, possibly holding the testament you are searching for."

"How could it still be there, after all these years? Surely somebody else has gone looking for it." Even as she spoke the words, and even before she saw the light dancing in the eyes of the storyteller, who would most certainly report that, yes, of course, the book was still there, Angelica could feel it in her heart.

It was there. It was in that ship.

Angelica needed to get to it before it was too late.

She stood, "I need to get to Anchorage. I need to go now."

"Such a hurry. Such a worry," the old woman said, laughing and waving a gnarled hand. That ship has lain there through 4 centuries, I don't think it will go anywhere now."

"You don't understand. If I don't bring the new testament back to my village before the festival of unleavened bread, my grandfather will die."

Angelica pulled her still damp clothes on despite Leah's protests, then hugged the old woman and hurried to find Joseph.

She found him and several other villagers, including Mary and Elizabeth, near the beach, sitting around a fire.

"I need to get to Anchorage."

"I thought you might feel that way" Joseph replied. "I have already begun the arrangements. We leave at first light."

Angelica nodded respectfully, but silently she wondered how she would possibly endure the wait for morning to come.

"We will stay with my brother and his family tonight," Elizabeth said.

Elizabeth's brother lived near the river, in a large cabin, with several rooms with beds stacked on top of one another called bunks. Angelica, Mary, and Elizabeth shared one such room.

"You take the bottom," Mary said to Angelica as she put her pack on a top bunk. After depositing their things, they went into the main room where they were offered hot tea and a place around the fire.

The room was warm and the furs soft. Angelica found herself drifting back in her mind to a time she and Petra had found a lost bear cub when they were ten years old. Angelica, upset, had wanted to take it home, but Petra had held her back.

"His mother will hear him crying and come for him," Petra said.

Angelica had yanked her arm out of his grip.

"She won't come, she'll never come," Angelica yelled at him, unable to stop the tears

A bellow from the woods proved her wrong. Petra grabbed her arm again, and, together, they backed away, Petra pointing to a large tree with low branches. They climbed almost to the top, hoping the mama bear wouldn't be angry enough to climb after them. They watched her storm into the clearing. She stood on two legs and sniffed the air, bellowing her disapproval. Down on all fours again, she charged the path along which Petra and Angelica's hiding spot was planted. Angelica held her breath.

"Where are you," said Mary.

Angelica jumped and looked over at Mary who was sitting with both elbows on the table and her chin in her hands.

"Just thinking."

"Are you homesick?"

"A little."

"If I had a chance to go on an adventure, I would go in a heartbeat,"

Angelica could see herself, sitting on the ridge and staring at the southern horizon with a longing she couldn't explain. She smiled at Mary and patted her arm.

Joseph sat at the head of the circle and the rest of the family followed, gathering around, and settling in to listen to stories. It was warm by the fire and the furs were soft. Already Angelica's body felt heavy and her eyelids drooped.

She looked around at those gathered. At the spot closest to Joseph sat a small boy, cross-legged with a finger buried in his nose. His sister tugged at their mom's sleeve to draw her attention, but she was too involved in a conversation with Elizabeth to pay attention. Mary sat in front of her mom, chin in hands, elbows on knees, and submitted to having her hair brushed. Elizabeth used long, slow strokes. The tender way Elizabeth's slender fingers caressed her daughters head filled Angelica with longing. She couldn't remember a time her own mom had brushed her hair, although she surely had done so. Without thinking, Angelica reached up and ran her hand over the short growth of hair on her scalp. The lack of memories of her mom made Angelica realize the weight of what she'd lost.

Heaviness covered Angelica like a blanket as the information she'd received from Joseph fell upon her anew. It took all her effort not to lie down. The hope she'd held onto for so long was gone now.

She squeezed her eyes shut to block out the scene before her. Her shoulders shook. She breathed a silent prayer.

Please God, it hurts.

She pulled her knees into her chest and hid her face in her arms so the others wouldn't see her crying. Joseph's voice rang through the room, deep and clear, almost like music, but the words he spoke could not penetrate Angelica's thoughts.

Suddenly, the hairs on the back of her neck stood up. Her

arms broke out in gooseflesh. The sound of Joseph's voice faded as though he were walking away from her down a long corridor.

Angelica stood in a dark room. There were two angels standing behind a figure of a woman. They shone with a white light like fire and each held a sword across their chests. There was something familiar about the woman. Angelica stepped forward, squinting to see through the bright light, but all she could make out was a silhouette.

"Help me, Angel," the woman said.

"Mama!" The familiar voice of her mother sent waves of joy and longing through her heart.

"Mama, where are you?"

But even as the words left her mouth Angelica felt herself being pulled backward. The room faded into the distance and the sound of her mom's reply was barely audible. Angelica thought she'd heard her say, "come," and, "find me."

Angelica wanted to stay there, but she was snapped back into reality. Joseph knelt before her, and she collapsed forward into his arms as the last of her energy fled.

"Are you okay?" Joseph asked.

"She's alive, I have to go to her! She needs my help."

Angelica tried to stand, pushing against Joseph's chest for leverage, but her legs were wobbly, and her head was spinning.

"I saw my mom," Angelica whispered as Joseph scooped Angelica up and carried her into a bedroom.

"We will discuss it when you've rested," he said.

Then Elizabeth was there, tucking her into the furs and stroking her hair. She was speaking, but the words were far away and muffled. Unable to think another thought, Angelica turned away, and fell into an exhausted sleep.

THIRTY

"Angelica wake up!" Angelica rolled over and looked at Mary through sleep filled eyes.

"It's not even daylight yet," she complained.

"Grandfather says you must wake up now. He is waiting for you in the kitchen."

The room was icy cold, but it was warm under the covers. Angelica wanted to just stay under them and go back to sleep. Mary stood by the door waiting, so she threw back the covers, and slipped her feet into her fur lined moccasins. An involuntary shiver shook her frame.

"It's warm in the kitchen," informed Mary.

Angelica reached up to pull her hair back, forgetting for a moment they'd shaved it. She ran her fingers over her scalp. Her hair had grown a little, but if it weren't for the dress she wore, she would still like a boy. The thought of her shaved head reminded her of why she was on this journey to begin with, and the events of the night before flooded back into her mind.

Angelica hurried out to the kitchen, where Joseph sat with a mug of steaming tea in his old weathered hands.

There were two other men with him. Angelica recognized one from when she'd first arrived. The other stood warming his hands over the stove and talking to Elizabeth in hushed tones.

Joseph set his cup down and motioned for Angelica to sit next to him. Elizabeth set eggs, meat, and fry bread in front of her.

"When are we leaving for Anchorage," she asked Joseph.

"Finish your breakfast," Joseph replied. "Then pack your things and go. Eli and Ivan will take you to the river where you will travel by canoe to the port at Bruin Bay. From there you will catch a ship to Anchorage."

Angelica's stomach lurched and her appetite vanished as reality hit her. She was really doing this. Really going to Anchorage. She fingered her Eagle pendant. She had three weeks to get to Anchorage and back home again. Was it even possible, or would she end up lost, wandering the forest alone?

Joseph motioned to the other two men, and they all went out on the front porch where she could hear them speaking in muted tones through the door.

Elizabeth set a packet wrapped in sealskin on the table in front of Angelica.

"I packed you some provisions for your journey," she said.

"What's going on," Angelica wondered out loud. "Did something happen?"

"I will leave that for Joseph to tell," Elizabeth said, but the way she was wringing the corner of her apron in her hands told Angelica that it was serious.

"Thank you, Elizabeth, it was delicious, but I couldn't eat another bite." Elizabeth picked up the plate with a worried smile.

"Do you need help packing your things," Elizabeth asked.

"No, I don't have that much, I can manage."

Angelica made her way back to the room and began to pack. She was so grateful to them for replacing all her lost supplies; she said a quick prayer for God to bless them for their generosity and kindness. When she walked back out into the kitchen, Elizabeth wrapped her in a teary hug.

"We will pray for you on your journey. Please know that you will always be welcome in our home."

"Thank you," Angelica said.

"Where's Mary, I want to say good-bye," said Angelica, realizing she hadn't seen her since before breakfast.

"I'm not sure, maybe she went to do her chores. She's not good with goodbyes," said Elizabeth.

"I'll try to find her," Angelica said. But Mary wasn't in the yard. She wasn't in the shed, or the barn either. Angelica called out her name several times but there was no answer. When Angelica returned to the porch Elizabeth was standing outside, wringing her apron. "I can't find Mary, will you tell her good-bye for me?"

"Yes, of course. Please don't be upset. The more she cares for someone, especially since her father... it's just, the more she hates to tell them good-bye. I am sure she will regret running off and missing her chance to wish you well."

As Angelica followed the group out of the village, she was disappointed about missing the chance to say goodbye to Mary, but she understood. She'd left home without saying good-bye to Grandpa, after all.

And I've regretted it every day.

She hadn't said good-bye to her father, nor to her Grandmother, and she wondered what they must be thinking. Were they angry with her? Father probably was, but Grandmother was more difficult to understand. Often, she seemed to be just as rigid as Angelica's father, but then she would surprise her with a moment of kindness and unexpected mercy. Like the time Angelica had been late for the sabbath meal, and

Grandmother had told Father it was her own fault for sending Angelica on an errand so late in the afternoon. It hadn't been true - Angelica had been in the forest, sitting on the ridge, daydreaming, and had lost track of time. Angelica sighed. It was hard to know for sure what Grandmother would think, but outwardly she would back Angelica's father up; she was sure of that. The group walked silently westward for quite some time, each lost in their own thoughts, until the sun began to rise, painting the snow-covered mountains with soft pink. When they reached the river, the sun was above the mountains and the water shimmered with light. Several canoes sat close together on the small pebbly beach, some empty, some packed with goods for trading. Eli put Angelica's pack into an empty canoe, along with his and Ivan's. They would all three travel in one canoe, Angelica and Chugiak in the middle.

There were other men there, some making plans in small huddles, some looking at the sky to determine the weather and at the river to gauge the roughness of the water. Still others were checking the cords that held the packages to the canoes, and kissing the women and children who'd come to see them off.

Joseph took Angelica aside.

"My men returned from across the lake last night," he said. "We found some of those men who were chasing you."

Angelica shivered; the picture of Petra's broken body cemented in her mind.

"Their leader was killed," Joseph continued.

Just the leader? What about Petra?

"They asked for our help. Some have already gone north to report the incident to the high priest."

Angelica's stomach flopped like a hot fish. Was it possible that Petra had survived the fall? She tried not to hope it too much - so that the disappointment of the reality of his being gone might not sting as badly - tried to swallow down the hope around the huge lump that had suddenly formed in her throat. "And what about the other man who died?"

"They said nothing about another man, but they talked about a curse. They believe the curse of the boundary is at fault for what happened, and they are afraid."

As Angelica climbed into the canoe, she blinked back tears.

I knew it. I just knew it.

Chugiak settled in front of her and put his chin on her knee, looking up at her with eyes that seemed to share her sadness. Angelica scratched his ears and tried not to think.

The motion of the river and the soft sounds of oars in the water made Angelica drowsy. The sun warmed her, and she succumbed to the heaviness of her eyelids, her head bobbing with the boat's gentle listing as she dozed.

The sun on the water shimmered like diamonds, but the trees lining the shore were shrouded in a gray mist, swirling in the breeze. A darker mist appeared, mixing in with the gray and eventually overcoming it. Dark shapes broke free, flying above the surface of the water toward Angelica. She saw momentary flashes of bodies within, which seemed to be shaped like men one moment, then cat-like creatures with faces of vultures the next.

She wanted to cry out, but the words stuck in her throat. Frozen, she watched in horror, her heart hammering in her chest, as the dark figures surrounded her, their bottomless black eyes boring into hers. One broke away and flew straight at her, its fangs dripped black drops of blood, its throat a fathomless pit.

She prepared for the blow. Regrets flooded her mind. Regret over taking her mother's necklace, regret over not trying harder to be a good daughter for her father, and regret over not telling Petra the truth of her feelings.

Soon, she would stand before God and answer for her many failures.

"I'm sorry," she breathed up to heaven as she steeled herself.

She had always imagined death would be more terrifying. Above her the eagle soared, a silhouette against the sky, its wings outstretched, it's eye on Angelica as always. Slowly it turned, riding the air currents, floating ever closer. Angelica felt her hair move, feather-like across her cheek, as the breeze kissed her skin.

A high pitched scream flooded Angelica's mind. Light, like a sunburst, flashed, causing her to turn her head away from its brightness. Her view of the creatures in the dark mist was blocked by clouds of light. She held her hand over her eyes and attempted to peer through the clouds. As she did shapes appeared among them. A wing. A head of long flowing hair. A sword that burned with fire. Sunbursts flashed as the swords found their marks. The screeching of the dark creatures filled the air and then, as quickly as it began, it was over.

The river flowed. It's surface rippling, the sun sparkling on the waves. Squirrels chattered in the trees, and birds sang out their choruses. The eagle turned again, swooping low over the river as if to lead Angelica onward. Its cry echoed off the mountains like a song of victory.

Angelica breathed deeply to calm her racing heart. The men silently worked their paddles, oblivious to the battle being fought around them.

"Thank you," Angelica breathed heavenward once more. She knew there was so much more she wanted to say, needed to say, to God, to her father, to Petra, but a heavy blanket of exhaustion pressed down on her, and before she could complete the thought, sleep overcame her.

THIRTY-ONE

Two lakes and several rivers later, they arrived at the Bruin Bay trading post.

It was located on a river delta beyond a gap in the snow-capped peaks of the Aleutian Range. There were several wooden buildings built near the docks where two ships were moored. Dozens of bald eagles perched on the rails nearby, waiting for the fisherman to come in.

Ivan spoke to the captain of one ship, pointing to Angelica as he did. The captain was a strange looking man with pale skin and fiery orange hair. After talking to the man for several minutes Ivan gestured for Angelica to come, and she joined the two men.

"This is Ahab," said Ivan, "Captain of the 'White Whale'."

Angelica nodded at the man. "Nice to meet you," she said. "This is my dog Chugiak." Chugiak wagged his tail at the mention of his name but stayed close to Angelica's side. He cautiously sniffed Ahab's offered hand and then allowed the man to scratch him between the ears.

"He's a beautiful animal," said the captain, "and obviously very protective of you."

"We've been through a lot together," Angelica replied, smiling down at Chugiak.

"We sail at first tide."

Her quarters were a tiny room with a bunk and a small table. There was just enough room for her bag on the top bunk and for Chugiak to curl up on the floor. After depositing her bag, they made their way up on deck, much preferring the fresh sea air to the musty room below decks.

She headed for the prow. There was a small deck there where she wouldn't be in the way of the men as they prepared the ship to sail. The sails made flapping sounds as they danced in the wind from the north, which carried with it a bite of cold. Angelica shivered as it found all the secret openings in her garments. Her eyes watered. She stroked Chugiak's head, which had been promptly deposited into her lap, while she watched the men work.

The captain labored alongside his men, securing lines, and pulling sails into position. She decided his hair was the color of a salmon's flesh, and she noticed he had bright blue eyes. His pale skin was covered with freckles above his bushy red beard. Once again, Angelica was fascinated by his coloring.

"High tide."

The words were shouted by a man in a basket atop a very tall pole. The captain began barking orders, which the men obeyed almost before he spoke to them. Soon the ship was moving away from the docks.

Angelica noticed the Eagles. They weren't only on the docks but were also roosting in the tall spruce trees that lined the shore. Hundreds of them, bowing, shifting as the wind toyed with the branches upon which they perched, and every eye of every one trained on a single lone eagle, which soared above them, It's long finger-like feathers fluttering in the wind. Angelica could swear the bird was looking at her and maintained eye contact even as it turned and swooped down, zooming toward her. Closer it came, until angelica could see the tough yellowing skin between the eagle's eye and his beak.

It's going to hit me. Just as Angelica had the thought the bird changed course, veering upward, sending a shiver of excitement through her. Up went the majestic bird, circling the ship three times before veering toward the east

"An Eagle seeing us off means good luck for our journey," said a sailor.

It wasn't long before they reached the mouth of the bay and entered the larger body of the inlet. Angelica stared in awe. She had never seen water so big before, she'd only heard about it in stories. It was more beautiful than she'd imagined.

"What is that mountain," she asked a man, pointing to the peak that stood above the others to the northeast.

"The volcano, Iliamna," he said. "When the land gets angry, she spits smoke and ash. It is said that if man continues to mistreat the land, she will one day rain fire down on him. It will gather from her bowels deep below the earth, and explode from her mouth, high into the air."

Angelica stared at the mountain in wonder, imagining smoke and fire spewing from it, and wondering if that's what had caused the great catastrophe. She stayed on the deck until the sun touched the horizon and the sky was painted with vivid reds and purples.

"Galley's this way," called one of the men. Angelica entered a warm room that smelled of food and wood smoke. The men sat around a long table, talking, and laughing as they waited for dinner to be served. The only empty seat was next to the captain, so Angelica took it. Chugiak lay at her feet.

Steaming bowls of stew were placed in front of them, and they all tucked in to their meal. Cookie, as the men called him, even gave Chugiak a bowl of the delicious stew, full of vegetables and salmon. Soon Angelica's belly was full, and the warmth of the room made her feel relaxed and sleepy.

"If you don't mind me asking," Angelica said hesitatingly. "From where do your people hale? I've never seen light colored skin, or eyes the color of the sky, and your hair..."

The captain grinned at her.

"Our ancestors are from the east. A land called "Russia." I am told it is a land of snow and vast forests, much like here. I am also told that fiery red hair is a common thing, and some of the best Kings of Russia had hair just like mine."

"Do you ever wish to go there?" asked Angelica.

"Yes," he said wistfully. "Someday I will make enough money to take my ship across the great ocean to the homeland of my people. But, for now, I work so we can eat."

"Things were easier for my wife Laura in the city. She may be lonely for womanly company at the trading post, but at least she is safe."

Hot worms wriggled in Angelica's belly.

"Are you saying Anchorage is unsafe?"," she asked, hoping he would say no.

"I don't know what your business is there, but I would caution you to think twice about going. A young girl like yourself, alone - I would not advise it."

Just then the door opened, and Mary was blown into the room. The wind grabbed the door and yanked it from her hand, slamming it against the side of the galley wall. Wind and rain blew in along with her. She stopped in her tracks, eyes darting around the room.

One of the men jumped up and wrestled the door shut.

"What are you doing here, girl?" the captain asked.

"I... well..." Mary stammered. She looked at Angelica with pleading eyes. "I just wanted to go with Angelica."

"You stowed away on my ship?" The girl did not answer. "Well, do you have payment for your passage, or shall we throw you overboard?"

Angelica turned to him, shocked, but immediately saw the gleam in his eye. Mary, however, didn't see that gleam and started to cry.

"No. I'm sorry, please don't throw me overboard."

The captain chuckled.

"I won't throw you overboard," he said with a smile. Then, his expression turned serious. "I am sure that Cookie has some dishes to wash or some vegetables to peel. You can pay for your passage that way."

Cookie held up a rag and motioned toward the swinging kitchen door.

"I'm afraid the only spare bunk is in your quarters," the captain said to Angelica.

"We'll make it work."

The captain nodded and stood.

"Well boys, get your bellies filled quickly and your bones warmed with hot tea. Seems like we have a storm upon us."

Angelica looked at the captain, the hot worms wiggling anew.

"Don't you worry," the captain said, returning her with a comforting gaze, "This is just a small storm, we've weathered much worse. Feel free to stay in the galley as long as you'd like. It's warmer here than below deck, and dryer than out there." Angelica sat near the wood stove, half dozing, half thinking about her journey, and what waited for her in Anchorage. She pictured herself getting off the ship in port, Chugiak by her side, Mary following close behind...

No. No way.

The very thought was enough to snap Angelica back to

full wakefulness. She couldn't take Mary along on such a dangerous mission. This stowaway situation was a complication that Angelica didn't want nor need. What had possessed the girl to stow away on the ship in the first place?

Eventually, Mary came out of the kitchen and collapsed beside Angelica. Angelica frowned at her.

"Not a very smart idea," she said to Mary. "Your parents and grandfather must be quite worried."

Mary only looked at her hands as Angelica continued.

"The journey I am on is full of dangers, not only from wild animals and nature, but from evil forces you don't understand."

"I do understand," Mary protested. She glanced up, as though she expected Angelica to interrupt, but Angelica stayed silent, and listened as the girl revealed her heart.

"All my life, I've heard my Grandfather tell his tales of the battles between the invisible forces in the world, He spoke of the adventures, the heroes God has used, the miracles. I am tired of only hearing heroic tales," Mary said, bringing her heel down on the floorboards. "I want to be part of one."

"It's too dangerous," Angelica said. "If anything happened to you, your mother would never forgive me."

Mary looked up at Angelica, her face a study in stubborn determination. "Try to stop me," she said, then rose and pushed open the door, fighting against the wind, letting it slam shut after she'd slipped through.

Angelica sighed. Mary needed to go home. It was the only option. Angelica had no idea what awaited her in Anchorage. She only knew she needed to find the book, and that her mother was there, in a dark room somewhere. How would she find them both in the short time she had left and keep Mary safe at the same time? How would she keep herself safe for that matter? Then it dawned on her. She couldn't keep herself safe. It was the angels protecting her the whole time.

Would they extend their protection to Mary? Angelica bowed her head and said a prayer for Mary before heading below decks to sleep.

Angelica tried several times over the next few days to broach the subject of going home with Mary, but she refused to discuss it. With Anchorage looming ever closer, Angelica knew she was running out of time. She decided she would simply put her foot down, and force Mary to stay aboard and return home.

The next day Angelica approached the captain.

"Angelica, how can I help?" the captain asked. "I hope your quarters have not been too uncomfortable."

"Oh, they are fine," she assured him. "After weeks of sleeping on the cold ground, to have a bunk and a room, no matter how small, is a luxury."

"Good, good," the captain said, returning his gaze to the water.

"I do have one small problem though," Angelica said hesitantly.

"Oh," the captain said, turning to face her, concern in his eyes.

"It's Mary. She needs to return home, but she insists she's coming with me."

"I see," said the Captain.

"I have tried several times to discuss the matter with her, but she refuses to listen. My only option is to refuse to allow her to leave the ship when we arrive in Anchorage, and I'm hoping you'll back me up on that."

The captain raised his eyebrows at Angelica, rubbing his beard with a weather-beaten hand as he considered her words.

"I must confess, it probably would be a good idea for her to go home, but it is not as simple as that," the captain said.

"What do you mean," Angelica was beginning to get a bad feeling about what the captain would say next.

"Well, holding anyone on my ship against their will, especially a young girl, is problematic at best, and at worst..." he let the sentence hang between them for several moments before continuing.

"Then, there is the problem of food. The fact of the matter is, if she stays, we will run short of food before we return home. As it is, I've had to decrease everyone's rations due to feeding an extra mouth the whole way there."

Angelica realized that not only was the captain not going to back her up, but he would most likely not agree to take her back even if Mary wanted to go. Angelica frowned, searching for a solution.

"I'm sorry," the captain shrugged. "Mary will have to disembark when you do. I can have provisions enough to take her back upon our return, and I will contact her family about paying for her passage while back in Bruin Bay."

Angelica brooded over the situation with Mary. She racked her brain for a solution but the more she thought, the more it became clear that she was meant to take Mary with her. After all, God had provided no alternative arrangements. Perhaps, Angelica thought, listening to the girl's slow breathing in the darkness of their berth, I can find a safe place for her to wait while I search the city for The Book.

One morning the silhouette of the City appeared above the trees - tall black wigwams reaching into the sky. Mary came on deck and sat beside Angelica on their favorite old rusty pulley. They sat in silence; Mary finally spoke.

"I'm sorry, Angelica. I know you're angry with me, but please don't stop talking to me."

"I am angry with you Mary," Angelica took a breath, then started again, softer this time. "I don't think you realize just how much danger you've put yourself in. I am responsible for keeping you safe, and I'm not even sure I can keep myself safe." Angelica threw up her hands. "I don't know what I'm going to do."

Mary stood, placing her hands on her hips, her expression hard. "First of all, I am responsible for myself. Nobody put you in charge of me, or said you were responsible for me. You took that on yourself. I chose to come to Anchorage, and I choose to remain here. If something bad happens, it will be on me, not on you."

"And what will your parents say, if I have to go back without you, and somehow explain to them what happened?"

"The note I left them explained this was completely my decision, and if something went wrong, I would bear the blame."

Angelica shook her head sadly. "And yet, I still feel responsible."

THIRTY-TWO

Angelica and Mary walked between cliffs that reached into the sky on their right, and a short drop to the inlet on their left. They followed the remains of an ancient road. Its black surface was broken and uneven, tilting to one side or the other, some pieces jutting straight up. Trees and bushes grew through the cracks, widening them, and forming strange islands in the middle of the crumbling road.

It gradually turned toward the north. Marshes filled in the increasing spaces between the road and cliffs. Mary pointed to the white Dall sheep high up on the face, on outcroppings that seemed too small to hold them. They stood regally in the crags of rock, their curved horns a strange crown on their royal heads. Chugiak ran circles around the girls to sniff as many things as possible as they passed by.

The day was cloudy, but the sun would occasionally peak through, shining silver on the narrow waterfalls that fell at intervals from the cliffs. Mary turned in slow circles as they walked, pointing out animals, birds, flowers, and the glaciers filling the crevices of the snow-capped peaks across the water.

Angelica couldn't share Mary's enthusiasm. She couldn't stop thinking about Petra at the bottom of that cliff. Had he survived the fall? She was afraid to let herself hope. Was her mother alive also? If her vision was true, she was, and she was locked away in a room somewhere and needed her help. If only Angelica knew for sure and could find that room. What about grandpa, was there time to find the book, her mom, and still make it back in time? Her stomach twisted in knots at what may lay ahead.

The road gradually rose in elevation, and the girls crested a rise. Angelica gasped. A vast city lay before them - rumbling buildings among the trees, bushes and broken roads, strange metal hulks which looked to be some sort of transports littered the roadsides, and in the distance, tall buildings stood black against the sky.

"Wigwams that touch the sky," murmured Angelica.

"It's so big, how will we know where to go," asked Mary.

Angelica hesitated. "The Spirits will guide us," she replied, but she wasn't sure if she was trying to convince Mary or herself. She gritted her teeth and concentrated on steeling herself against the overwhelming feeling of being tiny in a great big world. Even as she said it, doubt niggled at her mind.

They continued along the road leading into the city. The remains of many old buildings were only piles of rubble overgrown with vegetation, but some still stood, gray stone amidst the trees and bushes. The black voids of missing windows and doors appeared like faces looking back at them. They didn't see any people. It was as if everybody had just walked away and left their city to crumble.

Where are they all?

Was Anchorage just a ghost town, rising into the sky amidst a backdrop of majestic mountains?

The answer to Angelica's musings came as the sound of a stone clattering across the ground. It echoed out from between the buildings to the right. Angelica thought she saw movement out of the corner of her eye, but when she turned to there was nothing there. Chugiak headed in the sound's direction, his tail wagging, and disappeared around the back of a building.

"Do you think it's a person?" asked Mary, her eyes wide. "Or something else?"

"I don't know," replied Angelica. "There doesn't seem to be any people around here, but perhaps they're just hiding."

"Hiding from what?" asked Mary.

Angelica called Chugiak but there was no sign of him.

"I've got to go find Chugiak," she said.

Mary followed. When they rounded the corner of the building, several children were kneeling beside Chugiak, petting him. An older boy stood just behind them, holding a rope attached to Chugiak's harness.

"Finally," said the older boy. The other children stood, and she saw that they each had a knife in their hands. The older boy wore a scabbard at his belt.

"C'mon hurry, it isn't safe here," the boy said, gesturing for her and Mary to follow him.

"Who are you? Let go of my dog," Angelica said.

"There's no time, let's go," he called, and he turned and headed back through the maze of decrepit buildings pulling Chugiak along with him.

"Hey, I said let my dog go," Angelica called out.

One of the smaller children, a little girl with dark brown eyes and apple cheeks turned and looked with imploring eyes at Angelica.

"If you don't be quiet, they'll catch us," she whispered. The little girl grabbed Angelica's hand and began pulling her after the others.

They plunged into what appeared from the road to be nothing more than a tangle of thick bushes and trees, but which was actually an escape route with a path winding through it. The children led them through the maze of buildings, finally stopping near a wall covered with vines. The oldest boy stuck his hand through the vines, and they parted like a curtain, revealing a door in the wall which opened from the inside. Everybody filed in. It took several minutes for Angelica's eyes to adjust to the gloom. They were moving through a long hall with doors on either side. Occasionally a curious head would pop out, staring at Angelica as if she were an alien.

"It's her," one of the children whispered.

They entered a large room with tables and chairs arranged down the middle. There were several doors along an opposite wall and the oldest boy knocked on one and slipped inside. The children seemed excited and kept peering at Angelica with looks of wonder on their faces. Angelica wondered who they thought she was, but she didn't have time to think very long. The door opened again, and the boy gestured for Angelica to enter. She grabbed Mary's hand, but the boy stopped her.

"Just you," he said.

The room was dark. A hooded figure sat in a chair silhouetted by the light from a small window above.

"This is Mother."

"Thank you, Joshua. You may go." The woman's voice was deep and husky.

Hello Angelica, we have been waiting a long time for you."

"What do you mean? How could you know I was coming?"

"I've seen it. In my visions," Mother replied.

Something hot sliced up through Angelica's insides. Her knees felt wobbly and she was afraid she may crumble to the floor.

"Don't be alarmed my daughter," the woman said.

"Who? Are you..." Angelica sputtered?

"Hush now. There will be time for questions later, first we must eat."

Angelica wanted to protest, but as if on cue, Joshua entered the room with bowls of food. A young girl followed him in. Her long dark hair hung in a braid down her back. Paint in strange patterns of brown black and green covered her face, and she held a spear in her hand. She spoke softly to Joshua before slipping back out of the room.

"What is it Joshua?" Mother asked

"We led the men away and lost them in the trees. I don't believe they saw the girls. If they did, I suspect they will be back for another search."

Mother nodded, and he too slipped from the room.

"What men? What's going on?" Angelica spun around, unsure if she should simply run to find Mary and get out of this place.

"Please, calm down," Mother said. "The danger has passed."

"What danger? What men? Who are you really?"

"Angelica," Mother said firmly. "Take a deep breath. Count to three as you inhale." Mother counted for her and Angelica took a shaky breath, blowing it out and then taking another.

"That's better," Mother said. "The men were nothing. It was just the Militia patrol. They come through at the same time every day. We have it under control. You are safe here."

"Militia?" Angelica rolled the word around in her mind.

"They are the men who control the city, and the people who live within."

"And they're dangerous?" asked Angelica.

"Yes. They rule with an iron fist, and for those of us who are less fortunate, they take us away to work in their oil camps."

"Like Hooligan camp?" Angelica was confused. Did the people not want to catch the Hooligan?

"No, this is nothing like Hooligan oil. This oil is black as night and found under the tundra far to the north. Sometimes it floats in pools above the ground. The oil was once very precious, and with the right knowledge it could be again. It could be turned into energy."

"Energy?" Angelica asked. "Energy for what?"

"For machines that power vehicles and weapons."

Machines and weapons? Angelica had heard stories about the evil of the past when machines and powerful weapons were used by evil men, but she'd believed those days to be over long ago.

For so long she'd sat on the ridge and dreamed about going south and discovering the world she knew nothing about. Now she just wanted to go home. Hug her father and grandmother and spend their entire lives in the village, untouched by evil.

Then she realized- it wasn't untouched, the evil just took a different form, the form of an old man being thrown in a cell and threatened with death for speaking the truth. It took the form of two brothers fighting over a stupid journal and falling to their deaths, and the form of a little girl stealing her mother's special necklace. Finally, the evil in her village took the form of a mother leaving a child behind and dying alone in the wilderness. Her hand reached for her necklace and she twisted the jade eagle in her fingers.

Mother's gaze moved to Angelica's necklace. "What is that you have there," asked Mother.

Angelica shrugged, "Oh this, it's nothing, just an old necklace," she replied.

"I need to get into the city," Angelica said with new resolve. "Of course," Mother said. "But first, come, let's eat."

Although the sun was at its Zenith in the sky, it was dark inside the main room, which was lit only by candles and the light of the fire in the hearth. The warm room and Angelica's full belly made her drowsy. She sat on one of the stuffed chairs. A handle on its side caused a footrest to pop up. She pulled a blanket over her and happily dozed in this newfound comfort.

She could hear the soft murmuring of Mothers words as she talked with the children. It reminded Angelica of a bubbling brook and she smiled as she thought about the valley where she'd played as a child.

She remembered traveling that bubbling brook in her first kayak she made with her grandfather.

She expertly dipped the paddles into the water, controlling the direction of the vessel as she moved around submerged rocks and fallen trees. The brook widened and suddenly she was small in her little kayak, being pulled along by the current of the rushing river, and working hard to control the boat with her paddle. Angelica's vision wavered.

She was above herself now, floating on air currents that pulled at her outstretched wings as she looked down through the eyes of an eagle. She saw that the river was almost as wide as the entire land. On and on it ran, spilling out into the body of water she recognized as the inlet she'd just traveled on.

She watched her tiny kayak shoot out onto the waters of the inlet and then turn east toward the black silhouette of the city.

Then she was back in the kayak, paddling against the waves of the inlet, sweat dripping from her brow. A great volcano rose into the sky on her left, and a range of snow-capped mountains lined the distant horizon on her right. She paddled for what seemed an eternity until the black city rose above her. She skirted the shore until she came to the ancient harbor. Several ships lay partly submerged in the water, but she ignored them - her target was the big one at the center.

As she came closer the walls of the ship's hull became transparent, allowing her to see the small rooms and passageways inside. The rooms were filled with old rotten beds and water dripped down the walls. Her eyes were drawn to one particular room in the middle of the first floor below the deck. There was a door in the wall with a round wheel on the front. Light shone through the cracks of the treasure box, illuminating the room it was in and beckoning to Angelica.

Angelica's eyes opened back in the warmth of the common room, in the recliner near the fire. She looked around at the faces of the children who were standing all around her with looks of wonder on their faces.

"Come over here child," Mother called to her, "and tell me of your vision."

Angelica sat beside Mother and wrung the edge of her tunic between her hands. Would Mother think she was crazy after she'd recounted her dream? She took a deep breath and closing her eyes, recounted as much of it as she could remember.

"You must go retrieve this book," Mother announced rather abruptly. Angelica didn't know what to say. She'd been expecting to have to argue her case. She should be relieved, but something in her spirit didn't feel right.

Mother said something to Joshua, and he ran from the room, returning shortly with a scroll under his arm. "You'll need a plan," Mother said, "and a guide who knows the city." She sat, palms together, tapping her forefingers against her lips.

Beneath Mother's hood Angelica could see a scar. It pulled at one side of her mouth, holding that corner slightly open, showing a canine tooth. It gave Mother the appearance of a snarling animal. Angelica immediately thought of

Grandfather's scar. Had this woman also encountered a bear? Angelica wanted to ask, but it seemed rude to do so.

Joshua unrolled the scroll and laid it out on a table. It was a map of the city.

"This is us," he said, pointing to an area west of the city along a long black line.

The road Mary and I traveled on, thought Angelica, as her eyes followed the curve along the shoreline of the inlet the map called the Turnagain arm.

"Here is the city line, and the gates. Going through the gates is not an option. We will follow this route and go through a break in the wall here."

He pointed to a spot northwest of their current position. "We will then make our way here, to the Conoco building. From the top floor we will hang glide over the most dangerous parts of the city to the Port of Anchorage, where, with a bit of luck, we will land safely on the ship's deck."

"Very good," Mother said, nodding in approval.

"I'm sorry," Angelica said. Joshua and Mother both turned to her.

"What does 'hang glide' mean?"

Joshua grinned. "When we're done here, I'll show you what a hang glider is."

As they finished up the plans Mother said, "I will be praying that the Lord will bless your endeavor and that you will accomplish this feat."

"Thank you." Angelica said, but deep down in her gut something about it all didn't feel quite right. She needed the help though, so she decided to proceed with the plan, and pray the Lord would protect and guide her as he'd done so far on the journey.

"I trust you God," she prayed silently. *"Help me to trust you more."*

THIRTY-THREE

"Welcome to Tanglewood Mall," said Joshua.

"Tanglewood Mall," Angelica repeated in wonder as she peered into the rooms as they passed them. They were covered with strange metal gates. Most of the rooms were empty, but some of them had shelves arranged in rows throughout them.

"This is where the ancestors came for shopping."

"Like a market," Angelica said.

"Sort of, but they didn't buy food or supplies here. This was a place to buy luxuries, things they didn't need, to fill their meaningless lives, and keep them from getting bored."

"How do you know this?"

"From reading what they called, "magazines." Some were preserved from decay by being encased in a clear waterproof wrapper."

"How strange," said Angelica.

"Yes, they were strange. They didn't hunt to eat, because they ate a lot of artificial food. They hunted for fun. Some believe this is why the catastrophe happened. They believe the earth was punishing our ancestors for disrespecting her creatures."

"Do you believe that?" asked Angelica.

"Me? No, I don't. I do believe it may have been punishment, but not from the earth."

"From whom then?" Angelica asked, but her heart said the two word answer at the same time Joshua's lips formed the words.

"From God"

"God punished the ancestors for being evil you mean?"

"For rejecting him and his ways, yes."

They walked in silence for a while, leaving Angelica to mull over Joshua's words. She tried to fit it in with everything her Grandfather had told her about what he believed was in the second part of the book. Could the aftermath of the catastrophe be what God was sending someone to save them from? That didn't sound right to Angelica. Why bring a catastrophe on evil men and then send someone to save them from it?

Angelica hoped that when she found the book, she would also find the answers to these questions. They neared the end of the mall, and it widened into an atrium. There was a third floor, and the ceiling was high above them. Joshua led her through a door and up a flight of stairs.

"Over here," Joshua called excitedly, as he approached a strange contraption hanging from the ceiling. It was made of a strange colored cloth and the frame was of a material she couldn't name.

"What is it," Angelica asked.

"This is a hang glider," Joshua gestured dramatically as he spoke. "You strap yourself in, and it allows you to fly," he exclaimed.

"It allows you to fly," Angelica repeated with wonder and confusion. "That's crazy."

"Crazy in a wonderful kind of way," Joshua laughed.

"How will I ever learn how to use it in time, it looks so complicated," said Angelica.

"You don't have to learn how to use it - just how to hang on. We'll fly tandem."

"Tandem?"

"Yes, we'll both strap ourselves in. I'll fly and you'll ride along."

"I can't ask you to do that," Angelica protested, feeling the weight of one more person she would be responsible for.

"You didn't ask me," he said firmly. "God did, and you can't keep me from doing what God asked me to do."

Angelica sighed. She didn't have an argument for his reasoning. As she gazed up at the contraption, a feeling of peace came over her. Was that a sign from God? She wasn't sure, but she took it as one and if she was wrong, hopefully God would warn her.

"How are we going to get that thing down from there," she finally asked.

"Oh, we're not using that one. I have a replica I built out of modern materials."

"Modern materials?" Angelica asked, rolling the strange words over her tongue.

Joshua laughed, "something I read in a magazine. Essentially, the fabric on that thing," he pointed at the glider, "would probably tear or even disintegrate the moment we touched it. I doubt it would hold air to allow us to fly. So, I built one out of spruce and moose hide. It is very sturdy, and it flies like you wouldn't believe."

As they re-entered the atrium Angelica looked out front. There was a vast field of concrete. Weeds and bushes grew up through the cracks.

There was a broken rock sign in the middle. It's faded words read, "Tanglewood Park Mall,"

As they reentered the quarters Angelica could see that it was a part of the mall. One of the many stores, as Joshua called them, only larger and at one end.

"What kind of store was this," she asked Joshua.

"This is what they called a Department Store," Joshua replied. "This area was where the offices were, for the people who ran the store. The area where we have the bigger rooms used to be one big open area. That is where they sold things and customers would come to shop. We built our own walls to make the rooms"

Angelica had noticed the walls didn't reach all the way to the ceiling. A store that big must have held thousands of items. The people who lived back then must have been incredibly wealthy.

When they reached the common area, a girl approached. She had red hair that hung in two long braids down her back. Her pale skin was covered in freckles and she wore an apron over her simple Moose Skin tunic.

"I'm supposed to tell you they have assigned you to the kitchen, and it's time to prepare dinner," the girl said, smiling shyly. Angelica followed the girl to the kitchen where she saw a decidedly grouchy-looking Mary, who'd apparently also been assigned to the kitchen. "Is there something about my face that screams domestic, and not warrior?" she grumbled.

"Warrior?" Angelica laughed. "You are still a child."

"Shows what you know," Mary retorted. "David fought the giant when he was even younger than me."

"You know the scriptures," Angelica said with surprise.

"Yes, of course I do," Mary said, throwing Angelica an irritated glance. "My Grandpa is the village Shepherd after all."

"Shepherd," Angelica asked in confusion. "You mean someone who raises animals for the sacrifices."

"No, no, no," Mary said. "We don't make sacrifices

anymore. A shepherd is like a priest, but since there is no temple, and I guess calling the Rabbi was decided against, they are called shepherds, like King David was a shepherd."

"What about your sins, if you don't make sacrifices anymore?"

"We just go to the shepherd, he prays for us, and we do penance."

"Penance?"

"Some kind of good work. Helping in the village, with the elderly, the sick, things like that."

Angelica pondered what Mary was saying. What would it have been like to grow up in a world where you served people to atone for your sin, instead of killing innocent animals? The poor would be cared for, not stuck in camps, and labeled unclean. The elderly wouldn't be pushed aside or forgotten.

She wondered if anybody was ever stoned in Mary's village. She decided not to ask. She doubted they did, but she didn't want to appear any more ignorant to Mary than she already did. She sighed at the thought, realizing that wishing for a different past was a fruitless daydream. She turned her attention to the carrots they'd given her to chop, and determined not to think about anything but what she was doing for the next few hours.

When dinner was done Mary and Angelica and several others were given the task of serving it. Angelica carried the bowls of stew carefully, one in each hand, not wanting to spill any. The other children, however, lined three, sometimes four bowls up on each arm, and carried them as if they were attached there.

Angelica watched as Mary attempted to carry two bowls on an arm, but as she moved to deliver them, they both clattered to the floor, spilling stew everywhere. The girl in charge of the kitchen came and glared at Mary, hands on her hips.

"That's good food wasted! What a mess!"

"I'll clean it up." Mary started for the supply room, but the girl stopped her.

"Never mind, I'll get it. We've got a lot of hungry people out there, and the sooner we get them fed the sooner we can eat ourselves."

Angelica decided that one bowl per hand was good enough for her, and returned to her task. As she set a bowl down in front of Mother, the woman reached out and took hold of Angelica's wrist.

"Tomorrow morning it will be time for you to finish your quest. Get some rest. Joshua will wake you before dawn."

"We leave in the dark?"

"There will be light enough for you to see by. The midnight sun will ensure that."

"Our warriors will escort you as far as they can, and then you and Joshua will continue alone." Mother gave Joshua a fond smile.

"What about Mary and Chugiak?"

"We will make sure they get to the rendezvous point on time, until then, they will be safe with us." Mother glanced at Joshua again. Did her amiable smile slip for an instant, or had Angelica imagined it?

THIRTY-FOUR

In the morning, Mary's bed was empty. A folded piece of paper sat on her pillow. Angelica opened it and her heart sank.

"Angelica, I'm sorry I wasn't honest about my reasons for coming on this trip. I came to find my father. He is somewhere in Anchorage, and I've been longing to meet him for so long, I had to take my chance when it came. If I'm not on the ship in time, go back without me. Please forgive me, Mary."

Angelica sat down hard on the bed. Her father was in Anchorage! Had Mary even mentioned her father? Angelica couldn't remember.

How had she missed it? She thought back over the last few days. Had Mary seemed quieter, more distant than before? Angelica was so wrapped up in her own problems she hadn't been paying attention. Deep down she'd felt annoyed at the added complication of having the girl tagging along. Had that fact kept Mary from confiding the truth?

Guilt enveloped her. She should have been paying more attention instead of being so wrapped up in herself.

Just then the young girl with the painted face came into the room. They'd since learned her name was Kayla, and the militia had taken her parents.

"She's gone," Angelica cried. "I've got to find her."

Kayla took the note from Angelica and frowned as she read. "Foolish girl," was her only comment.

As if Kayla isn't just a girl herself, Angelica thought.

"Come," Kayla said.

Angelica followed Kayla down the maze of hallways to where Joshua and Mother stood waiting for her.

Kayla handed the note to Mother, who read it and handed it back to Angelica.

"I have to find her," Angelica said. "I can't leave her out there in the city alone."

Mother took Angelica's hand into her own and held them for a moment. Then she said. "You finish your quest. Come back here when you're done. Kayla will find Mary and bring her back here. Then, when we are all here, I will go back with you, and together we will save your Grandfather."

Angelica looked at Kayla, who stood with her spear at her side and her shoulders back. Mary was her responsibility. Mary leaving without a word was her fault. It wasn't fair for someone else to have to chase after her.

"If Kayla can't find her nobody can," said Joshua.

Mother squeezed Angelica's hands. "I have a good idea where she may have gone. Kayla knows those streets better than anyone and will find her before she gets far."

Angelica gave the confident girl one last appraising glance. Then she said, "Okay." She wished she could pull Kayla aside and have a private conversation with her but there was no time. She met the girl's eyes. They had a somber but determined look in them. Kayla gave Angelica a slight smile. It was a small reassurance, but it was all that Angelica would get - Joshua started giving final instructions and Angelica refocused her mind on what he was saying. Dread grew inside her. Then they were out the door.

They moved through the shadows of trees and bushes, along paths the children knew well. The sky was crimson and purple as the sun touched the horizon. As the light faded to dusk Angelica's eyes adjusted. Soon she could see almost as well as if it were daylight.

They ran in a single file line, Kayla in front and Joshua in the rear, twisting and turning down paths and ancient roads lined with the crumbled foundations of old houses. The remains of what had once been a giant city was a strange contrast against the natural beauty of the mountains and sky.

Occasionally they would slow to a walk, catching their breath, before running again.They stopped several times and Kayla sent two of the older boys to scout the area ahead. They would return and nod to her, and they were off again, the tall buildings that stood black against the sky looming ever closer as they ran.

When they reached a certain point the others stopped, bid Joshua, Kayla, and Angelica safe journeys, and turned back.

"Things get more difficult from here." Joshua said. "We'll have to move slowly and watch for others. Stay close behind me, if I run, you run. If I hold my hand up like this, you stop." Joshua showed her several other hand motions and Angelica did her best to commit them to memory. Her stomach was full of hot fish, wriggling and jumping. She swallowed hard and steeled herself as Joshua began to move. Kayla took up the rear.

Occasionally Joshua would pull them into an alcove or

doorway and they would watch as others passed. They also seemed to be wary of being seen, keeping close to walls and peering surreptitiously around corners. At one point the sound of hooves clopping on the road echoed all around them. Joshua frantically started pulling at doors, trying to find one that would open. The fourth door opened even before he touched it and they tumbled through. As they entered, a man pushed the door firmly shut and secured it with a metal bar.

As Angelica's eyes adjusted to the dark, she could see that the room was filled with people, their eyes wide with fear as the sound of hooves came closer. A child whimpered and his mother quickly picked him up, putting his face against her chest to muffle the sound and quietly shushing him. Everybody held their breath.

The clopping sound stopped.

"Did you hear something," said a gruff voice.

"No," another replied.

There was silence for what seemed like forever. Angelica stood still as a statue, trying not to move, her heart pounding in her ears.

The sound of metal clambering came from somewhere outside followed by a feline screech.

"Just a dog chasing a cat," the first man grumbled. Then the clopping hooves started up again and moved away from their position, slowly fading into the distance.

Angelica realized she'd been holding her breath. She sucked air into her lungs and then breathed out slowly, willing the tension to leave her body. Her heart was pounding and she could feel her pulse in her temples. Part of her wanted to curl into a ball and stay hidden, but instead she steeled her shoulders and willed herself to keep going.

"Thank you friend," Joshua whispered to the man at the door. "Your kindness has saved us." The man at the door only nodded, before removing the bar and opening the door for them to leave.

"Thank you," Angelica whispered as she moved out the door. The man smiled at her, warmth in his eyes. "May God bless you on your journey," he said. Angelica wanted to stop and ask him what he knew of her journey - the knowing in his eyes made her wonder, but then they were back out on the road, the door closed again behind them, and they began to move.

The closer they got to the city center, the more people they saw. They began to hide less and less as the sun started its descent toward the western horizon. Everyone else seemed to be in a similar state of hurry. The tallest building soon loomed above them and Joshua was prying open a door for them to enter.

"This is where we part ways," Kayla said.

THIRTY-FIVE

Chugiak watched Angelica leave. He sat obediently next to the boy who held his lead. Angelica had told him to "stay", and Chugiak was always obedient to her. When she was gone from sight, the little boy pulled at the lead, but Chugiak stayed where he was. The boy tugged harder, but Chugiak was much bigger than him.

A creature made of light hovered above the road near the path where Angelica had disappeared, and beckoned to Chugiak. He stood for a moment considering. It wasn't in his nature to disobey a human, but he knew in this case he should follow the creature of light.

Chugiak picked up a stick and dropped it at the boy's feet, wagging his tail and barking excitedly. The little boy grinned, threw the stick, and then unhooked the lead from Chugiak's harness. Chugiak took off after the glowing being, picking the stick up on his way just for the joy he felt at having it in his mouth. He kept going, crossing the road, and flying into the trees, pursuing the glowing creature that hurried ahead, leaving the little boy, still shouting, behind.

A malamute, Chugiak's body was bred more for hard

work than for speed, but still he could run faster than a human, and following Angelica's scent was second nature. Though he heard no words, the creature of light bid him "be cautious," so Chugiak slipped into the trees, unseen.

Angelica had left him accompanied by many, but now had only two companions, the tall boy, and the girl with the painted face.

Chugiak followed the group into the city, the light being hovering just ahead of him. He didn't like the heavy darkness that hung over the people and buildings here. The hair on the back of his neck bristled, and he tucked his tail between his legs, keeping his head down. Most people ignored him, or moved away cautiously when they saw him. A large brown stray with black eyes and short hair eyed him from across the street.

Alarm coursed through Chugiak when he heard the clopping of hooves. He moved behind some barrel-shaped containers the color of fish skin, and watched the men approach on giant long legged beasts. Angelica and her friends slipped into a doorway. The sound of a child coughing behind the door reached Chugiak's ears. The men stopped and looked around, their gaze moving to the door.

Chugiak pushed over the container in front of him. It made a loud sound when it hit the ground, and the cat who had been rummaging within streaked down the alley.Chugiak pretended to give chase.

"Just a dog chasing a cat," one man said, and they moved on.

Soon Angelica and the two others emerged from their hiding place, and Chugiak continued to follow unseen. They stopped near another doorway and spoke for a few moments. Angelica and the tall boy moved through the doorway, but the girl with the painted face stayed back. After waiting for several moments, the paint-face girl moved from the doorway and strode down the center of the street further into the city. She motioned to someone in an alley, and a group of men burst out, running toward the doorway Angelica had just gone through, shouting, and banging on the door before going through it. The dark creatures that had followed Angelica since they left fish camp surrounded the girl and grinned, their gruesome teeth snapping together in their large black mouths. Chugiak growled. He wanted to follow Angelica, but the door was closed. He didn't trust the tall boy with the dark creatures around him and Angelica needed his protection, but the light creature beckoned him to follow the girl. Disobeying a creature of light would be like disobeying the Alpha Spirit, so Chugiak followed the girl, whining and looking back at the door only once.

Chugiak followed the girl for a long time. The buildings around them got shorter and more spread out. There didn't seem to be any people around anymore, and any animals they encountered skittered away. They crossed a strange metal roadway with rails and crisscrossed beams and turned toward the east on the other side. Following a road alongside a creek, before eventually turning north again, crossing a bridge over the creek, and turning east once again. A smaller bridge over the creek led them to a small island full of trees and bushes. There was a fence surrounding an encampment full of dwellings made of stiff cloth. This cloth smelled nothing like the moose hide villagers used at home to make dwellings. Chugiak hung back while the girl walked up to the gate and spoke to the men standing guard. They opened the gate, and she walked inside, greeting a man wearing all black and a hat with something resembling a beaver tail sticking out in the front. Chugiak spotted Mary, hiding behind one of the dwellings, listening to what the man and girl were saying.

Chugiak didn't know a lot of human words, but he recognized Angelica's name, and the urgency with which it was spoken. He sensed the fear that came over Mary as she clamped her hand over her mouth, and then ran into the trees behind her, one creature of light pulling her by the hand, the other following behind with its hand in the small of her back. Chugiak followed the fence line around the encampment. The creature of light moved ahead, guiding him.

At a place where the fence line was damaged, Mary pulled back on the woven metal and slipped out of the encampment. When she saw Chugiak, she knelt and wrapped her arms around his neck. Words and tears poured from the girl. He didn't know what she was saying, only sensed that she was afraid. He licked her face to comfort her.

The creatures of light beckoned to Chugiak, and together they led Mary away from the encampment. Wading through the creek to avoid the bridges, they made their way unseen back through the city and into the forest on the other side.

They traveled long into the night, and when Mary was too tired to go any further, they stopped within a grove of spruce trees. Crawling under the large branches that brushed the ground, they curled up together on a bed of pine needles, hidden from the world.

THIRTY-SIX

Angelica and Joshua stood in what appeared to be an atrium with hallways leading off to the right and left. Directly in front of them were several doors made of metal with no handles. They overlapped each other where they met as if they would slide open, and a great arch bridged them all. Angelica walked over and put her hand on the metal, then pushed to see if it would slide.

"The elevators don't work," Joshua motioned to another door. "We'll take the stairs."

Angelica peered up the staircase that twisted with sharp angles, spiraling higher than Angelica could ever imagine going. As they climbed her thighs burned, and it was hard to breathe. The pack on her back bit into her shoulders and she stopped frequently to adjust it.

"I need to rest," she called to Joshua.

"Only for a minute, we need to get to the top before the sun touches the mountains. Any longer than that and we won't be able to see where we're landing."

Angelica had climbed mountains all her life, and she ran through the woods constantly. She was in great physical condition. This stairway was unlike anything she'd ever seen, however, and by the time they reached the top she was aching everywhere, and her breath was coming in gasps.

When they pushed through the door onto the roof, the scream of the wind was deafening. It flattened the fur of their parkas, and bit into their cheeks. As Angelica struggled to catch her breath, her nostrils burned with the crisp clean scent of promised snow.

She could see the harbor to the east, bathed in the crimson of the sunset. Silent, like a ghost town, the rest of the city was spread out before her. The Sleeping Lady mountain lay across the inlet just as she had for centuries, content in her slumber. The mountains to the south of the city stood guard, their slopes covered with the remains of winter snows. The inlet that separated the lady from the city glowed with the reflection of the setting sun. The high-rises stood like black steel skeletons above the ruined skyline; and a black destroyer languished in the harbor to the east, long dead in its watery grave.

"Sit down and catch your breath." Joshua began assembling the hang glider he'd made. The framework, made of wood, had made up the skeleton of his pack, and he began to lash it together with leather cords. Angelica wondered if it was wise to trust such a thing to carry her through the sky like a bird. Joshua didn't appear to have any such worries.

"Done," he finally announced, standing back to peer at his handiwork. The sky had turned pink with splashes of purple and crimson as the sun stretched its edges to try to touch the mountain peaks.

Joshua picked up the harness, and motioned Angelica over so he could put it on her. A shout of a man's voice echoed from the open stairwell door. Joshua ran into the stairwell, peering over the railing and down into the long shaft. He closed the door and tried his best to secure it with a metal pole that was lying on the floor.

"Who is it?" Angelica asked.

"I don't know, but I don't plan to stick around and find out." He hurriedly put the harness on Angelica, checking to be sure it was secure before getting into it himself. As he worked, the sounds of men shouting grew louder from the stairwell. It felt like it was taking forever as Joshua secured them to the glider. Finally, Joshua picked up the glider and nodded at Angelica.

The door behind them rattled. Men shouted.

"Go!" Joshua began to run toward the edge. Angelica wanted to scream for him to wait, what if it wouldn't hold them both? What if they plummeted to their death? The door crashed open behind them and she heard shouting voices close behind her. She squeezed her eyes closed and willed herself not to scream. Her feet left the ground and they were floating. She opened her eyes. They were above the city. Joshua was shouting. Whether it was Joshua's contagious enthusiasm, or the adrenaline, Angelica didn't know, but she found herself caught up in the moment's exhilaration. She grinned, the men in the high-rise, her grandpa, her mother, all momentarily forgotten.

All too soon, they were approaching the big black ship that sat at an angle in the water. Before Angelica could even wonder how they'd ever land, they were there, Joshua's feet landing with a thud as he ran across the deck with the momentum. Angelica ran along with him, doing her best not to lose her footing, until they finally came to a stop.

When the harness was unstrapped, they both collapsed to the deck, lying on their backs and laughing.

"That was close," Joshua exclaimed.

"I can't believe that worked," laughed Angelica.

As the adrenaline wore off, a foreboding feeling filled

Angelica's chest, the pounding of her heart in her ears was no longer from the thrill of flying. A dark fear swirled in her mind, of what, she wasn't quite sure. She opened her eyes. The dark ones were all around them, flying over them, their black mouths open in silent laughter, or screams, it was hard to tell. Angelica couldn't move. She tried to call out to Joshua, but her voice wouldn't work. Finally, she turned her head toward Joshua, and she saw that the dark ones were all over him, grabbing on to his limbs and sitting on his torso.

Angelica squeezed her eyes shut again. What was she going to do? Images of being torn apart by those gruesome teeth sent shivers up her spine. Worse yet, what might they do to her soul? She felt powerless, her legs felt like rubber, and she couldn't see any Angels anywhere. Tears escaped her eyes.

This is hopeless.

She'd made it this far but now she'd reached the end. The quest would go unfinished, she would die here on the deck of the ship, with her objective so near. She felt herself surrendering, then she heard someone calling her name.

"Angelica, come on, get up." It was Joshua. He was on his feet, pulling her up. She let herself be drawn to her feet. It felt as if she were far away watching it happen. Then she saw the light ones amidst the dark ones, fighting them with their gleaming swords. Three of them surrounded Angelica and pushed back against any of the dark ones who tried to come near her.

"The Book Angelica, where is it?"

Realization began to dawn in Angelica's mind. The dark forces wanted the book just as much as she did. If they got a hold of it, they would destroy it. She prayed silently for help to know what to do, chiding herself for not doing so sooner.

Why do I always seem to wait until things feel hopeless to call out to you? As she prayed, a light began glowing through the iron walls of the ship from below, straight down from where she stood.

"It's somewhere below us," Angelica told Joshua the impressions as they came to her. There's a room with a safe, the Bible is inside the safe."

"Where should we start?"

"We follow the light," Angelica said, pointing to a large structure in the middle of the ship. "It's just below there." She said.

They made their way to the structure, found a door, and stepped inside. It was dark, cold, and stank of dead fish. Water dripped from the ceiling, running down the walls. Angelica hesitated, swallowing fear that threatened to rise back up.

"What's wrong?" Joshua asked.

"Nothing," she said. "Let's go."

There was a stairway just inside the door. Joshua pulled out a lamp and turned the dial that caused the ember within to light into flame. Angelica descended, their feet on the metal stairs making sounds that echoed back at them. The lamplight cast shadows on the gray walls. She turned left at the bottom. The light was coming from behind the door directly in front of her, making the door appear to be a spectre, itself.

Could it be this easy?

Angelica hesitated, uneasiness fighting for control of her mind. She pulled on the door, but it wouldn't budge. She pulled harder, but it did no good.

"I BET we have to turn this," said Joshua, tugging at a wheel attached to the front of the door. It didn't move. *Of course we do,* thought Angelica, chiding herself for not realizing the obvious sooner.

"I think it will open the door, but it's not budging," Joshua said between gritted teeth. Angelica looked around. There were other doors with wheels as well, and some with bars that crossed the door at an angle. She found one door that was ajar. She had to tug hard to get it to move. It made a screeching sound as it slowly gave way.

"Well, everybody knows we're here now," Angelica said. The room appeared to be a kitchen of some sort. It looked as if scavengers had been there. Angelica found a pipe amongst the debris and brought it back to Joshua.

"Try this," she said.

Joshua put the pipe through the spokes of the wheel and pulled, hanging his whole weight from the pipe. Angelica moved in front of him and also grabbed the pipe. It started to bend slightly. Joshua yelled, a loud guttural yell, and bounced up and down. The pipe bent more. The wheel moved just slightly, and then a little more, screeching, like a scream, echoing through the bowels of the ship. Then it gave way, dropping Angelica and Joshua, onto the floor. Joshua jumped up and turned the wheel. After a few turns, they heard a loud click, and the door popped open.

For Angelica, light shining through the wall panels once again rendered solid material translucent, and completely illuminated the room. Joshua held up the lamp. Angelica followed. There was a bed to the right, a desk on the left, and several small doors in the far wall, each with a panel of keys numbered zero to nine.

The source of the light was coming from the largest one at the bottom. Angelica knelt and looked at the panel, punching several of the keys. Nothing. Joshua knelt beside her.

"According to a book I found in the library, you punch in a special code and it unlocks the door. All of them are dead. They need special power called 'electricity' to work. I'm afraid that's something we don't have." Of course, thought Angelica, running her fingers around the edge of the door.

Her fingers snagged on something. "What's this?" she asked, indicating an oddly shaped hole in the safe door.

It's a keyhole," said Joshua.

Joshua started rummaging through the desk drawers. Angelica sat on the bed and breathed a silent prayer.

What do I do? Finding nothing in the drawers Joshua started banging on the wall around the safe with the pipe, but all that did was make a racket.

"Stop, I need to think," she said.

Joshua dropped the pipe, throwing his hands up in mock surrender. The pipe hit the floor with a clanging sound. Angelica grabbed the pillow and threw it at him. A small ring with a single key on it fell out of the pillowcase, landing with a 'ting' next to the pipe.

"The key," exclaimed Joshua, grabbing it and turning to the safe.

Angelica held her breath as Joshua inserted the key and turned it.

The door popped open, revealing the contents of the safe. There was a stack of old papers, yellow and cracking with age. A dish of coins. A magnet held a yellowed picture of a woman and a small boy to the inside of the door. In the back of the safe was a leather pouch. A light, shining from within, made the leather translucent, almost invisible.

Angelica hesitated. The hot fish flopped in her stomach. This is what she'd come for. This was the thing that would save her Grandpa's life and change her village forever. Her father wouldn't be happy. Angelica took a deep breath and reached for the pouch. The moment her hand touched it, the light, which had beckoned so ardently to Angelica, disappeared. It was strange how shadowy the room seemed, the lantern light barely dispelling the gloom. She longed to hold the book in her hands - to read its words - but a new sense of urgency made her slip the pouch over her shoulder and head for the stairs.

"Angelica wait," Joshua called. "Shouldn't we look inside and make sure it's what we came for?"

"I'm sure," said Angelica. "We need to get out of here."

Back on deck the midnight sun lit the sky crimson and purple, making the air seem shimmery. Angelica ran toward the rail opposite the shore, peering over the side, hoping to find some means of escape. Sure enough, there was a canoe secured to the hull by a rope. She pulled another rope from her pack and tied it to the railing. She took a deep breath to calm her nerves.

"C'mon Angelica, you just flew off of a giant wigwam, this is nothing," she whispered to herself.

She climbed over the railing and pressed her feet against the side of the ship the way Joshua had described, then let herself slowly lean backward as the rope slid through her hands. Then she was walking down the side of the ship, and before she knew it, she landed in the canoe. It wobbled. She threw her arms out to steady herself. She sat down hard in her seat and watched as Joshua followed, rappelling down the side of the ship as if it were second nature.

He untied the rope and pushed the canoe out onto the water. A while later she looked back. The silhouette of the ship and city were black against the colors of the sky. Smoke rose into the air, forming ominous clouds she knew weren't clouds at all. She also knew, without seeing them up close, that the demons were angry.

THIRTY-SEVEN

The dim light of dusk covered the water and bathed everything in shadows. Angelica's arms were strong but eventually they began to ache. She kept paddling, knowing the feeling would pass and she would get a second wind. She leaned into the motion, putting in extra effort to get through the fatigue. As they came around a spit of land, Joshua motioned toward a small beach along the shore - their landing point.

As the tip of the canoe slid onto the beach with the swishing of wood on sand, Joshua jumped out to pull it further up on shore. Mary and Chugiak burst from the trees. Chugiak jumped into the canoe and licked Angelica's face, his tail wagging furiously.

"Quick," cried Mary. "It's Kayla. She's hurt and needs help."

"Where?" Joshua asked.

"Back there, about a quarter mile up the trail."

Joshua took off running. Mary pushed the canoe back out and jumped in.

"Hurry. Grab your paddle. We don't have much time."

"What's going on?" exclaimed Angelica.

"It was a trap," said Mary. "The whole thing was a trap."

Further explanations would have to wait as the two girls put all their energy into paddling. They sliced through the choppy waves, far out into the inlet, until they saw the shape of the White Whale appear in the dusk.

They pulled up alongside the ship, and the crewmen threw a rope ladder down. The girls climbed up onto the deck. Angelica's arms were like rubber as she pulled herself over the rail.

One sailor motioned toward the galley.

"They are waiting for you in there," he said.

Angelica almost ran to the galley, bursting through the door, eager to see the captain, but nobody was there. She ran back up on deck toward the stern of the ship where the Captain liked to walk in the evenings. She'd accomplished her mission and was bursting with desire to relay the wonderful news. However, the words died on her lips as she rounded a corner to find Mother walking alongside the captain, her hand tucked into his elbow.

"Did you find it?" Mother asked. "Where's Joshua?"

"Don't tell her anything," Mary, who had been following close to Angelica cried. "She's a liar. It's all a lie. She wants the book for herself." Angelica met Mary's eyes. They were full of urgency and something else that hadn't been there before. A kind of resolve, as if she'd been unsure and now she wasn't. Angelica's own instincts had warned her about Mother from the start.

"Don't be ridiculous, Mary." Mother said, her voice was smooth, her smile benign.

"I want what Angelica wants - to bring the book back to our village and save my father, side by side with my precious daughter." She reached her hand out toward Angelica.

Mother's face wore a hesitant smile, and her eyes seemed to be pleading and encouraging at the same time.

Angelica knew the truth, and her fingers went unconsciously to the jade eagle around her neck. She hadn't had time to think about where her mother might be, and how to find her. Without Joshua and the children to help her how would she survive another trip into the city? Deep inside something snapped. Angelica realized she wasn't going to find her, at least not this trip. Could her mother hold out that long? A tear slid down her cheek.

"You're not my mother," Angelica said softly. "My mother is a prisoner somewhere, but I suspect you know that. I also suspect you know exactly where she is." The accusation had flown from her lips without thinking. Mother began pleading again, "Angelica, it's me. Please believe me." How the woman could make real tears flow like that was beyond Angelica's understanding.

The Captain held up a hand, "Ladies, let's all sit down and discuss this. Angelica, what if she is your mother, shouldn't you at least let her plead her case?"

Angelica lifted her gaze toward the sky and prayed aloud.

"Reveal the truth," she cried. "And send your armies of Angels to protect and guide me. I will do what you will me to do."

The wind picked up and began to swirl around the ship. The sails snapped and the rigging clanged together. Men began to run to their positions, shouting to each other, scrambling up into the sails.

The demons appeared then, swirling around Mother, one of them crouched on her shoulder, whispering in her ear. Mary leapt at Mother, yanking the hood from her head, revealing short white hair and eyes the color of the sky in spring.

"You're not her mom," Mary shouted. "You're my sister. My half-sister."

Shock came over Mother's face, followed by anger,

making her scarred mouth even more sinister. Her blue-gray eyes were as hard as the steel hull of the naval ship.

"You're controlled by the demons," Angelica shouted. "They're all around you. I can see them. They have a hold of your arms, and one is on your shoulder, whispering in your ear."

Mary stared at Angelica. "You can see them?" she asked, her eyes wide with shock.

"What exactly are you saying?!" the Captain exclaimed.

"These dark spirits are evil," Angelica said, unable to take her eyes from the sinister creature perched on Mother's shoulder. It seemed to smirk at Angelica, as if it knew she sounded crazy to Captain Ahab. "I know it sounds crazy, but it's true." She wrenched her eyes away from the demonic scene and locked eyes with the captain - it was vital that he believe her.

"They want to destroy the book. They have been trying to stop me this whole journey. I can see them. I thought nobody else could." She looked over at Mary.

"I couldn't," she said, "until I was fleeing my father, and I prayed for God's help and protection. Suddenly I could see the demons, and angels with flaming swords, who showed me the way through the city as I fled."

"You found your father?"

"He is the leader of the militia," Mary said, her shoulders drooping as she spoke the words.

"I overheard him and Kayla talking. They believe the book has the power to heal Mother's wounds, and they want it for themselves."

Mother's face was close to purple now. She moved toward Angelica.

"I need not listen to these ridiculous, and may I say, unbelievable, accusations from this child. I am Mother. I am to be respected and obeyed." She wagged a finger at Angelica as she moved closer. The captain held out his hand to stop her. She turned her angry gaze on him.

"Do not interfere between me and my daughter," she spat.

"Stop calling me that," Angelica said. "You are not my mother. My mother is being held prisoner."

"You're evil is exposed, big sister," said Mary, linking her arm with Angelica's. Chugiak growled low in his throat. Mother shot them a piercing glare.

The Captain motioned for Angelica and Mary to move behind him.

"Thank you for having tea with me. I am sure you will be eager to be on your way. I would appreciate you not delaying," He said, his voice getting stronger as he spoke.

He motioned to two men wearing scabbards on their belts, they moved to stand on either side of her, hands on their weapons. Angelica saw the trepidation in their eyes but still they obeyed their Captain.

Mother glared at the girls. "Very well," She said through clenched teeth, "but this isn't over. She turned away, yanking her arm from the grip of one of the men and strode to the ladder at the rail. "My father is not somebody you should cross. You will come to regret it," she said just before she disappeared over the side.

"Go to my quarters," the captain said, handing Angelica a key. "Lock yourselves in. As soon as Mother is well away, we sail."

THIRTY-EIGHT

The Captain brought them their dinner that evening and ate with them in private. As he put his empty dish on the table, he cleared his throat.

"I want you to bunk in here for the trip home. My bed is large enough for two girls."

"Captain, we can't deprive you of your comfortable bed," Angelica said. The captain held up his hand and shook his head.

"YOUR SAFETY IS MY PRIORITY." Angelica and Mary exchanged concerned looks. The captain continued. "When Mother came on board, there were several of my crew who greeted her warmly, as if they knew her. I hate the idea that I'm not sure where these men's loyalties lie. I can't risk having you vulnerable, which is what another night below decks would mean. There are a handful of men I trust. They can escort you on deck for air, but otherwise I need you to stay here, with the door locked. I will bring you your meals. This is not a request."

After the Captain left, Angelica let out a long sigh. "Well Mary, it seems as long as you're around me, I'm afraid you're exposed to danger."

Mary pierced Angelica with her eyes. "Do you really think you're that important?" Angelica's eyes widened in surprise at the girl's tone. "The dark ones have always been around," she continued. "They're always working against those who do God's will. My Grandpa has been fighting them my whole life."

"How does he do it? Fight them, I mean," Angelica asked.

"He doesn't, the angels do. That's their job. He prays, that's his job. He prays them up, and the angels fight the battles"

"How do you know this?"

"Grandpa told me. And I've watched him. Since I was this high." She held a hand low to the ground.

Angelica thought about the times she'd seen the dark ones. It was as Mary had said - when she'd called out for help, the angels had appeared, bursting with a power that completely overcame the dark creatures. She felt a little silly that she hadn't made the connection before now.

"God sent me Angelica. He sent me so I would find my father and discover the truth."

"Thank you, for telling me." Angelica whispered. "I've been so confused." After a moment, she swallowed hard and added, "and afraid." Mary came over and knelt at Angelica's feet, taking her hands, and smiling.

"Let's thank Him together."

Mary prayed out loud and Angelica listened in wonder. There were no recited verses or memorized words. There was repentance, but it was simple and sweet, a basic, "forgive us for our sins," spoken with a certain confidence that the forgiveness was a guarantee, there for the taking for anyone who asked, a confidence unlike any Angelica had ever witnessed, and certainly had never possessed, no matter how much blood was shed on her behalf. On and on Mary prayed, pouring out her soul. She not only asked for forgiveness, but boldly asked for divine protection, as well. It was unlike anything Angelica had ever seen - it was as though Mary was having a conversation with a most intimate friend. As Mary continued, Angelica's heart lightened, and all the pressures of her quest seemed to melt away. She realized then just how much she'd been carrying - the worry about her grandpa, the need to find her mother, the guilt over Petra's death, the responsibility she'd felt for Mary, and the fear of failing. She let it all go as Mary prayed, asking God to take their burdens into his hands. When Mary finished, with a sweetly whispered, "amen," the girls sat in silence, basking in the feeling of peace.

After a while, Angelica pulled out the pouch and turned it over in her hands, a shiver coursing through her as she thought of the little boy who'd given his life to protect its contents.

Thank you for your sacrifice, she thought.

"Here goes," she said. With delicacy, and care, she opened the flap, then reached in and pulled out the book.

On the back, the black leather cover was cracked. The binding was loose. On the top were only dry flimsy pages. The first page was printed with a large bold type that read, 'The New Testament'. Angelica's heartbeat quickened. The remaining pages were thin like birch bark and appeared to be barely hanging on. She would need to continue to handle this treasure with care.

Angelica opened to a page near the center of the book and began to read.

"For our battle is not against flesh and blood, but against the rulers, against the authorities, against the powers of this dark world and against the spiritual forces of evil in the heavenly realms."

"The demons and angels that have been constant throughout this whole trip," Angelica said. "They are the real enemy."

"Does it say how to win the battle?"

"It says put on the whole armour of God." Angelica replied. She read the next section out loud. Mary tapped a thoughtful finger on her chin.

"The belt of truth, the breastplate of righteousness, the gospel of peace. What does it all mean?" she asked.

"Maybe we should start at the beginning," Angelica said, turning to the first page.

"This is the genealogy of Jesus Christ, the son of David, the son of Abraham," she began. As she read the list containing so many familiar names, Angelica's heart sang with joy, and she forgot Mary was even there.

A KNOCK on the door reminded Angelica of their circumstances. She frowned. There was a battle raging outside the door. It was time to go back into it.

Mary took Angelica's arm. "Don't worry. We are protected."

Angelica wanted so badly to share her confidence. How small her faith must be that the joy she'd felt only moments before had faded so quickly.

"WE SHOULD PRAY for God to reveal which sailors to be wary of," Angelica whispered to Mary as they walked around the deck on their scheduled time in the fresh air, with their escorts staying only a few yards behind them.

"Can't you see them?" Mary whispered back.

"See who?"

"There, hovering around some of the men."

Angelica looked. Sure enough, the dark creatures were swirling around three of the men as they shared a hunk of cheese. The sunlight flashed on the blades of their knives.

Angelica sighed. "I'm so glad you're here, you make me stronger." Mary squeezed her arm. They circled, Chugiak running ahead. As they approached the men, Mary squeezed Angelica's arm tighter. Angelica studied them. They were young, not much older than Angelica. Their clothes weren't as nice as the other sailors', and they weren't as brawny. Their hair hung in strings and the scrub on their faces could barely be called beards. They were barely more than boys.

One of them caught her gaze. Angelica detected displeasure in his eyes.

ANGELICA CAME to dread going up on deck. Her stomach was tied in knots as they circled the deck, and her heart pounded each time they passed one of the three men. Even Chugiak seemed nervous, hovering near the girls. One of the men tried to talk to him, kneeling and holding out his hand, but Chugiak growled, his hackles raised. The man quickly stood, frowning at the girls as they passed. Angelica wondered if he knew she and Mary could see the dark ones hovering all around him. For that matter, did he even know the demons were there?

The third day was drizzly and gray. The wind blew cold air in from the north. Angelica walked the deck with Mary, the hood of her parka pulled over her head with the ruff out to protect her face from the wind and rain. They were following their usual route, past the handful of trusted men the Captain had assigned to protect them, when Mary's arm flung out and stopped Angelica, who looked at the girl with questioning eyes.

"New guy," she said, flicking her chin in the direction of three of Ahab's men. Sure enough, there was an unfamiliar face among them - likely one of the usual workers had taken ill. It took Angelica only moments to see what she was sure Mary also saw, the demon circling the head of the interloper.

He and two other men leaned against a barrel, passing a cheroot around as they huddled against the elements. As the girls passed, the demon lashed out with its long black claws. Angelica jumped and cried out, "God". The moment she spoke, a light flashed, blinding her. When her vision cleared, the men were shouting and throwing a floating ring over the rail into the water.

"Did you see that?" Mary whispered.

"All I saw was a flash of light."

"The angel hit the demon with such force it knocked that sailor right off the ship," Mary whispered with wide eyes.

The Captain approached. "Get inside. You shouldn't be out here with this commotion." He ran to where the men were pulling the shivering sailor back onto the deck. Someone immediately covered the rescued man with blankets. Another pressed a hot mug of tea into his shaking hands. The sailor took the mug and said nothing. He only stared at Angelica. Back inside the cabin, after the door was securely closed and locked, the girls curled up on the bed and Angelica pulled the New Testament from its pouch.

"Matthew chapter three," Angelica read aloud, "In those days John the Baptist came, preaching in the wilderness..." As Angelica read her whole being filled with wonder that God would send a baby - not a warrior, not a mighty King on a throne, not a great prophet - a baby.

"Now here comes John the Baptist, dressed in camel hair and eating insects." Angelica wondered what a camel looked like. Was its fur short like a moose's, or long, like a bear's? Soon, she was reading about Jesus coming to be baptized.

"Suddenly the heavens were opened, and He saw the Spirit of God descending like a dove and resting on Him. And a voice from heaven said, 'This is My beloved Son, in whom I am well pleased!' Angelica paused, pondering the verses in her mind.

"It says the Spirit of God, singular, so that would be different from the spirits we see, the angels."

"It seems so," Mary agreed.

"I want to see that one," said Angelica, tapping her finger where the word "dove" was printed on the page. She smiled as she tried to picture it. Before they knew it, the Captain was bringing dinner. "You girls look like a couple lynx with pheasants," said the Captain as he ate. "What have you been doing here all day?" He looked around the room as if searching for evidence of some kind of mischief.

"It's the New Testament," Angelica said. She began to tell the Captain the whole story from the beginning.

"...AND then the King cut off John the Baptist's head, put it on a platter, and gave it to her." She paused, looking up at the captain who had his chin on his fist and was looking at her with rapt attention.

"You mean to tell me; this Mary was a virgin?" He slapped his palm on the table. "Who ever heard of such a thing?" He looked at Mary. "Are you going to pop out a baby now?"

Mary's horrified expression was all the answer he needed. His belly started to shake. Soon he was laughing so hard there were tears streaming down his face.

"Captain," Angelica protested. "Will you stop?" Angelica's face was hot as he continued laughing. She stood, crossed her arms, and stalked over to the bed, turning her back to the mirthful Captain.

. . .

"What's wrong with her?" the captain asked.

"I think she's upset that you're laughing at a story we consider sacred. It's a miracle that the baby was born to a virgin. It was foretold in the prophecies of the Old Testament. It's also a miracle that we even have these Holy scriptures."

"So, you think God has no sense of humor then? Whereas I think God has a great sense of humor. I have heard some of the stories that have been passed down. Have you heard the one about the talking donkey? Now that is a God with a sense of humor." Angelica heard the captain rise, cross the small cabin, and open the door.

"I meant no disrespect to God, or to you Angelica," he called just before pulling the door shut. "But I do believe if God can make a donkey talk, he can make a virgin have a baby."

Mary sat beside Angelica, wrapping an arm around her.

"He doesn't get how important this is," Angelica said.

"No, but you do, and that's what matters." By the time they reached Bruin Bay Trading Post Angelica had read through almost four of the named sections, Matthew, Mark, Luke, and John.

"It's incredible," she told Mary. "Jesus took them through the Old Testament scriptures and showed them how they were all about Him. I wish I could have been there for that!"

THIRTY-NINE

The harbor was mostly empty when they disembarked in Bruin Bay, but Joseph stood near the end of the gangplank, waiting for the girls. He grabbed Mary and pulled her to his chest, holding her tightly and looking up to heaven. Angelica saw his lips mouth the words 'thank you'. The guilt she'd struggled with when she first discovered Mary had stowed away tried to capture her thoughts, but she dismissed it. Mary had been instrumental in the Journey's success.

After several moments of quiet conversation with his granddaughter, Joseph turned to Angelica.

"I am so glad that you have made it back safely." As he spoke, his eyes fell upon the pouch.

"Come, let's not linger here." He glanced up at the sky. Angelica followed his gaze. In the east, dark clouds roiled and churned, moving closer as they watched. Sailors on deck turned and pointed. The clouds grew darker by the minute. Joseph grabbed Angelica by the arm.

"We must go."

They hurried to their canoes. Chugiak pressed his ears

flat against his head, and his hackles stood straight up as he followed close to Angelica.

The rain came suddenly, pouring down in great sheets. Storms in this part of the world were so common that the men paddling simply continued. They couldn't see the dark clouds, these not part of the storm, that were amassing all around them. Angelica's heart was pounding in her chest. She wanted to shout out - paddle faster - but she sat frozen in her seat, bracing herself for what was coming. She looked over at Joseph and Mary in the other canoe. They were praying. As they prayed, Angels surrounded them in greater numbers, the flames on their swords flaring. Angelica chided herself, why didn't she ever remember to pray until all seemed lost?

She lifted her face to the rain; water running in rivers down her face as her lips moved. She closed her eyes and pictured a cloud of Angels. She imagined they were bigger and more powerful than the demons, throwing them back as if they were puffs of cotton-weed. The canoe slowed. Angelica opened her eyes. The men were staring at her, their paddles still, their mouths hanging open. Thousands of angels surrounded them. The light they emitted was almost blinding.

Can they see them? Angelica wondered.

"Why have you stopped," she asked, turning to face one and then the other.

"You're all..." began one.

"... lit up," another continued. "It's like you're sitting in sunshine but..." He moved his hand to indicate the rain that was still pouring from the sky.

"All is fine," Joseph assured the men. "Angelica is a chosen one, and God is shining his light on her. We should continue on." With that, the men continued their paddling, as if this kind of thing were normal. It all seemed a little surreal to

Angelica. She didn't know what lay ahead, but she was feeling far more confident about things working out than she ever had before.

The light shone through her closed eyelids with a reddish glow, and her face felt warm, as though the sun were shining on it. A feeling of peace overtook her, and she let herself settle into it. It was a welcome change from the anxiety she'd lived with for so long. It rained the rest of the day, and when Angelica looked at the clouds, they were only normal rain clouds. She wondered at the thought that her prayer was answered exactly as she'd envisioned it.

Could the air south of the border be truly poisoned? Had she gone insane? She didn't feel insane. Everything she'd experienced felt real.

But, isn't that what insanity is, thinking things are real when they aren't?

When they arrived back at the village, Joseph led her to the main building at its center. People stopped to stare at her when they passed, talking excitedly to each other, and then moving in behind to follow. She pulled her cloak up over her head, trying to disappear within. A small crowd had formed behind them and followed them right into the building. Joseph pointed Angelica to a chair on a raised platform along the western wall. He sat beside her and soon several other men and women ascended the platform and took the other chairs, each one stopping to introduce themselves to Angelica.

The air had a shimmery quality, and it was as if her feet weren't touching the floor. The strangeness of each moment was dizzying, and she thought she may faint. It was difficult to register what was being said, and the urge to run outside into the fresh air was strong, as it was too hard to breathe in here.

Why were they all gathering anyway? Shouldn't Angelica

be on her way north? She was running out of time. She turned to say as much to Joseph, but he stood and walked to the edge of the platform. The crowd grew silent. They covered the floor, seated in groups, children filling in the front row. Some were standing near the back. One man had a bandage wrapped around his head and was leaning on a walking stick. He seemed familiar. She squinted her eyes to see better, but Joseph began speaking, pulling her attention away.

"I know that you can all see the light that illuminates our friend and daughter Angelica. This is because she's chosen by God and the light bears witness to that fact. When she speaks, we can trust her words as true, and we should all hear and heed them." With that he turned and motioned for Angelica to join him. As she came alongside him he said, "Tell them".

"Tell them what?" she whispered, trying not to stare at the crowd of faces looking up at her. Joseph took her shoulders gently and turned her to face those in the chairs behind her.

"Tell the elders your story. All of it. From the beginning." With that, he left her standing alone. Angelica's scattered thoughts began to gel in her mind, and the spinning sensation began to fade.

From the beginning.

"I was born in the north, in a village beside the Turquoise river..." Once she started, the words flowed from her, unbidden. She almost forgot where she was, reliving the journey in her mind as she spoke.

"All my life I have been unworthy," she said. "I tried to be better, tried to make my father proud, but I failed, again, and again. My mother left when I was small, and never returned. Even God turned from me, or so it seemed."

Angelica looked out at the crowds, they listened in a

silence that seemed to fill the room louder than any sound ever had.

"God chose me to fulfill his purpose. I have no idea why. He guided and protected me on my journey, and in the end, he led me to the missing half of our Holy Book, called 'The New Testament'. Angelica smiled then, fresh waves of peace washing over her.

"This New Testament has revealed the Truth to me. A truth that offers redemption for all my failures, and hope, that I can be better with the help of God's son. He is the one whose story I want to tell."

She told them what she'd read. From the virgin birth to death on a cross. The elders were all leaning forward, listening intently. She watched the tears in many of the people's eyes change to gasps of joy at hearing of Jesus raised from the dead.

"...and Jesus told them all who believed should be baptized in the name of the Father, the Son and the Holy Spirit." She stopped. Suddenly, she had no more to tell. She looked at each of the elders, then turned toward the crowd. "We need to be baptized," she said, realizing it herself for the first time, "all of us who believe." Then she returned to her seat. Her whole body thrummed with energy. She was forgiven! She no longer felt the heaviness of guilt inside her! The words in the New Testament weren't just words. It was true! The only blood sacrificed that could save her was the blood of Jesus! Finally, the right sacrifice for all her sins had been found!

There were several moments of silence. Nobody moved. Nobody spoke. Angelica fidgeted with excitement. Finally, Joseph stood again, and turning to the elders, said, "I propose that all who choose to do so should be baptized as Angelica advised. I will volunteer to be first." He turned to Angelica. "Will the river be sufficient, or do you require some other accommodation?"

Angelica looked at him in surprise. "Me? How can I baptize you? I need to be baptized myself."

Joseph smiled at her. "Well then, you baptize me, then I will baptize you, and together we will baptize the others."

They made their way to the beach with the crowd following behind. Angelica and Joseph ventured out into the cold, waist deep water.

"I'm not sure how to do this," Angelica whispered. Joseph pointed up. Angelica lifted her eyes. There were angels all around them, their light so bright she couldn't tell if there was any darkness beyond.

"What do I do?" she prayed.

Then she turned to Joseph. "Do you believe in all we have learned today about Jesus; that He became the sacrifice for our sins; that He died but rose again, and now sits in heaven with the Father as our advocate?" she asked loudly, so the crowd could hear.

"I do," replied Joseph. Angelica grabbed his arm and shoulder. "Joseph of Iliamna, I baptize you in the name of the Father, the Son and the Holy Spirit." When Joseph came up out of the water, his face was glowing, transformed by a smile that pulled dimples out she'd never noticed before. "Your turn," he said. As Angelica went under, time stood still. She saw herself in another river, being submerged under the water, her head newly shaven. This cleansing ritual required no scrubbing or shaving of hair. There was no shame. No people looking on with judgment in their eyes. This one was an acknowledgment of guilt, but it was a joyful acknowledgment, because when she went down under the water it reminded her, and told everyone watching, that it was all washed clean now. Instead of judgment, the onlookers rejoiced at her joy, and many of them shared in that joy for themselves that day. Angelica came up from the water with a smile she imagined must rival the one on Joseph's.

"Who's next?" she called, and the villagers started to come forward, one by one, to be baptized. Angelica barely registered the cold water, and she never once felt fatigued. Soon, the last one was entering the water.

Later that night, after everyone was dry and warm in the central building, and a celebratory meal was served. One of the elders moved to the front of the hearth. She was an older woman, with long gray hair that hung in a braid over one shoulder. Her Parka was a patchwork of black, red, and tan furs. Her Dark skin was weathered but clean and free of wrinkles.

"This is the part of the night when we tell stories of old," she said. The crowd nodded and murmured their agreement and anticipation. "However, today has been a day of new things - new hope, and new beginnings." The crowd was completely silent, waiting for her next words. "I propose that instead of telling stories of old, we listen to the words of the New Testament." The crowd roared their agreement with her proposal. She turned to Angelica. "Will you read to us?" Angelica pulled the Bible from the pouch at her waist and opened it. She waited for the crowd to quiet, then, clearing her throat, began to read in a loud, clear voice.

"In the beginning was the Word, and the Word was with God, and the Word was God."

Angelica read late into the night. Nobody moved. Her voice never got tired. Some of the children fell asleep in their parents' laps, but the eyes that gazed back at her were bright and eager. It wasn't until the first light of dawn peeked through the window that she closed the book and placed it back in its pouch. The people rose silently, almost reverently, and made their way back to their homes. Angelica wondered if she could even rise from the chair. Her eyelids closed and refused to open. She heard Joseph beside her. "Let's get her to bed." She felt herself being carried and was asleep before her head ever reached the pillow.

"Angelica."

Her mother was calling her inside for the sabbath meal. Angelica ran excitedly to the door. Sabbath was her favorite time. She loved the cozy feeling of the family around the table and mother and father saying the prayer together. She skipped into the house and stopped short. This was not the house she grew up in. It was dark and musty, and she could hear water dripping. One small barred window let light in from the top of the wall. Her mother lay on the floor, curled up under a thin ratty blanket. "Angelica," she whispered in a raspy voice. "Come for me. It's time."

Then her father was standing at the cell door, a cruel smile on his face. "You'll never leave here. You're a slave to the law."

Angelica sat straight up in her bed; the dream vivid in her mind. What did it mean? Was her mom being held prisoner somewhere by her father? If she were, there was only one place it could be. The temple.

Only a few days earlier, if somebody had used the phrase "slave to the law," it would have meant nothing to her. Now, her mind spun with the meaning of those words. That's what she'd been, that's what everyone in Turquoise still was. Suddenly getting the New Testament back to the village was about more than just saving her grandpa; it was about restoring the truth that was lost centuries ago. Her people literally had been slaves to the law, and it was time to set them free.

She scrambled from her bed and dressed hurriedly. She found Joseph in the dog yard rubbing ointment into one of the dog's paws. Chugiak ran happily through the yard, greeting each dog as if they were old friends. Joseph looked up at her.

"So, it is time," he said. Come, let's talk."

Angelica followed Joseph into the house where he stoked

the fire and put a kettle on to boil. As they waited for the tea Joseph took Angelica's hands in his.

"This New Testament you have found is beyond price, and something everyone needs to know about."

"I'm not sure what you're trying to say Joseph, but I have to go back to my village, and I have to take the testament with me. I can't leave it here with you, and I won't let you stop me from going." Angelica tried to hide the irritation in her voice.

"That is not my intention," Joseph said. "Please, just hear me out."

"Fine, but you won't change my mind," she said, leaning back in her chair and crossing her arms.

"What I was trying to say, is that everybody who wants to, needs to be able to read this. Copies need to be made."

Angelica opened her mouth to protest but Joseph held up a hand.

"What I am proposing, is that, I and a couple other men who are scribes, travel back with you and begin copying. Once we have several copies between us, we can return here and get others to help with distribution. It will take time, I know, but eventually we can give copies to all who want one."

Angelica sighed. "That would be a great idea Joseph, but you don't know my father."

"I do not," Joseph replied, "but I know my God, and I think by now you do as well."

"It is urgent that I leave as soon as possible."

"I must talk to the others, but we will be ready to go by midday."

FORTY

It seemed like the whole village had gathered to see them off. Elizabeth held Angelica in a tight hug, then kissed her forehead, the way a mother would. Her eyes were shiny with tears.

"You're in my prayers," she said.

"Thank you, your kindness has meant more than you know." Then Mary approached.

Angelica didn't want to say good-bye to Mary. They'd been through so much together, they'd discovered the truth about their savior, and the grace he offered them, together. They had knelt side by side and asked for mercy together. That kind of thing bonded two people in a way no other experience could. Mary hugged her.

"I wish I could come with you," she said.

"This will not be good-bye," Angelica promised. "It's just, until I see you again."

"We really must go," Joseph said gruffly after hugging his daughter and granddaughter, his eyes bright with tears.

Angelica joined Joseph and the others, following them

toward the lake. She couldn't stop the tears, nor the quiet sobs that shook her shoulders as she walked.

"You will see them again," Joseph stated.

"Is that a prophecy?" Angelica asked.

"A confidence in my heart," he replied.

As they stepped into the canoes and headed back across the lake, Angelica prayed that Joseph's confidence would be a reality, and the reunion would occur sooner rather than later.

ON THE OTHER side of the lake, some men met them leading several bridled moose.

"We ride from here," Joseph said. Angelica stared at him, unsure if she'd heard him correctly.

"You want me to ride a moose?" she stammered.

"It'll be okay," he laughed. "We raised these moose in captivity, and they are highly trained."

Angelica stared at the animal; she'd never really thought about how high off the ground a moose's back was before.

"Come on. Don't be afraid."

ANGELICA APPROACHED SLOWLY, climbing onto the log beside the giant beast. She still couldn't believe they expected her to ride it. Her heart hammered in her chest. After all the challenges she'd faced on this journey, why was she afraid of this? All her life she'd treated moose with a healthy dose of respect, knowing they were volatile, unpredictable, and incredibly fast. In her village, moose were considered the most dangerous animal in the forest. If a moose got it in its head that someone or something was a threat, it wouldn't stop stomping with their long powerful legs and sharp hooves until they eliminated that threat. A bear would run away most of the time, but one never knew what a moose may do. Stomp first, ask questions later was the moose way. She took a deep breath and put her foot in the stirrup.

"That's it," the man helping her said. "Now, grab that horn in the middle of the saddle and transfer all your weight on that leg."

Angelica took a deep breath and then did as he said. The beast didn't even flick an ear.

"Now swing your other leg over her back and sit in the saddle."

Angelica swung her leg over. She was in the saddle. She let out a shaky breath. She gripped the saddle horn; her knuckles turning white.

"See? Easy." The man grinned up at her.

Angelica tried to smile back, but she felt as if she might throw up. The ground seemed so far down. Then the animal moved, and Angelica let out a shriek, causing the beast to toss its head back and shake its antlers from side to side.

"Calm down," James said. "If you're afraid, Comet will sense it, and be afraid also."

Angelica took a long breath and loosened her fingers a bit from the saddle horn.

"There you go," said James. Comet let out a snort, and Angelica gripped the saddle horn tightly again, but she managed not to cry out.

"All set James?" Joseph asked from the back of his own moose.

"Sure am, boss," James replied. He rode up alongside Angelica and took the reins from her.

"I'll lead him 'til you get used to him, then I'll show you how to ride for yourself," he said.

By afternoon, Angelica's nervousness was almost gone. James showed her how to hold the reins and use them to control her mount. The trees whizzed by in a blur, but the powerful beast beneath never seemed to tire. By evening she was comfortable enough to forget she was in the saddle and enjoy the scenery. She even had a conversation with the others as they rode.

On the second day, they came to a fork in the trail. Angelica got an uneasy feeling when she looked down the trail to the left. She studied the sky, trying to see any sign of demons. She realized she'd seen none, nor any angels either, since the baptisms.

"I feel my spirit telling me not to take the left path," said James.

"I feel that too," said Angelica with wide eyes.

"As do I," agreed the other elder, Peter.

"I agree," said Joseph. They took the right path. It took them up onto a ridge that followed a small rushing stream below. From their vantage point, the path to the left could be clearly seen as it followed the other side of the stream on lower ground.

As they rounded a bend, there was a Mama bear with three cubs at the water's edge. Mama was drinking, and the cubs were playing nearby. They tumbled and rolled, chasing each other onto the path and then back to the riverbank to catch a quick drink.

It was a beautiful scene, and the cubs were unbelievably cute, but Angelica knew there were few more dangerous situations than to come upon a mother bear with her cubs. It could have been a bad situation if they'd gone that way, but somehow Angelica knew there was something far worse than a bear sow and her cubs that was the reason for them all choosing the other path.

A warning.

That was it wasn't it? The feeling she'd had was a warning. The Words she'd read only that morning came to her mind - the ones about being led by the Spirit.

"It was the Holy Spirit," Angelica blurted. "It warned us not to go that way."

The elders all nodded their agreement. "The words you read to us said, 'be baptized and you will receive the gift of the Holy Spirit'," stated James.

Angelica realized it was the moment she was baptized that she stopped seeing the spiritual world. Perhaps she didn't need that sight anymore if she had the Holy Spirit to guide her. Angelica wished there were someone she could ask. She'd always gone to Grandpa with questions about scripture, but there was nobody to ask now. As far as she knew, she was the first one to read the New Testament in 400 years. She vowed to pay more attention to those little nudges on the inside, that small voice she was beginning to recognize was the Holy Spirit.

That evening they reached the wall. The wind was moving the gate, causing a squeaking sound as it protested against the gusts on its rusty hinges.

"It was locked before," Angelica told them. "There was a big lock and a chain on the gate. I had to climb under through a hole dug out by an animal.".

"Here," Peter called, picking the lock out of the grass nearby.

"There's a rusty chain lying over there," said James pointing to the other side of the gate. Joseph took the lock from Peter and turned it over in his hands, moving the looping bar back and forth. "Somebody had a key," he said.

My Father.

Angelica's father must have known about the wall and had the key all along. Did he know the New Testament existed? Did he know the law was incomplete? Did her father know where her mother was? Was he her jailer?

"What is it Angelica?" asked Joseph with a frown.

"My father," she whispered. "Before we go past this wall,

we need to pray. He is on the other side, and I am afraid he won't be happy to see me. And we must pray for my mom." She told Joseph about the dream she'd had, and her suspicions about her father.

He put his big, weathered hand on her arm, his eyes full of compassion

"You're right, the forces of evil will stop at nothing to prevent you from bringing the truth back to your people. We must fast and pray."

They decided that they would set up camp right there, fore-go dinner, and spend the night in prayer.

FORTY-ONE

The morning dawned in its usual lazy way, the sky slowly lightening as the sun, which was only hidden behind the mountains for a few hours, rose once again into a blue cloudless sky. The group silently saddled their beasts, the only creatures among them who'd had a meal the night before or that morning, and mounted up, moving through the gate with solemn prayers moving silent lips.

They soon approached the tall spruce that marked the southern boundary, still standing proud upon its island. The eagle alighted from its nest, circling over their heads several times, its cry echoing through the valley and bouncing off the mountains, as if announcing their arrival. Angelica wrapped her fingers around the carving at her neck.

"I don't need you anymore," she whispered.

The eagle pivoted, riding an air current to a higher altitude, then glided off toward the horizon, until it was just a speck against the blue sky.

Angelica was in familiar territory now. The trails and landscape felt like a part of her that had been missing. She was at once elated and nauseous when she saw the line of the tabernacle peek out above the trees. The village was oddly quiet as they rode between the cottages. Where was everybody? As they approached the square, sounds of raised voices and shouting reached her ears.

She looked at Joseph in alarm. And spurred her beast forward, riding into the middle of the square in a cloud of dust. Joseph and the other men followed. They broke into the market square and the crowd stopped shouting. Some had their fists in the air, their faces screwed up and eyebrows furrowed. Some were weeping and shaking their heads. But they all turned, and stared in silent disbelief at the sight of the riders on the backs of moose.

Angelica's father stood before the great doors of the tabernacle, a scroll of the law in his hands. The high council stood on either side of him, making a half circle around her grandfather, who knelt in the dirt before them. Grandpa's shoulders slumped and his dirty clothes hung on his emaciated frame. He had a cloth hood on his head. Two royal guards stood over him as if he might try to get away. Angelica slid from the moose's back, her fear of the drop forgotten, and approached, kneeling to remove the hood from her grandfather's head.

Her stomach was in her throat, but she swallowed hard and faced her father.

"Grandfather told you the Holy Book was not complete. It was torn, and the back half was missing."

The crowd began to murmur and stir. "Blasphemy," somebody shouted.

"Stone her, too," another voice called.

Angelica turned to face them. In as even a voice as she could muster, she said, "My Grandfather was telling the truth, and I have the proof right here." She held up the pouch, opened the flap, and pulled the New Testament out, holding it so they could all see the words written on it. Some in the crowd cried out. "Stone her."

"What does it say?" shouted others.

Joseph stepped forward and held up both hands.

"Please listen," he spoke in a calm voice, waiting several moments and then repeating the request. After the third time, the crowd quieted and Joseph lowered his arms, addressing them now with loud authority.

"What Angelica has said is not blasphemy, but the truth." He turned toward Levi and the elders. "You are about to stone a man guilty of nothing more than getting a revelation from God and passing it on."

Levi's face was pale. His eyes darted from Angelica to Joseph. James and Peter stood on either side of Joseph, hands hooked in their belts, their feet wide apart.

"What are you doing here, this is private village business?" Levi demanded.

"We have come as scribes, to make copies of the 'New Testament' to take back to our people."

"The 'New Testament?" Levi's voice sounded weak, tired. His normally stern expression cracked. He seemed unsure of himself, and Angelica was shocked to see that he looked frightened also. She couldn't remember a time her father had ever been anything but solid, resolute, and incredibly strong. She'd always thought of him as invincible. She saw now that he was just a normal person, just like everybody else, and just as much in need of the hope she'd found as she had been. A new determination blossomed inside her. She stepped forward and met her father's eyes while addressing the crowds.

"Do you see here, where the spine is torn?" she asked the crowd. "The Holy Book in our tabernacle is also torn. If we put these two books together, you'll see they are the same."

The crowd began to murmur.

"Bring out our Holy Book," somebody shouted. "Let her prove what she says is true." The crowd began to voice their approval of the idea, others shouting the same suggestion again and again, until the whole crowd was chanting in unison, "Prove it. Prove it. Prove it."

Angelica turned to her father, watching his eyes dart across the crowd, his skin pale.

"You'd better get it," Angelica told him softly. "The truth is out. Don't fight it."

Angelica saw sadness, fear, and worst of all, surrender in her father's eyes. After several moments he shook his head sadly and said, "Very well." He turned to Eli and nodded. Before Eli could move, another priest, Benjamin, ran to the door, yanked it open and disappeared through it. The pounding of running feet inside the courtyard echoed into the square.

"He's trying to get the Holy Book," Angelica shouted.

Levi, Eli, and several other priests took off after him. Angelica followed, and almost collided with her father's back when he halted.

"Give it to me Benjamin," Levi said, inching closer to the man.

Benjamin held the Holy Book above his head. He moved in a slow circle, eyeing the priests surrounding him. He scooted to the left as he spun; the priests moving with him but keeping him within their circle.

"He's trying to get to the brazier. He's going to try to burn it." shouted Angelica.

"We need to stop him," Levi said.

"We need to pray," said Joseph. They all joined hands. Angelica took Joseph's hand and held the other out to her father. He looked back at Benjamin, who was pushing against the priests as they tried to hold him back. Levi hesitated, then grabbed Angelica's hand as well as James's. The circle completed; Joseph called out in a loud voice.

"O Lord, we ask that you intervene, and preserve your Holy Word so we can prove your truth to your people."

There was a crack, a sound like thunder striking a treetop. The group turned and saw Benjamin sprawled, unmoving, on the ground. One of the priests gingerly took the Holy Book from Benjamin's lifeless fingers. He carried it over and handed it to Levi, bowing slightly.

"What happened?" Levi asked.

"The fire from the brazier reached out and struck him." the priest replied, his eyes wide, as he backed away, glancing nervously toward the brazier. The others began to back away also, their eyes darting all around, and their shoulders hunched as if ducking from an unseen danger.

"He's alive," one of the other priests called, "but badly burned."

"Get him to a cell," Levi said. "Fetch the healer."

Levi turned to Angelica. His mouth stern.

"Let's test this theory of yours," he said, reaching to untie the sealskin wrapper around the Holy Book.

"No," Angelica said. "Do it out there, in front of the people. Let them see."

Levi hesitated, the fear returning to his eyes.

"They deserve to know the truth," she persisted.

Levi nodded reluctantly, and they headed back to the square.

Grandpa was sitting on a barrel with a chunk of bread and a skin of water. He tried to stand when he saw them, but Levi motioned for him to remain seated.

"This Holy Book has remained in its sealskin wrapper for decades, to protect its delicate pages," He announced to the crowd. "Those who preserved it," he gestured to Grandpa

Christopher, "only took it out to transcribe the scriptures, and then only in a closed room by special priests trained in its handling. Correct?" Grandpa nodded, verifying the statement.

"Is it your will that I should unwrap it now?"

Someone in the crowd shouted, "Open it." There were calls and murmurs of agreement from the people.

One of the priests ran forward with a podium and placed it in front of Levi. Another set the package on the podium and Levi stepped forward. He began to unwrap it. It was a slow and delicate process, but after several minutes of utter silence from all watching, Levi pulled the Holy Book from its wrapper and turned it over.

The crowd elicited a collective gasp when Angelica placed her half of the book on top of the other. It was a perfect fit. Joseph came forward then, lifting the New Testament and peering at the page beneath.

"The last page number on your half reads, 1,345 and the first page number in ours reads 1,346," he announced.

"I knew it," exclaimed Christopher.

The crowd grew quiet. All eyes turned to Levi. Angelica held her breath, barely daring to let the hope that swelled inside affect her expression. Why did he hesitate? What was there to think about? She could see the struggle on his face. Finally, he said to the guards through clenched teeth,

"We will not stone Christopher. Release him for now." The crowd began to cheer and then chant, "Christopher! Christopher! Christopher!" Levi's face grew red, his eyes narrowing as he watched the crowd.

Angelica watched the emotions at war on her father's face. She could see that he was afraid, but eventually anger overrode the fear, and she could see that it was taking effort for him to not respond to the crowd.

What right did he have to be angry, Angelica thought to herself, her own ire starting to rise? He was wrong, about everything, and when he knew he was wrong he'd tried to hide the truth. He'd known all along the book wasn't complete, and that Grandpa wasn't guilty of heresy. She could see it all clearly now. Was it all just a desperate attempt to hold onto power? To retain his position of High Priest and the control it gave him over the people? Release him for now, he'd said. For now?

"What do you mean, for now?"

Levi's expression softened when he looked at Angelica, but she was sure it was just an attempt to appease her. She could still see the anger seething behind his eyes.

"I will admit that Christopher was correct about the Holy Book being incomplete. However, what that missing part actually says remains to be seen." Levi began to wrap the sealskin around both halves of the book, but Angelica put her hand on the New Testament.

"I've read it, I can tell you what it says."

"Not in front of the people. Not yet," he said, glancing at the crowd to see if they'd heard. Some in the front had and were beginning to shush those behind them so they could better hear what was being said. Angelica took the New Testament and held it up for everyone to see.

"This book says God sent his only son to earth as a man. His name is Jesus. He came to become the final sacrifice for our sins. He has saved us from the Law."

The crowd began to murmur, getting louder each moment.

"Enough," Levi shouted, quieting the crowd. "I will read this 'New Testament', then I," He pointed to himself, "will tell you what it says... and what it means."

"No," Angelica said, her voice resolute. "It should be read publicly, for everybody to hear, just as we did in the village south of the boundary."

The crowd erupted then.

"Praise God for the book," some shouted.

"Blasphemy," insisted others.

"You've been south of the boundary?" Still others asked in horrified tones

"Go on then, read it to us," one man shouted.

Levi frowned at Angelica. "Daughter, your lungs are filled with the cursed air from south of the boundary, which has made you even more disobedient than ever."

"There is no "cursed air." The boundary is a lie." Angelica continued to address everything she said to the crowd. "The only thing I've been filled with is the Holy Spirit of God, a gift which is promised to everyone who believes in His son, Jesus."

The crowd grew even louder, shouting for Angelica to read to them.

"We are finished here," Levi shouted back at them. "You will be notified when this "New Testament" will be read to you."

"No. We are not finished here," Angelica said, lowering her voice now. She felt a courage she'd never known before as she stood before her father, confronting him. His discomfort was apparent, but she took no pleasure in it. Her heart ached for the father she'd wished she had all those years. Instead she'd gotten a hard man, a cold man, who seemed unable to feel. His feelings were so obvious to her now. He was a frightened man trying desperately to cling to power. He was afraid of losing control. The revelation struck her like the cold of the river when you first plunged in. She realized then that it was the Holy Spirit allowing her to see these things. Similar to the ability to see the spiritual world, this new vision allowed her to see the truth, and at the same time see her father with eyes of compassion. What hurt had he endured that made him so afraid to lose control? The thought led her naturally to her next question.

"Where is my mother?" She said loud enough for all to hear. It was a simple question, but when it was asked, all the world, even the birds, grew silent, as though waiting for Levi's answer.

His face grew pale, he looked around for a way of escape. "I don't know." Angelica had never seen her father this way. He seemed...

Vulnerable.

The word popped into Angelica's head as though inserted there by divine force. That was it - all her life Angelica had known this man to rule with an iron fist, to be certain in his decrees and proclamations. Now, here he stood, looking for all the world like a shame-faced little boy who'd been caught sneaking sweets. Angelica, afraid the sight of her Dad in such a weakened state would rob her of her courage, turned to address the council of priests, "I've had a vision of my Mother being held prisoner, here, in the tabernacle."

The priests formed a huddle and whispered to each other. They glanced Levi's way several times. Eli pushed his way to the middle of the group. They all listened as he spoke. Angelica wished she knew what they were saying but their expression revealed nothing. They all stood straight with their hands clasped behind their back as they always did, their body language revealing nothing. Finally, after a dozen agonizing minutes, the priests all returned to their places, and Eli stepped forward.

"I know where she is," he said, matter of factly. "I will take you there."

FORTY-TWO

Angelica's stomach rolled within her, but not for the same reason it usually did when entering the tabernacle doors. This time, instead of spilling the blood of an innocent animal, she would be reunited with her mother for the first time in twelve years. She swallowed the lump in her throat and followed through the gate into the courtyard. Eli took her across the courtyard to the back corner, and then through a doorway in the outer wall.

"This section wasn't part of the design given for Moses' original tabernacle," he explained as they traversed a long hallway lined with doors. "These rooms were built to house the priests, but over the years we have used some rooms for other purposes. Most of the priests live with their families in their own dwellings these days. Sadly, the most common use for these rooms now is to house prisoners while the council decides their punishment."

Some of the doors were open. Angelica saw each simple square chamber was identical - furnished with a simple log frame bed, a straw mattress, a rough hewn table, and an oil lamp.

. . .

Eli turned to the right, leading her down the hall that ran along the western wall.

"Nobody comes down this way much anymore," Eli said, a note of sadness in his voice.

Coming to a door near the middle of the hall, Eli stopped and fumbled with a ring of keys he'd produced from his belt.

Angelica's heart was pounding, and her stomach was in her throat. Tears pushed at the back of her eyes. How had her mother changed in twelve years? Would she still be beautiful? Would her smile still look as sweet? Would her hair smell the same? Angelica knew these were the memories of a child, but it had been all she had for so long. Now she was afraid. Perhaps her memories were only wishes, dreams of a five year old missing her mom. What if her mom wasn't how she remembered her at all? What if her mom was hard and unfeeling like her father now, from being locked up in a cold, dark, cell for so long?

Something squeezed Angelica's chest making it hard to breathe. She suddenly couldn't think. It felt as if her arms and legs were frozen, unable to move. Everything within her told her to run. She closed her eyes, concentrating on each breath. Inhale, she felt the air fill her lungs. Exhale, her breath made a soft sound as it left her lips. Her heart rate slowed. She opened her eyes to find Eli waiting expectantly, watching her with eyes that spoke of understanding. He stood to one side, the door opened, the soft light of the oil lamp making a hazy orange circle on the floor. Angelica took a shaky breath and willed her feet to move forward, one step at a time, until she stood before the figure of a woman, who lay on a thin mattress in the corner. Angelica rushed forward, as she ran, her fingers and thumbs wrestled the clasp of the eagle necklace, removing it. Hannah's skin was pale, and her shorn hair was growing back in patches of gray. There were dark circles under her eyes.

Mom.

Angelica had prepared herself for the fact that her mother would not be as she remembered her, but never had she imagined the bone thin figure in rags that lay before her, pale with blue veins prominent beneath the skin, with her hair shorn from her scalp. Tears poured down Angelica's cheeks.

"Mom, it's me Angelica." As she reached to put the medallion around her mother's neck, her fingers brushed warm skin. *Too warm.* Angelica placed a hand on her mom's forehead.

"She's sick, she has a fever!" Angelica exclaimed, looking up at Eli, who nodded sadly.

"She has been sick off and on for some time. I have kept her hydrated, and I sneak medicine into her tea, but I'm afraid it hasn't been enough. If you hadn't come when you had..."

One of the priests, who had followed them, now entered the room, and gasped when he saw Angelica's mom.

"She is gravely ill, we need to help her," Angelica said, pulling off her parka and covering her mother with it. The priest knelt down and picked Hannah up, cradling her like a child, and the company made its way back to the village square. The people fell silent when they saw the limp figure in the priest's arms. By the time Angelica reached the square she had hot tears pouring from her eyes. She marched up to Levi, not bothering to temper the anger that came flooding out of her at the sight of him.

"What have you done to her?" Angelica demanded. "How could you lock her away like some animal? How could you lie to everyone - lie to me - and say she'd run off and never come back? I always knew you were a hard man, a cold man, but I was a fool not to realize just how evil you really are. If she dies, her blood will be on your hands!"

Levi opened his mouth to speak, but Angelica whirled away from him.

"I need to get her home and into a warm bed, she needs caring for. She needs the healer." Angelica's grandmother appeared out of the crowd. "Bring her to our house, I will care for her," she said.

Angelica narrowed her eyes at the woman. "Did you know about this?" she demanded.

"No, Angelica I did not. I wish that I had. Come, let's get her home." Angelica peered into the old woman's face looking for any sign of deception. There was none.

"No," Angelica was shouting now in spite of herself. "I will not bring her into his house." She flicked her head in her father's direction. "If she ever enters that home again, it will be by her own choice." She turned to her Grandpa. "Can we bring her to your place?"

"Of course," Christopher said, in a voice that cracked with emotion. He gently took his daughter from the priest's arms, who bowed to him in respect. Christopher began walking away toward his cabin on wobbly legs. Angelica fell into step beside him.

"Let me carry her Grandpa," Angelica said.

"No, I must do this." Angelica heard the resolve in his voice and let him move on ahead of her, her mother's head nestled snugly in his neck.

"Wait," her father called. "The Testament."

"It stays with me," she replied, giving him a cold look before turning and leaving the square. The people began to mumble to one another - the volume and pitch slowly rising - but Angelica ignored them, and soon they were far enough behind where they could no longer be heard.

At Grandpa's cabin, they placed Hannah on the bed, and

covered her with furs. Angelica stoked the fire while Grandpa put a kettle on to boil.

Grandpa set up a cot beside the main bed. "Lie down and rest," he said.

"No, Grandpa, you take the cot," Angelica said, then crawled into the bed next to her mother, lying as close to her body as she could.

How often as a child had she dreamed of this? Except, in her dreams, her mother would wrap her arms around Angelica and kiss her forehead. She would smile with loving eyes and tell her she loved her. She would sing her a lullaby.

Angelica could remember the melody of that song but had long ago forgotten the words. She pushed down the lump in her throat and started to softly hum the melody she remembered.

Her mom's mouth began to move, and the words of the song came out. Her voice was cracked and weak, but to Angelica it was the most beautiful thing she'd ever heard.

As the Eagle soars on feathered wing,
As the grass grows green in the early spring,
As the river, and salmon run,
ever faithful, on and on,
So my love for you will be,
ever faithful, eternally.

Her mom patted Angelica's arm softly. Angelica smiled at her. "I love you Mama," she said.

And I'm sorry I stole your necklace, she almost added.

"And I you, Angel" she replied. "Always."

FORTY-THREE

Three days later, Angelica's mom was stronger, sitting up in bed, while Angelica prepared breakfast. Grandpa was working in the yard, and Chugiak had gone with him, running eagerly into the trees he'd known since he was a little lost pup who'd wandered into Grandpa's yard.

Angelica was starving, and soon emptied her bowl of porridge. She realized her mom had taken only a few bites. She was still so thin and frail, and Angelica couldn't help but worry.

"You should eat. You need to regain your strength."

Hannah pushed the bowl toward Angelica. "That's all I can eat for now. I'll try again later." Angelica set the bowl aside. Hannah reached up and touched Angelica's head. Angelica closed her eyes, relishing the feel of her mother's hand.

"Your hair? What did you do?"

"I went into the peasant camp to care for a sick child."

Hannah laughed, the shoulders of her frail body shaking.

"You didn't fall far from this old tree," she finally said. "I did the same, many times. I'm afraid I was a great disappointment as a wife of the high priest."

"You're right, as apples go, I was a great disappointment as a daughter of the high priest as well."

Angelica reached up and touched her mom's hair, which wasn't much longer than her own.

"Hey, at least we match."

ANGELICA WAS DRAWN to the door by the sound of someone calling her name. Mary was running into the yard.

"Mary. What are you doing here? How did you get here?"

"No time," Mary gasped, her hands on her knees as she attempted to catch her breath. "You've got to go. They're coming."

"Who? Who is coming?"

"Mother." The single word was enough to cause Angelica's heart to race and rise into her throat. This couldn't be happening. She'd just gotten Grandpa out of a cell, and finally found her mom. They'd had no time to enjoy the victory.

"She's brought the militia," Hannah added. Grandpa appeared; his eyes wide with alarm.

"They're speaking to your father right now. I don't know what they're saying, but whatever deal they make, they won't abide by it. They attacked our village, even after we assured them you'd moved on."

"Oh no," cried Angelica. "Is everyone okay? Your mom?"

"I don't know. When the attack began, we knew we had to warn you, so we took two of Grandpa's fastest Moose and headed north in the midst of the battle. I can only pray that my mom, Grandpa, and everybody else, is okay."

"What are we going to do?" Angelica asked her grandpa. Christopher shook his head, then took off behind the cabin.

"Who is with you?" Angelica asked Mary. "You said 'we' took two moose."

Mary turned to look behind her, and Angelica saw a figure coming up the path. He was riding a moose and pulling another behind him. He looked so much like Petra Angelica had to blink her eyes and look again.

"He looks like..." She began.

"Petra," Mary answered at that moment, inadvertently finishing the sentence.

Then Angelica was running, and Petra was sliding off the moose, leaning awkwardly against its flank on one good leg, the other wrapped in a splint. It was all Angelica could do not to fling herself into his arms. She managed to slow her pace to a walk about three feet from where he stood.

"I thought you were dead." Her voice sounded shaky and thin, she suddenly didn't know what to do with her hands.

"Nope, not dead yet," Petra replied, wincing in pain when the moose shuffled away from him.

"Come into the house. Rest after your long journey," Angelica offered, chiding herself for acting like a hostess in the middle of crisis. Petra had a way of jumbling up her thoughts.

"There's no time," Petra winced again. "Mother made a deal with your father. She claims you stole the New Testament from her, and your father has promised to return it."

"What? He can't do that."

"You need to get it away from here."

Joseph, James, and Peter came running up the path.

"They're coming," Joseph shouted.

Grandpa came back around the cabin with his arms full.

"I have two canoes standing by," he said, motioning toward the river with his head. "I have several packs, and provisions to last us a few days."

"Where will we go?" asked Angelica, her head spinning.

How could her father make such a deal with Mother? More importantly, how could she tear herself away from Petra, from her mom?

"I know a way through to the Kuskokwim that isn't marked on any of our maps," Christopher explained. "Once we make it there, we can either go Northeast toward the Yukon, or southwest toward the sea. Once we find a safe place, we can start copying the New Testament. "I have parchments here, somewhere." He gestured with the jumbled armful of items.

"There is no time to waste. We must go now," Joseph said.

"My mom," Angelica said. "I can't just leave her."

"Well then, give me the Testament and you can stay with her."

"No," Angelica said. "Without the proof in the New Testament to protect us, my father will be able to convince everyone we belong in a cell. We have no choice - Mom has to come with us."

They packed provisions and packs into the canoes as quickly as they could. Joseph carried Hannah down to the river, gently placing her in the center of one of the canoes and covering her with furs. Angelica knew what her mom needed was rest and a warm bed, but she had no choice now, she would have to trust God to protect them all.

"They are just down the path," Petra said. "The people from the peasant camp caught wind of what they are up to, and are blocking their way." He grinned at Angelica. "They put the sickest ones in the front." His face straightened and his eyes widened again. "But you better get out of here right now. I don't know how long they'll be able to keep them away."

Joseph, James, and Peter piled into one canoe, Angelica, her mom, and Grandpa, in the other. Chugiak jumped in too, his paws on the bow, barking excitedly.

"What about you two?" Angelica said to Petra and Mary.

"We'll be fine," Mary said, already slipping her foot into the stirrup to mount her moose.

How Angelica wished Petra could come with them. It tore at her heart to think of leaving him, but she had a responsibility, not only to her mom and grandpa, but to the Lord, and to the book.

"We'll see each other again soon," Petra said, his eyes stormy.

"They'll arrest you," Angelica replied, but they were both already on their beasts' backs and turning them toward the southern trail.

"God will keep us all safe," Petra called. Before Angelica could reply, they disappeared into the trees.

Unable to stop the tears that coursed down her cheeks, or the shaking of her shoulders, Angelica succumbed to the sobs that escaped her throat.

"We are all in God's hands now," Joseph said with a sad smile. "We have to believe, as the New Testament teaches, that He will work everything together for our good. Come. We must leave before your father gets here."

They turned their attention and their backs to the task at hand. The paddles sliced through the turquoise water as they headed upstream. Just before they reached the bend which would take them out of sight, Angelica looked back at her Grandpa's little cabin on its patch by the river. It was home to her - it had been her safe place as a child, a place where she was loved and accepted. Now she found herself leaving it again. She wondered if she'd ever return.

"We will return one day," her grandpa said, as though reading her thoughts.

"From your lips to God's ears," Angelica replied. She looked down at her mother, whose eyes sparkled with the reflection of the sun dancing on the water. The eagle medallion hung in its rightful place. Funny, her mother had not said a single word about it, though she fingered it now in a way angelica recognized. For a moment she wondered if others had seen her mother in her as she had done so.

Tears slipped from her eyes as she noticed the straining muscles of these brave men in this boat with her, and those in the other canoe, and the fullness of what they were doing dawned within her heart. These men were risking imprisonment, death, or both, to protect not just herself and her mother, but also the actual living Word of God.

With a whispered prayer of thanksgiving, Angelica put her mind back on the paddling as she fought the current to round the bend, before turning north toward the Kuskokwim river.

EPILOGUE

Levi stood in the yard outside Christopher's cabin.

"They aren't here," he said, spitting on the ground, his ears red, and his eyes hard.

Mother stood on the dock and peered upstream. The wind blew the tail of her coat out behind her, and made her cheeks ruddy in stark contrast to her short white hair.

"I thought you were the leader of this village," Mother said. Behind Levi stood at least a dozen men with large spears strapped to their backs. The Militia, she'd called them. The spears were not like the spears made for hunting they had in the village. These spears were weapons of war, made for controlling and killing other men. "Your people murmur against you, defy you, and prevent you from doing what you will." When there was no response from Levi, she scoffed, and looked around the empty yard. "Where could they go from here," she asked.

A man appeared from behind some barrels near the dock. Neither Levi nor Mother could know that this was the man whose ptarmigan Angelica had replaced with her own, so many moons ago.

"I know where they've gone," he said, "if you can spare a scrap of meat, or bread." He held out his hand.

"Tell me," said Mother, "and I shall be sure you have a feast you won't ever forget."

"They went south." He pointed. "They rode on the backs of moose, and they had big mean dogs with them; ferocious, snarling beasts."

Mother placed a hand on the man's cheek and then patted it gently. She could not know how much the man was tempted to recoil from her touch.

"Good boy," she said. She nodded at the militiamen who quickly disappeared down the trail. Then she turned to Levi.

"Do you want your rebellious little girl back dead, or alive?"

FREE BOOKS AND MORE

Receive free book offers, get exclusive behind the scenes content, and be the first to hear updates about upcoming books, release dates, and events.

Join Christina Cattane's mailing list at christinacattane.com

YOU CAN MAKE A DIFFERENCE!

Book reviews are valuable tools. They are extremely powerful and effective in bringing books to the attention of other readers. They are the number one thing you can do, (other than buying the book) to support an author that you love.

If you've enjoyed this book I would be so grateful if you would spend a couple minutes to leave an honest review on whichever platform you purchased it from. It doesn't need to be long or detailed.
Thank you so much.

ACKNOWLEDGMENTS

One cannot write a work of Christian fiction and not acknowledge the Lord first and foremost. He is the creator of all things, including the ability of mere mortals to create things, beautiful things, works of art that flow from the heart of the artist onto canvas, clay, instrument, or page. He is the inspiration for all things, but most of all, for this novel. The grace and mercy He bestows on each of us through the sacrifice of His only begotten son is incredible, unbelievable and beyond anything mere words on a page could ever express. Yet, this work of fiction is my attempt to do just that. Inspired by His Word, and led by His Spirit, I hope that I have not fallen too short of giving him His due glory.

I would also like to thank my parents, Jim and Maggie, who moved us to the state of Alaska when I was two years old. They made sure I got a great education, and encouraged my passion to learn and to create. The beautiful vistas that surrounded all sides of my childhood home, and the many Winnebago trips we took into them, played no small part in my need to express through words the beauty in the world all around us.

I would like to thank my husband for supporting me in this profession that offers no quick and easy rewards, but requires perseverance in playing the 'long game'. Not to mention he doesn't complain, much, about the money I've spent to make sure my finished product is the best it can be.

I don't want to be remiss in thanking my children; Amber, Mike, James and Chris, who were instrumental in making me the person I am today. (I little crazy and a lot loved)

Last, but certainly not least, I need to thank my writing group girls. Without the ladies from F.L.A.W.S., (The Fellowship for Ladies and Accountability in Writing Society) I would never have treated my writing as anything more than a hobby. I would have only taken my manuscript out, dusted it off, and done any work on it during National Novel Writing Month, once a year in November. It was because of these wonderful ladies, Barb, Gina, Jamie, Jennifer, Rhonda, and Vicki, that I decided to take my writing more seriously, treat it as my job, and finish my book. The final result was hitting that 'publish' button. I love you all!

ABOUT THE AUTHOR

Christina Cattane is an Indie Author who writes in several different genres, including Christian Fiction.

Her first novel 'Lost in the Land of the Midnight Sun' was as an idea that came to her while teaching a Bible study about the life of Moses. The idea, *"What if we lost the New Testament and reverted back to living under Old Testament law?"* took over ten years to come to fruition as a completed novel. Her next novel, Lost Book 2, should not take nearly as long.

Upon deciding to treat writing as her profession, Christina did some freelance writing (about garage floor oil mats, infant car seats, and other boring stuff), and ghost writing. Now, she works part-time on her own book(s), and part time as a Web-Search Evaluator.

In addition, Christina also homeschools her 17 year old son, is a pastor's wife, teaches the Wednesday night Bible Study, and has three other grown children, as well as one granddaughter.

She currently lives in Flint, Michigan with her husband and the youngest son.

Made in the USA
Monee, IL
13 November 2020

47338272R10167